BENEATH THESE LIES

MEGHAN

NEW YORK TIMES BESTSELLING AUTHOR

MARCH

CONTENTS

Copyright	v
About Beneath These Lies	vii
Chapter 1	1
Chapter 2	5
Chapter 3	11
Chapter 4	21
Chapter 5	29
Chapter 6	55
Chapter 7	61
Chapter 8	76
Chapter 9	79
Chapter 10	81
Chapter 11	84
Chapter 12	98
Chapter 13	106
Chapter 14	119
Chapter 15	125
Chapter 16	127
Chapter 17	129
Chapter 18	134
Chapter 19	138
Chapter 20	143
Chapter 21	152
Chapter 22	155
Chapter 23	158
Chapter 24	161
Chapter 25	168
Chapter 26	177
Chapter 27	187
Chapter 28	192
Chapter 29	196
Chapter 30	205
Chapter 31	226

Chapter 32   229
Chapter 33   236
Chapter 34   242
Chapter 35   252
Chapter 36   264
Chapter 37   270
Chapter 38   272
Chapter 39   278
Chapter 40   283
Chapter 41   289
Chapter 42   290
Chapter 43   294
Chapter 44   297
Chapter 45   299
Chapter 46   302
Epilogue   304

Author's Note   313
Acknowledgments   315
Also by Meghan March   317
About the Author   321

ABOUT BENEATH THESE LIES

Look, but don't touch . . . she might as well wear a neon sign that says it. It just makes me want her more.

She might be above me in every way, but I still want her under me.

I've got no business touching her rich-girl skin, but that won't stop me from stealing a taste. Because rules were meant to be broken—especially when the prize is so fine.

In a world where nothing is as it seems, what's buried beneath these lines?

ONE

VALENTINA

"I'm in love. It's official."

My head jerked up from the invoice I was scanning at the sighed words. Lowering my pen to the blotter, I stared at one of my gallery employees as she wiped down the front glass door, letting the bright sun of the French Quarter glitter through without tourists' fingerprints marring the surface.

Trinity had been wiping down that door for two years as an employee, and before that, from time to time when I'd bring her to the gallery as my "Little" in the Big Brothers/Big Sisters program.

"Excuse me?" I said.

Trinity was all of eighteen years and three days old, and I was pretty sure she didn't know any more about love than I did. At thirty-two, I'd given up on the concept. Well, I'd given up on men in general, and since I wasn't into the ladies, that ruled love out of the picture.

"I'm in love. With Derrick. He's the one."

Her tone was emphatic, hopeful, and incredibly naive to my thinking. If she were a cartoon, there would be stars in her eyes and a giant red heart pounding from her chest.

She'd been with this Derrick guy for almost four months, and I didn't know much about him except the fact that he was *so different from the boys in school.* Different wasn't always good, so it wasn't shocking that I was rather skeptical.

"Well . . . that's exciting." I wanted to be supportive. Trinity hadn't had the easiest upbringing, and I wanted nothing but the best for her. Including the full-ride scholarship she'd earned to art school in the fall.

She tilted her head and crossed her arms over her chest. "You need to take that *down with love* and *I don't ever need a man* attitude and keep it on your side of the room. Not all of us want to be crazy old cat ladies when we grow up."

From my perch at my minimalist desk, I winced. *Ouch.* That stung. *I don't even have a cat,* I wanted to argue. But that was a moot point.

"I just haven't found a guy worth my time. That's all."

"Maybe if you'd talk to men, you might actually decide to give one a chance." Trinity's gaze was sharp on me, and as usual, she missed nothing.

"I talk to plenty of men."

Her dark eyebrow arched. "Hate to break it to you, but customers don't count, Valentina."

"They have penises, so I'm saying they do."

But her point was well taken—none of the customers I interacted with spurred the least bit of interest. The tourists were transient, and I wasn't getting involved with someone long distance. The local guys who came in here and thought they saw something they liked had a tendency to flash their money around. I was happy to take it because it kept my bottom line healthy, but there was nothing attractive about a man who felt the need to use money to get my attention.

How about a flirty conversation that actually got my blood

pumping? Witty banter? Apparently that was too much to ask. Hence, why I'd given up on men.

Trinity's mouth dropped open. "You said *penis*. At work."

A smile tugged at the corner of my mouth. Eighteen years and three days did not an adult make.

"And you're eighteen, as you've informed me a dozen times in the last few days, so I'm assuming this isn't a new word for you."

"No, but . . ."

At least I knew I could still scandalize my employees by throwing out the word *penis* on occasion. "Face it, I've seen more of them than you, and I'm really not impressed with what comes attached to them."

Especially because you couldn't tell whether the man attached to the package fell into the category of man or monster —or a combination of both. My humor fled at the thought, but Trinity didn't pick up on that.

"Well, if you saw Derrick's package—"

I covered my face and groaned. "No, thank you. I do not need that visual."

A husky laugh interrupted us.

Crap. I cringed as I thought about a customer overhearing this particular conversation. But when I jerked my hand away from my face and caught sight of the person in the doorway, relief flooded through me, along with the reminder that I really needed to get that door chime fixed.

Yve Santos smiled as she strolled inside on fabulous red platform sandals and a retro yellow dress. Actually, it was Yve Titan now.

"If you're talking about packages, I'm down for this conversation."

I pushed away from my desk and stood with a smile. "I bet you are. What brings you in today?"

Trinity eyed Yve with awe. My friend had become something of an idol to her. Yve had also grown up in less-than-ideal circumstances, but now owned a successful shop in the Quarter and was married to Lucas Titan, a rather infamous businessman.

Yve crossed the wide wooden planks of the gallery to meet me in the middle. "I came to invite you to my belated bachelorette party. Tonight. Sorry for the late notice. I wasn't going to have one, but Elle badgered me into it. As soon as I said yes this morning, she had it planned in about five minutes. I think she's afraid Lucas is going to find out and kidnap me before she has a chance to start ordering shots."

That sounded about right. If ever there was a man likely to kidnap his wife, Lucas Titan would be at the top of the list.

"Then by all means, we should go out and celebrate while we have the chance."

Warmth filled my chest at the happiness Yve had found. She and I had come to know each other after facing the same monster—although it had been infinitely worse for her because he'd been her husband—and we'd both held our heads high and survived. Thrived even. And for that reason, I would go out and celebrate.

"Good! I'm so glad you're coming. We both deserve to celebrate." Yve squeezed me with a quick hug and pressed a kiss to my cheek. "We'll come by and get you at your place tonight around eight."

"Perfect. See you then."

As soon as Yve left, Trinity looked at me with a big grin on her face. "Bachelorette party? Sounds like the perfect opportunity for you to find yourself a man."

TWO
VALENTINA

"**M**ore shots!" Elle yelled, swirling her hand in the air.

The shot glasses lined up on the table seemed to multiply, and I didn't know if there were actually more or if I was seeing double. Rubbing a hand across my face, I stared at the glasses again.

Seeing double wasn't usually a concern for me. I never let myself get more than a touch tipsy because I hung on to my control with an iron grip.

But tonight had been different. My vision was hazy, and my legs had been less than steady the last time I'd made the trek to the bathroom with Yve and Elle and another one of their friends. Girl posse, Elle called it. I'd never had one of those before, but I liked it.

"Glad you're having fun, Val," Elle said, bringing over one of the newest round of concoctions.

"We can be a girl posse, but only if you don't call me Val," I said, accepting the shot.

"Fair enough." She raised her shot glass and we clinked

5

before downing them. When we both slammed them on the table, she added, "I'm also glad you're losing that whole prim-and-proper thing you had going on. We need to find you a man to help you lose it the rest of the way."

Yve joined us. "What's this about finding Valentina a man?"

"She needs a big bad alpha of her own so she can find out just how good it is on the other side."

I scrunched my forehead and considered. "I'm not sure I can handle a big bad alpha. Maybe a beta. Someone nice who likes wine tasting and *Masterpiece Theatre*."

I always figured if I was going to start dating for real, that was the kind of guy I'd go for. Someone safe. Nonthreatening.

Both Yve and Elle screwed up their faces in disgust.

"Van, get your ass over here. We need you!" Elle called.

We do?

Vanessa, a gorgeous blonde, came over and snagged another shot off the table.

"I should probably stop after this one." She tipped it back. "But Con likes it when I get a little tipsy. The man lets me climb all over him like a jungle gym. And that's just the beginning."

Hearing those words from the woman wearing YSL and Judith Leiber was a little more than shocking.

Elle took in my surprise. "See, alpha all the way. Tell her, Van."

Vanessa sat and patted the seat beside her for Yve. Yve slid onto the chair. "I'm just gonna say it. The woman's lib move-ment can skewer me if they want, but there is something so fucking hot about a guy who isn't afraid to just toss you over his shoulder and carry you away."

Both Yve and Elle nodded in agreement.

"Damn, that does sound kind of hot." I couldn't believe I was agreeing too. It was the shots talking, not me.

Elle piped up again. "Because it is. Alpha all the way."

"So where does one find this species of man?" I asked. "Not that I'd even know how to handle one."

Vanessa waved a hand. "You find one, we'll teach you all the tricks."

When large forms blocked the neon lights from the bar, I blinked and looked up, fighting the urge to shrink back in my seat. I was stronger now. It had been over ten years. I was fine. I was with friends. And *that* was the reason I'd let go tonight. It was truly time to let go. Yve had, and that inspiration was what I had needed to start shedding the past.

It was over. He was dead, and I was not. It was long past time to start living again.

"Sweet thing, you don't need another shot. Hell, I don't think any of you needs another shot."

The man's voice was deep, and it took me a minute to put it together that he was Elle's boyfriend. Of course, the way she jumped up from the table and threw herself at him and then climbed the man like a spider monkey was what really gave it away. I could see the alpha thing stamped all over him from the way he lifted her up and grabbed her ass.

"You're not supposed to be here," Yve said, her happily slurring words directed at Lucas Titan.

"And yet I am. Your ride awaits."

I wondered if Yve would say she wasn't ready. I blinked again and the number of shot glasses shrank by half, and then doubled immediately on my next blink. *Yep, it's time for me to go.*

Yve rose and held out a hand. "Then take me home." Her gazed flicked to me. "After we take Valentina home."

Lucas glanced at me and nodded. "We'd be happy to."

I rose from my seat on tottering heels, once again marveling at the fact I'd drunk so much, and that I'd felt completely at ease doing it. Girl posses were awesome.

I reached out with my left hand to steady myself by grabbing the back of the chair I'd vacated, but I misjudged the distance. My balance faltered, and my right hand flew out and smacked into a hard body. An arm slipped around my waist, steadying me. If it hadn't been for the buzz, and the relief I wasn't falling on my butt, I would have jerked away.

"Easy there." His voice was equally deep as Elle's boyfriend's, but completely familiar.

Shock fighting with my buzz, I turned my head to stare at Detective Hennessy. Or rather, two Detective Hennessys.

"Had a few?" he asked.

"Maybe," I said. "You gonna arrest me for it?"

Where the words came from, I didn't know. I just knew being around Detective Hennessy brought back memories I'd decided to shake off completely, starting tonight.

"You done something you need to be arrested for?"

I shook my head, determined to keep the memories at bay. "No. But I do need to go home."

I watched as Lord led Elle out of the bar, and his brother, Con, swept Vanessa up in his arms. The gorgeous blonde was beyond walking in a straight line at this point. From the big tattooed Viking of a man's husky laugh, he didn't seem to mind. Another alpha.

I want that. Pea green was a horrible color on me, but that knowledge didn't stop the envy from taking up residence in my chest.

"Ready, Valentina?" Lucas Titan asked, his eyes moving from Hennessy to me.

"I can give her a lift. She's on my way home. It's no trouble," Hennessy replied.

"That okay with you, girl? If not, we'll take you," Yve added.

Say what now? My head was swimming with the constant swinging back and forth to follow the conversation. I just wanted my bed. And to make it there without getting sick. With the good detective, at least I'd be safe. He'd helped put the monster in the cage, and for that, I trusted him more than I trusted most people.

"It's fine. I'm good. I'm ready to go," I said, taking a step and almost losing my balance again.

Note to self: I need to wear flats the next time I go out with these girls.

Hennessy steadied me, and I waved to Yve as we walked toward the door. She blew me kisses and then Lucas grabbed her ass.

I want that, I thought again as we followed them out of the bar. That easy togetherness with a man who was all man. The kind who took care of his woman and made sure she and her friends would get home safely.

Stop, Valentina. I forced my thoughts back to the present.

Hennessy's bright green gaze fixed on me, and I couldn't help but wonder what he saw.

"Am I riding in the back of a cop car?" I asked, hoping to break the intensity of his study. I wasn't in any shape to be analyzed closely tonight.

"I don't drive a squad car. But even if I did, you wouldn't be riding in the backseat."

We rounded a corner, Hennessy's arm tucked around my back to keep me upright as I stumbled on the uneven sidewalks of the Quarter. Always a protector.

I focused on staying upright until he slowed and keys jangled. Lights flashed on some kind of SUV a few feet away.

Hennessy led me around to the passenger side, opened the door, and helped me up into the seat.

"I got it," I said, fumbling for the seat belt.

He backed away and waited until I clicked the buckle into place before shutting the door.

I was out before he put the key in the ignition.

THREE

VALENTINA

"Oh God, why did I drink so much?" My scratchy voice filled the room as my head pounded against the soft down pillow. "Never, ever doing that again," I said with a groan.

I hadn't felt this awful since Ash Wednesday my senior year in college. We'd gone to a fancy party, drinking with abandon because it was our last Mardi Gras before we hit the real world, and the booze had been free because of someone's parents' friends.

Last night hadn't been quite as crazy, but I was years out of practice at drinking like that. My memory was hazy, but I still recalled the highlights. Including . . .

Detective Hennessy, offering me a ride.

Detective Hennessy, carrying me to my door.

Detective Hennessy . . . handing me a washcloth to wipe the vomit from my face.

Brilliant, Valentina. Just brilliant.

I groaned again, burying my face in my pillow. Could I smother myself with embarrassment?

Why did it seem that there was always one person who

continually saw you at your worst? In high school, I was as poised and proper as any Catholic prep school girl could be expected to be, except when I saw the captain of the swim team, Kirk Ryan. I hadn't fallen down the stairs because I was flustered. No, it was the fact that I was staring at him and didn't see the piece of loose-leaf paper that someone had dropped at the top, and I'd slipped.

And then there was the giant puddle the janitor hadn't cleaned up from the leaking door seal and the epic rainstorm we were having. He'd been kind enough not to laugh when I'd fallen on my face. And the cafeteria tray incident? Billy Butcher ran into *me* and knocked the spaghetti down the front of my white shirt and all over my cardigan.

But regardless of the reasons for these unfortunate incidents, Kirk Ryan always saw me at my most disastrous. Which was why, when he asked me to the junior-senior prom, I had politely declined in favor of studying. No one likes being vulnerable, especially not in front of someone you'd prefer to impress.

Did I want to impress Detective Hennessy? That was a matter for another moment, because right now I needed to find my way into the shower and drag myself back to human status in time to get to work. I didn't want to leave Trinity waiting on the sidewalk like I'd done once before when I'd overslept.

Forty minutes later, I was slipping a shoe on and rushing out the door. I had three minutes to get to work, which meant I'd be late and she'd indeed be waiting on the sidewalk.

Except she wasn't.

I unlocked the door and turned off the alarm before slipping inside and crossing to my desk to stow my purse in a drawer. Trinity was never late. Never.

Then again, I wasn't usually late either, so maybe she was having a rough start to the morning too. But when I hadn't heard from her by noon, every internal warning bell I had was going off.

Trinity didn't pull a no-show without calling. Ever. She'd called in sick exactly twice since she'd started working for me two years ago, and one other time when she needed extra time to study for a test. She was as reliable as any adult employee I'd ever had.

I called her cell no less than a dozen times before I called her grandmother around three, and learned that Trinity hadn't come home last night and there was no word from her all day. I thanked her grandmother for the information and immediately started calling hospitals. The woman was used to Trinity coming and going as she pleased, sometimes staying the night with boyfriends, and had basically kept her out of the foster system but hadn't provided much else in the way of parenting. She'd seen it all and wouldn't share my fears.

Every possibility ran through my head while I talked to customers throughout the day and sold artwork. When the clock turned to five and I was locking up the gallery by myself, panic set in. Something was wrong. I felt it in my bones.

Trinity had graduated weeks ago, so calling the school wouldn't be any help. I'd exhausted the hospitals, didn't have any way to contact her friends or her boyfriend, and a second call to her grandmother returned the same conclusion as the first: Trinity was MIA.

So I was left with only one other option . . . the police.

Was I overreacting? Maybe. But when it came to Trinity, I wasn't taking any chances. I knew better than anyone what could happen when a girl went missing, and how quickly it could turn bad.

"Ms. Noble, I'm going to need you to calm down. Ms. Rodgers is eighteen years old and therefore no longer a minor."

Frustrated, I jammed my hand into my hair, and my ring caught. I was trying to free it when Detective Hennessy stepped out of an office and paused. His green eyes were on me, assessing, like always. Seeing my weaknesses, my flaws, my vulnerabilities. *Probably remembering the horrific display of last night.*

If this were just about me, I would have turned and walked out rather than face him, but my purpose was too damn important. Trinity was too important. And I was not above exploiting my connections to get help tracking her down.

I tugged my hand from my hair as discreetly as possible before raising my chin at Detective Hennessy, who was already walking toward me.

How is it possible I didn't know his first name? It showed just how little I actually knew about the man. He was taller than my five-foot-four-inch frame and if I stood behind his back, I'd disappear behind his wide shoulders. Every time I saw him, I remembered what it felt like to clutch the scratchy white sheets lining my hospital bed with my broken fingernails and nearly lifeless hands. I shoved the memory back down.

Detective Hennessy's long stride carried him toward me and the uncooperative officer within seconds.

"Is there something we can help you with, Ms. Noble?"

The officer I was speaking to, the bar on his uniform read L. JENKINS, decided to reply for me.

"She's trying to file a missing person's report, and the missing person in question hasn't been gone for even twenty-four hours yet. I keep explaining that because the girl is eighteen and Ms. Noble here isn't a close relative, she really needs to get a family member to report the girl missing, and it'd be best if she waited another day or two to make sure the girl is really missing."

"That's not acceptable," I said. "Trinity's only been eighteen for *four days*. She's barely an adult. Her grandmother is her only living relative, and she's not much for getting out of the house these days. I've been the closest adult in Trinity's life for years, and it's absolutely ridiculous that you won't file the damn report."

My temper was flaring, even though I was trying to keep my cool. This was ridiculous. Trinity was barely out of school, didn't live on her own, and when something was wrong in her life, she came to *me*.

"Jenkins, let me speak to Ms. Noble. You can carry on with your duties," Hennessy told the fresh-faced officer who wouldn't budge off his asinine rules.

Jenkins smirked at me, clearly pleased to be handing me off to someone else.

Fabulous. Now I'd have to make my plea directly to Hennessy when what I really wanted to do was have him hypnotized and order him to forget every interaction we'd ever had—especially last night.

Hennessy led me to a small room and shut the door behind us. He wasted no time before starting with the dreaded small talk.

"How are you feeling today?"

I swallowed back the urge to wish for some voodoo incantation that would handle the aforementioned memory wipe, and forced a placid smile to my lips. "I'm fine, thank you. I appreciate your assistance. I apologize for . . . everything."

Hennessy shrugged, as if my personal humiliation was really no big deal. And honestly, compared to my concern over Trinity, my personal issues were nothing.

"You have a missing person to report?" he prompted.

"Yes, one of my employees. She's the most responsible eighteen-year-old I know, and she's never done anything like this before. Her grandmother said she didn't come home last night, and she hasn't heard from her. She didn't show up at work today, and she's not answering her cell. This isn't like her. I've called all the hospitals, and Officer Ever-So-Helpful confirmed she wasn't in jail."

Hennessy's face, handsome in a rough-hewn and stubbled sort of way, didn't show any indication of his thoughts. "Have you called her friends? Boyfriend? Did she get into an argument with her grandmother or anyone else?"

"She and her grandmother aren't exceptionally close, and Trinity basically just comes and goes as she pleases. As far as I know, they don't argue about anything. She hasn't been hanging out with her friends ever since she got involved with her boyfriend."

Finally, Hennessy's expression changed. Skepticism was branded all over it now. "Have you checked with the boyfriend?"

Feeling like a moron, I shook my head. "No. I don't know how to get in contact with him."

"Do you know his name?"

The moronic feelings compounded. "Derrick. I don't know his last name."

"You know anything about him? How old he is? Where he works? Who he might hang out with?"

I shook my head as I kicked myself for not getting more details. I'd been listening to Trinity talk about him for months, but she mostly just talked about their dates, how romantic he was, and that she was sure he was the one, but she was still going to start art school in the fall. She certainly wasn't going to get knocked up—yet.

I sifted through all the details I could recall. "He worked for a guy. One guy, not a company. Sometimes she called Derrick 'D-Rock,' which I assumed was just some kind of pet name.

16

The guy he worked for had an odd name too. Rex or something like that."

Squeezing my eyes shut for a beat, I searched my memory for anything else I could think of. Why couldn't I remember the name? Why hadn't Trinity ever brought Derrick to the gallery? I'd assumed it was because he wasn't interested in art, but hadn't asked too many questions because she told me over and over how supportive he was of her going to college because he hadn't gotten a chance to.

"And he's older than her. Twenty-three or four, I think." I opened my eyes to see a dark expression settle over Hennessy's face. "What?"

"Was the guy's name Rix? The one Derrick worked for?"

I felt like I'd hit the jackpot. "Yes! Rix. That's it. Do you know him? Can you help me track down Derrick, and if Derrick hasn't seen Trinity, will you file a missing person's report and start investigating?"

Hope bubbled up inside me—and then Hennessy crushed it. He clicked his pen shut and flipped the little cop notebook closed. *Bad sign.*

"Your girl never mentioned that she hooked up with a gang-banger, did she?"

I blinked, trying to comprehend his words. "What do you mean?"

Hennessy crossed his arms and leaned back in the chair. "Rix heads up one of the biggest gangs in the city. I haven't heard of D-Rock before, but it wouldn't take me long to track him down, especially if he's been arrested before."

Shock ripped through me. "A gang? Like . . . *what*?"

Hennessy pushed his chair back from the table and rose. "Let me go run a search, and I'll see if I can confirm it. But there's only one guy I know named Rix in this town, and he and his crew are not people you should be messing with."

He was already halfway out of the room when I gathered my wits and shoved out of my chair. Marching after him down the hall, I caught up with Hennessy as he turned a corner and entered a room full of desks and cops. The noise hit me first—everyone was either talking to someone or yelling.

Hennessy pulled out a chair at a battered metal desk covered in stacks of manila files, and began clicking keys on a keyboard.

My mind was on Trinity's boyfriend and what that meant. She'd never once mentioned he was in a gang. It had to be a mistake. There could be more than one guy named Rix in this city. I dropped into the molded plastic and metal chair next to the desk without invitation.

"You should've stayed in the conference room, Valentina," Hennessy said without looking away from the computer monitor.

"Well, I wasn't just going to sit there and look pretty while you figure out if the girl I've known for years is caught up with something she probably doesn't even understand. Trinity is good people. She's bright, hardworking, and loves art, and she wants to paint and own her own gallery. She's not the kind of girl who falls for a guy in a gang. She's smarter than that."

Hennessy finally looked at me. "Are you sure? Some people say you can't choose who you fall for."

When I didn't address that comment, Hennessy's attention went back to the monitor as mug shots started to appear. One was of a very handsome young black man, and Hennessy clicked on it.

"Derrick Rockins, also known as D-Rock, is a low-level member of the New Orleans Down 'n Out, also known as the NODOs, which is the gang currently headed by Rix."

I straightened in the chair, disbelief warring with fear. *No. Way.* This had to be a mistake.

"Please tell me you're joking."

"Sorry, Valentina. Your girl got hooked up with a guy in the wrong crowd."

My concern for Trinity mounted exponentially. "So that's all the more reason to investigate that she's missing, right? I mean, who knows what could have happened to her? She's in danger. Clearly."

My voice was rising with every word, and I could only imagine what my face looked like right now as panic zipped through my system, but Hennessy never lost his unflappable calm.

"She's eighteen. She's made her choices. Keep calling her, and if you don't hear from her by tomorrow, get her grandmother to give us a call to file the report. For adults, it's usually best if a close family member is the one to report the disappearance."

"But—"

Hennessy stood, cutting off my words. "The girl is probably holed up with her boyfriend somewhere and will more than likely show up today. If she doesn't, then we can worry."

I shot out of my chair, crossed my arms, and stared down Hennessy. "You don't know her. This isn't like her at all. And I swear to God, if something happens to her, I'm going to rain down hell on this police department for refusing to take me seriously."

Hennessy's gaze dropped to the floor as he debated what to say in the face of my threat. Capitalizing on his inattention, my eyes shot to the computer screen where Derrick Rockins's information was listed—including his address. If the police wouldn't take me seriously, I'd do my own digging.

Without waiting for a response, I spun and took a step away from Hennessy. When his big hand caught my elbow and pulled me to a stop, I met his bright green gaze with my determined one.

"Don't do anything stupid, Valentina. This isn't something you want to get involved in. Get the grandmother to call me tomorrow, and we'll figure it out."

I hoped my face was set into an unreadable mask, because I had absolutely no intention of following his directive. Shaking off Hennessy's arm, I straightened my shoulders and gripped my handbag.

"I'll do whatever the hell I want. I care about her, even if it's clear that you guys don't."

Whatever Hennessy was going to reply was lost when the doors to the room swung open and a loud group of officers entered.

I slipped out behind them. I was on a mission.

FOUR

VALENTINA

I shouldn't be here.

I knew it the minute I drove into this neighborhood, and so did the men on stoops eying my red Tesla roadster. I had a feeling they weren't admiring its awesome engineering. But to find Trinity, I was willing to do whatever it took.

Driving slowly, I searched the fronts of the dilapidated houses for the address I'd memorized from Hennessy's computer screen. Most of the house numbers were barely hanging on. I checked the slip of paper I'd written the address on. I was in the right place.

Psyching myself up, I parked and pushed open the door to the car, locked it, and hugged my purse close to my body. I swore I could feel eyes on me from every direction.

Doesn't matter. I've got this.

Mental pep talk complete, I glanced back at my car, hoping it would still be there when I got back. Hennessy was right. I had no business being here, but that wasn't going to stop me.

Forcing confidence into my stride, I headed for the sidewalk and the gnarled chain-link gate blocking the walk up to the house. Luckily the metal latch was in good working order, which meant I probably wouldn't need a tetanus shot from touching it.

After opening the gate partway and sliding inside the yard, I took a deep breath and strode up the cracked concrete to the porch. At least the steps had been recently replaced, so I wasn't at risk of falling through them as I climbed up. The screen door also looked relatively new, but the doorbell I pressed looked ancient.

I listened for the telltale chime from inside that would let me know the thing actually worked, but heard nothing. Pressing it a few more times for good measure, I continued to wait. Nothing.

"Ain't fixed yet."

I spun around at the deep, rough voice coming from behind me. A man leaned against the inside of the gate, watching me. I hadn't even heard him come through it. Clutching my purse closer, I thought about the Smith & Wesson inside and prayed to God I never had to use it.

Something about this guy told me I might need it. Menace. It came off him in waves. But under it, he was also strangely gorgeous, which didn't make sense.

I took in his light caramel-colored skin, hair buzzed to a dark shadow, his T-shirt stretching across a broad, well-muscled chest. Intricate designs in black ink wrapped around thick biceps and forearms. I dragged my gaze back to his face, finding his piercing silver eyes assessing me as carefully as I did him.

Swallowing, I got to my purpose for being here. "Do you know Derrick Rockins?"

The man's carved features gave nothing away. Jesus. Was his going to be the last face I saw before I ended up in the trunk of a car and my parents had to file a missing person's report for me?

My heart hammered and my palms sweat where I held on to the leather of my purse.

After a long silence, he finally responded. "This ain't the kind of neighborhood you come to and start asking questions. Woman like you? It won't take long before someone decides not to let you leave."

I gritted my teeth, willing myself not to show fear. Instinctively, I knew that would only make things worse. I would face down the devil in hell to find Trinity; I just hoped I hadn't found him.

I tried again. "I'm looking for a girl named Trinity. Someone said Derrick Rockins might know where she is."

Something flashed through those silver eyes, and I was willing to bet my Tesla it was knowledge.

Resolve straightened my spine, overcoming the fear, at least until he pushed off the gate and crossed his arms. Jesus, Mary, and Joseph, they were big. The muscles strained against the cotton of his T-shirt.

"Who is she to you?"

Decision time. Tell him more or offer as little information as possible? I decided at this point, I had nothing to lose by going with the truth.

"My employee, and someone I'm very worried about." When he said nothing, I filled the silence instinctively. "She didn't show up at work and she's not answering her cell. Her grandmother hasn't seen her either, and since I care about her and the police won't let me file a missing person's report yet, I'm doing what I can to find her myself."

His expression hardened to granite as soon as I mentioned the police.

"You went to the cops?"

His ominous tone threatened my resolve. If he was connected to the same gang as Derrick, then obviously I'd just said the wrong thing. There was nothing I could do but brazen it out. Show no fear.

I lifted my chin. "Yes. And if you'll tell me where she is, you'll save me another trip to the precinct tomorrow."

His eyes narrowed. "Who the fuck goes to the cops when someone doesn't show for work?"

Squaring my shoulders, I infused my tone with all the confidence I could muster. "I did, because she's just a kid."

He uncrossed his arms. "She ain't no kid."

Bingo. He knew her. He freaking knew her. I latched onto that fact like a dog to a bone, and some of the apprehension of facing him down drained away in the face of my determination.

"You know where she is. Admit it," I demanded.

The thunderous expression on his face told me that no one demanded anything of this man, but I didn't care.

"Why should I tell you a goddamned thing?"

"Please," I said, my tone near to begging. "All I want to know is if she's okay."

He studied me for long moments. I didn't know if he read the desperation on my face, but he shifted.

"She's fine. He took her out for her birthday."

"It's not her birthday anymore."

"Well, it was, and he was out of town," the man countered.

That was true, but Trinity would have told me if he was taking her out. She'd been moping about him being gone before our conversation about love and penises, and Yve showing up to invite me to the bachelorette party.

"She didn't say anything about it."

"Not my problem."

He might as well have held up a sign that read *That's all the information you're getting from me.* But I wasn't satisfied.

"Where are they?"

24

His gaze drilled into mine as if he couldn't believe I was still asking questions. Which explained why he ignored it.

"I'm gonna give you a piece of advice and suggest you take it. Leave the girl a voice mail like any normal boss. Don't come 'round here knocking on doors. You might be the one needing a missing person's report if you're not careful."

Banked fear curled around my spine, but I refused to succumb to it. The last several years, my life had been a constant battle to try to sort "good guys" into categories of *actually good* and *pretending to be good*.

I'd never faced someone in my sheltered little world who was unapologetically bad. It wasn't inherently logical, but there was some comfort in the fact that he wasn't pretending to be anything but what he was. It was the *pretending to be good* guys who struck the most fear into me because they presented an unknown danger.

Take the monster—he'd been a "good guy" from a good New Orleans family. And he'd terrorized both Yve and me.

This man in front of me was unequivocally dangerous.

"Is that a threat?" I asked, idiotically testing my theory. The good thing about unapologetically bad guys? They were usually pretty honest. They had nothing to hide.

"Call it a warning. This ain't the job for you." He tilted his head and watched me for my reaction, but I didn't give him one. "You ain't lettin' this go, are you?"

"No."

He shook his head slowly. "She's probably holed up with D-Rock in some hotel room. The boy was going to take her somewhere romantic." He made air quotes around the word *romantic*, and suddenly he was a little less scary and a little more human.

"Romantic?"

The boy gangbanger was into romance? So Trinity wasn't

missing due to some malevolent deed, she was a young girl being swept off her feet by her boyfriend. Could I have really missed the mark so widely?

Glancing back at the man watching my every change in expression, I knew I didn't have a choice but to believe him. Which meant I didn't need to be in this neighborhood at all, and it was time for me to go.

I dropped my gaze to the ground and debated how I was going to get out of this yard. He was blocking the only exit. Nothing to do but brazen this out too.

He's not going to hurt me, I told myself. *I'll shoot him if he tries.*

I stepped down from the porch, head held high, not showing a trace of fear except perhaps with how tightly I gripped my purse. "I appreciate the heads-up. I'll be on my way then, if you'll excuse me."

When in doubt, choose manners. My mother would be so proud. Actually, she'd probably want to lock me up until I was fifty if she knew where I was.

He pushed off the gate, uncrossed his arms, and stepped toward me.

Good grief, he was even bigger up close. In my heels, I was nearly five eight, and I didn't think the top of my head came to his eye level. *Not important.* I stepped off the path, my heels sinking into the dry grass of the front yard as I attempted to get around him.

"You ain't leaving until I get a name from you." His hand shot out and wrapped around my arm.

I froze at the contact. Strange men didn't get to touch me. I waited for my skin to crawl . . . but it didn't. All I registered was the heat of his hand on my skin and the light grip that kept me from taking another step.

"My name isn't relevant," I said. It was time to retreat to the safety of my car, get home, and leave Trinity another voice mail to call me with a sternly worded reprimand.

"It's relevant as hell to me."

The deep timbre of his voice sent shivers up the arm he held, but these strangely weren't shivers of fear. My reaction surprised me, so I ignored it.

I tugged at my arm, but I couldn't free myself. "Let go. You wanted me out of your neighborhood, and I'm leaving."

"Give me your name, and you can walk right out that gate."

My tugging was getting me nowhere, and I wanted to be gone. In my head I labeled it a form of self-defense when I snapped out, "Valentina. Now let me go."

His touch was gone immediately, and the absence of the heat of his hand hit me.

"Valentina," he repeated. "Last name?"

"No way," I said.

"Don't need it anyway."

I said nothing, and I didn't look at him. I wouldn't look at him. And I absolutely wouldn't think about the change in his tone when he'd said my name. Nope. I wouldn't.

Keeping my gaze firmly glued to the cracked sidewalk as I walked, I reached for the latch. My fingers froze when he said, "This is my neighborhood. My world. You don't belong here. Don't come here again. You do, and you won't like the consequences. You get that, *Valentina*?"

I straightened my spine, and despite my vow, I turned to face him. "I don't plan on coming back. And as long as Trinity shows up at work tomorrow, I won't have to."

I stepped outside the gate and was pulling it closed when he dropped both palms on top of the chain link. "You're either fearless or stupid."

"Neither," I shot back, hackles rising. "I'm just worried about her."

I turned my back on him and walked to my car. Once I had my door open, I swung my head around toward him. I had no earthly idea what possessed me to ask the question, but I couldn't help it.

"All this hassle about my name, and you never even introduced yourself."

His lips quirked, but he didn't smile. Still, I thought it was humor I saw on his face. He was laughing at me. *Jerk*.

"Rix."

One syllable. That's all it took. Recognition slammed into me and I dove into my car, shut the door, and locked it.

Holy. Shit. That was Rix?

Pulling out of my parking spot, I couldn't help but stare out the window as I drove away.

He's the head of one of the biggest gangs in New Orleans?

I'd put him in the category of unapologetically bad, and I'd been right on the mark. *It's okay*, I told myself. *You'll never see him again.*

FIVE
VALENTINA

I drove directly home and left another voice mail for Trinity telling her to *call me, goddamn it.* After I'd stripped off the skirt and blouse I'd worn to the gallery today, I pulled my dark hair back into a messy bun and threw on a pair of leggings and a tank before covering it with an old dress shirt of my father's that was so worn from washing, his monogram was barely visible on the cuff any longer.

I had to paint.

I had no idea what, if any social commitments I might have tonight, but I didn't care. Everything could go to hell when the need to paint struck. It had been weeks since I'd picked up a brush, and even longer since I'd completed a single piece.

No one knew about my closely guarded hobby. Because if they knew, they'd ask me why I didn't show my own work at Noble Art. I was the owner, therefore I could do whatever I pleased.

The reason? While I had confidence in my ability to choose great artists and pieces to sell, I had no confidence in my own work. Instead, I held a piercing, blinding certainty that it was beyond terrible and not fit to be seen by human eyes other than

29

my own. I had no classical training, and those flaws I was so critical of in others' work while assessing its ability to sell were more than present in my own. But I didn't care because painting wasn't something I did for money or for show—it was all about the escape for me.

The night I was raped over ten years ago, my entire life had changed. One moment of bad judgment contaminated every day since like black paint tainted every color it touched.

I'd been torn apart on the stand by the defense attorneys, my reputation put on trial. Rape charges were ugly, and they were even uglier when your rapist was the son of a politician who had plenty to lose. I'd been barely twenty-two when it had happened, and I hadn't exactly been a choirgirl in college. At least the proceedings had been kept closed—again the benefit of the plaintiff and defendant being well-connected—and the general public never knew my humiliation.

I'd given up so many things after that. I was careful to keep any of the limited number of sexual partners I had completely off the radar, because of my hyperawareness of my reputation for the last decade. Instead of going out with friends and having fun, I'd locked myself away with my canvases. Painting had become my own personal salvation.

For years, I'd told myself I'd moved on, but I hadn't. I would have been living a normal life all these years if I'd really moved on rather than burying myself in work and paint.

I paused to take in the man I'd painted while the events of the day replayed in my head. Tall, broad-shouldered. His skin color strikingly similar to the man I'd met today. I dropped my brush and stepped back.

What the hell?

Painting him hadn't been a deliberate act, but it wasn't something I could deny had just happened. There he was. All rippling muscle and striking silver eyes.

The only things that were missing were the tattoos I didn't get a close enough look at to replicate.

But it was him. *Rix*.

His name didn't seem to fit him.

Stop, Valentina. Just stop. He's not important, he's not relevant, he shouldn't even exist to you.

I was just starting to believe the things I was telling myself when my phone vibrated from the side table where I'd left it. After quickly cleaning my hands and wiping them dry on a rag, I reached for it.

Two things struck me at the same time: I'd been painting for hours. It was after midnight. And the second was: *Trinity*.

I answered immediately. "Are you okay?"

Her voice, which I expected to be filled with excitement over what Rix had told me, was shaking when she spoke. "Can you come get me? I'm scared, V. Something's wrong here and I'm freaking out."

Protectiveness to rival a mama bear roared to life within me. "Baby girl, I'm coming for you. Just tell me where you are."

She rattled off an address, one that was almost the same as the one I'd already visited today, except for two transposed numbers. Apparently my memory sucked when I was sneaking peeks at a cop's computer screen.

"Is that Derrick's house?" I asked.

"Yeah, I'm in the bathroom. I just want to go home, but there are people downstairs and they're yelling, and I can't find Derrick. I don't know what to do. I tried to go out the back, but one of his friends wouldn't let me leave and told me to get out of the way."

I thought about the neighborhood she was in, and was happy someone didn't let her run out into the night by herself. I'd had no idea she'd been hanging out there the last few months, or I definitely would've had something to say about it.

She might only be my employee now, but I'd watched her grow up from awkward middle schooler to a bright and beautiful woman. I'd given her birthday and Christmas presents. I'd taken her prom dress shopping. I'd done all of the things a parent would have done that her grandmother was too old or too uninterested to do.

"It's okay, honey. I'll be right there."

I didn't bother changing except to toss off my smock and grab a light cotton zip-up hoodie. It was still humid and hot, but it was late and I wanted to be covered when I ventured back into the lion's den. Because this was the lion's den. It was Rix's world, and he'd made no bones about the fact that I didn't belong in it.

Well, dammit, I don't want to be back in it. But I had no choice.

My mind raced as I drove my Tesla back to the same street I'd parked on this afternoon, wondering how I'd flip-flopped the numbers of Derrick's address when I'd jotted them down. I could have circumvented my encounter with Rix altogether, but that didn't matter now. I just hoped I wasn't walking into another confrontation with him.

No lights were visible from the house I now assumed was Rix's. Good. He never needed to know I was here. In and out. Quick and quiet. Get my girl and go.

Every light was on in the run-down house two doors down, and cars with dark-tinted windows lined the street. It was the address she'd given me. I parked my car a few houses up and once again marshaled my courage. I'd texted Trinity when I was at a stop sign about a block away, but she still hadn't responded.

Did I wait or did I go? I waited for another minute. Still nothing. *Screw it.* I was going in so I could get out of here just as quickly.

With no plan other than to get my girl, I stepped over beer bottles and crushed cans to make my way up the front walk. The house was similar to Rix's but it hadn't been repaired. The steps were caving in, the screen door was falling off its hinges, and more blue paint had peeled off the house than stayed on.

I thought about knocking but didn't bother as the door flew open and two drunk girls stumbled out. Their mini skirts and tube tops revealed more than they left to the imagination, and their makeup was so dark and smoky, they'd almost assuredly look like raccoons in a few hours. But I could use them for information.

"Have you seen a girl named Trinity? She's got long, dark hair with a pink streak on the side, and she's about five seven."

One girl giggled but the other, seemingly a touch more sober than her friend, nodded. "Yeah. She's D-Rock's girl. I saw her in there."

Oh, thank God. A wave of relief rolled through me. This day was all going to be a bad memory tomorrow.

"Do you know where in there?" I asked.

The girl shook her head, and grabbed the top edge of her tube top before it slid down and caused a wardrobe malfunction. "Try D-Rock's room. It's in the back but it might be occupied, if you know what I mean."

She winked and grabbed the other girl's hand, and they tripped their way down the steps and the sidewalk to the street. They chatted as they lit their cigarettes, ignoring me completely.

Whatever Trinity had been worried about didn't seem to be troubling these girls at all, but still I entered the house with extreme caution—and my gun-packing purse tucked tight against my side.

Someone chose the moment I reached for the door handle to turn the music up to earsplitting levels. I pulled the door open, grateful the latch didn't come off in my hand, and stepped into a tiny entryway that connected to a living room and kitchen combination. The paneled hallway in front of me ran down the center of the house.

I got looks from people in both the kitchen and the living room, and I think a few catcalls, but I couldn't hear them over the music. One guy on the torn couch licked his lips and gave me a chin jerk, but I ignored him and made my way down the hall toward the back, where I hoped I'd find Trinity. I made it about five feet before someone—a very large someone—burst from a room and stumbled into me.

"Excuse me," I yelled, my voice getting lost in the noise.

The man, obviously drunk and about a hundred pounds heavier than me, jerked his head toward my voice. "You lookin' for me?"

What in the world? "Um, no. I'm actually looking for—"

"Don't care. I'm laying down claim on you."

He moved one arm and I tried to duck under it to escape, but all I did was get myself trapped against a big, sweaty body.

"Where you trying to go, baby? I'll take good care of you."

His words were slurred, but the sheer bulk of him pinned me to the wall. My mouth went dry and my fight-or-flight response kicked into high gear. I shoved at him with both hands, struggling to get away so I could reach into my purse for protection.

I will not let this happen again. My greatest fear, and I was trapped and helpless. He was immovable.

"Let me go!" I yelled. My voice was drowned out by the music as he reached a hand between us to grope at my chest.

Oh my God. No. No. No.

"You're a fighter. I like that."

Flashes of being held down by another man ripped through my brain, and I struggled harder. "Let go!" I screamed. His hot breath hit my ear, and the flashes of the past came stronger and faster.

"I like it when you scream. Gets me hard."

Heart hammering, static in my ears drowning out the sounds around me, I clawed at him frantically. Panic stole my breath, but still I threw elbows and twisted until my lungs burned, and all I could hear was his mocking laugh in my ears.

And then he was gone.

I tumbled to the floor, landing on my butt. Pain shot through my wrists as they caught the brunt of the impact. It was the pain that snapped me back to reality.

Wincing, I lifted my hands and reached for my purse, ready to defend myself against him, but a glance up in the direction of the man revealed an unlikely rescuer.

Rix.

Their voices were masked by the music, making it impossible to hear what they were yelling at each other, but Rix's face twisted into an angry expression as his fist flew. It connected with the man's jaw, and his knees bent as he crumpled to the floor. Out. Cold.

Holy shit.

The door to my right opened and a girl stumbled out. The bright light illuminated the pale yellow tile of a bathroom behind me, and I scuttled back into the room and slammed the door shut with my foot. I pushed up onto my knees, my hand shaking as I pushed in the flimsy button lock.

He'd told me not to come back.

Oh. Shit. Why was he here?

My brain flipped into survival mode and I scanned the room, looking for something to barricade the door. Nothing. Instead, I reached into my bag and wrapped my hand around the grip of my pistol and sagged against the water-stained wall, forcing the images of Jay out of my brain. Every time I thought

I was over it, something came back and yanked my past right up into my present.

I sucked in breath after breath, filling my lungs with oxygen as my heart slowed by degrees.

My present. *Trinity*. She might have called me from this very same bathroom, but she wasn't here.

I have to find her. Latching onto my sole purpose for coming here, I fought to gather myself. I couldn't stay locked inside. I had to go out, and when I did, I would have to face Rix.

I've got this.

I'm okay.

No, I don't. I'm screwed.

Someone banged on the bathroom door, jarring me from my thoughts. I slammed my head back against the wall in surprise. Thank God I had the presence of mind to keep my finger off the trigger.

The music died, and a voice came from outside the door.

"Let me in."

It was Rix.

Did I open the door? Aside from Trinity, he might be the only other possible ally I had in this house, no matter how unlikely. I was still debating whether to open the door when the button on the lock popped out and my choice ceased to matter.

Strangely enough, I didn't panic. Probably because I wasn't capable of panicking again so soon. Besides, now I had my hand wrapped around the grip of my pistol. If anyone tried to touch me, I'd shoot them.

The door swung open and Rix's tall frame and wide shoulders filled the doorway. His eyes were unreadable as he took me in, sitting on the bathroom floor, knees pulled up to my chest, one hand wrapped around my legs and the other hand buried in my purse.

He didn't ask me if I was okay. He didn't ask me what the hell I was doing there. I assumed he either knew or didn't care about the answers to those questions. Instead, all he said was, "He won't bother you again."

I thought of the man he'd knocked out with one punch. I couldn't be upset about it. If I could have, I would have done worse to him in that moment to protect myself.

It was a perfect reminder that I shouldn't even be here. As Rix had made perfectly clear this afternoon, this wasn't my world, and I probably shouldn't even know it existed. Trinity shouldn't be here either.

Rix's stare intensified, and he stepped inside the room and shut the door. The room seemed to shrink to half size, and I was hyperaware of his proximity to me.

"He hurt you?"

I mentally assessed myself. "No," I replied, shaking my head. "He didn't have a chance."

"He scared you."

Rix's words weren't a question. And nor should they be. Of course he'd freaking scared me. It would have scared anyone, even someone without my messed-up past. I could admit that without shame.

I nodded.

"He'll hurt for a week. If that ain't enough, you say the word, and I'll make him hurt longer."

I shook my head, trying to wrap my brain around what Rix had just said. Had he really just offered to hurt someone for me? The twisted side of my brain took strange comfort in that. He'd defended me.

Stilling my shaking hands, I babbled. "I'm fine. I guess I thought I was over it. Maybe I'll never be over it."

Rix's gaze sharpened on me. "Over what?"

Once again, my only reply was to shake my head.

37

"Over what, duchess?" The nickname caught my attention and drew me off the path that led down memory lane.

"Why would you call me that?"

"Answer my question first." He crossed his arms over his chest.

"A thing that happened years ago. It's fine. No big deal." Again, I sounded like I was babbling.

"You're talking about that politician's kid. The one you sent to prison. He fucked you up."

My eyes cut to his. "You know who I am." Shock colored my words and icy coldness spread through my limbs. He shouldn't know that.

"Didn't take me long to find out. And I'll call you whatever I want. You're back in my world. Thought we covered this already. You don't belong here."

I'd address his declaration another time, like when I wasn't cowering on a bathroom floor and needing to find my girl.

And enough cowering. Not in front of this man. No, since he was here, he was going to help me whether he wanted to or not.

"I'm looking for Trinity. She called me from here. Scared, said something was going on and people were fighting. She wanted to leave, but someone wouldn't let her."

A cold ruthlessness settled over Rix as soon as my words were out. "She called you and told you this?"

"Yes. Otherwise, trust me, there's no way I'd be here."

He held out a hand. "Come on." When I didn't reach for it, he snapped his fingers at me, his impatience clear. "Don't have time to wait around. Let's go."

"I am not a dog. Don't snap at me." As soon as the words were out, I remembered who I was talking to. The scary head of a gang. I needed to take more care before I spoke.

A deep rumble filled the tiled bathroom, and it took me a

second to realize it was laughter. Rix's whole body shook with it.

"Not many men would dare talk back to me like that, and sure as shit no woman would. You're something else. Now, come on. Let's go see if we can't find your girl."

I hesitated for another beat before I took his hand and he pulled me up. But he didn't let go when I was standing. Rix's fingers stayed wrapped around mine as he opened the bathroom door and led me out into the hallway.

I was stuck on how much bigger his hand was than mine. And how strong and capable his grip was. Heat shot through me as an image of his hands gripping my hips filtered through my brain. At the thought, I missed a step, stumbling into Rix's side.

He paused and looked to me. "Whoa. You sure you're okay?"

Forcing the image away, I nodded in response.

"All right then, let's do this."

Rix shoved open doors as we passed them—something that had seemed foolish and stupid to do by myself—and yet the house seemed so much less forbidding with him beside me.

That's when it hit me. I was with the most dangerous man in this house, maybe in this neighborhood, or even this city, my hand in his, and I felt . . . safe. My mind was trying to wrap itself around this foundation-rocking realization while I glanced in each room that we passed.

Each one was . . . occupied.

None of the girls were Trinity.

And he never let go of my hand.

He led us back down the hall and into the living room. He spotted someone and jerked his head. A younger guy came toward us.

"Where's D-Rock's woman?" Rix asked him.

He shrugged. "Don't know. Saw them both leave after we ran off those FiveNDown punks who showed their faces."

Rix stiffened, but his grip never changed. "You're telling me we had FNDs on this block and no one told me?"

The guy shuffled his feet and looked at the floor.

"What the fuck ain't you saying, Evo? Don't you dare think about covering for D-Rock if he had a damn thing to do with it."

The kid, Evo, dragged his gaze from the floor to Rix's face. "They were here selling some white. D-Rock wanted some, and they got pissed when he did three lines tryin' the product and then told them it was shit and to get out."

Rix's voice dropped even lower. "Those fucks were here sellin' blow on my block? They're done. D-Rock answers to me. Where'd he go?"

"Went to take his girl home."

I bit my lip. Even though I wasn't fluent in drug speak, I'd seen the movie *Blow* because . . . well, Johnny Depp. So I was 99.9% sure Evo was saying that Derrick did cocaine and then drove Trinity home, and that had to be totally unsafe.

My mama-bear-style rage burned off the remainder of the fear I was harboring. I really, really didn't like this D-Rock kid, and Trinity and I were going to have a come-to-Jesus talk tomorrow when she got to work. This was not the life that a girl who had a full ride to art school needed to be involved in.

"I need to make sure she got home okay," I said to Rix. "I have to go. Now."

Glancing at me, he nodded. "We'll make sure."

Looking back at Evo, he said, "You ever see the FNDs anywhere in this neighborhood, and I don't care who invited them or for what fucking reason, you call me ASAP. You don't wait two minutes, you don't pass go. You don't do a goddamned thing but call me so I can handle it. You get that?"

Evo nodded. "Got it, Rix. I got it."

"Good. Now, spread the word and make sure everyone hears it. Anyone has a problem, they take it up with me."

"Okay." Evo turned away and paused. "What about D-Rock?"

"Don't worry about it. He gets to deal with me too."

I didn't know what Rix was going to do to Trinity's boyfriend, but I also couldn't pretend I cared. I was on the *ship D-Rock to Timbuktu* committee from this day forward.

Evo headed back to the living room, and Rix tugged at my hand. "Let's go, duchess."

Wait, what?

"I'm good. I'm going." I pulled at his hand, but he didn't release his grip.

He shook his head. "*We* are going. Not you."

"Not necessary."

"I don't care what you think is necessary."

"Fine. Whatever. Let's go."

He studied me for a long moment before letting me pull him toward the door. I didn't know why he was still holding my hand, but it was like he didn't want to let me go.

Why doesn't he want to let me go?

The girls I'd seen when I was arriving at the house were leaning up against a dented gray Ford Focus, smoking and looking too young and too cool. When they caught sight of me and Rix, their demeanor changed instantly. Slouched shoulders instantly went back, hair was straightened, skirts were tugged up slightly, and boobs went out.

"Hey, Rix," one girl called. "We thought you might wanna party tonight."

I was clearly not labeled competition, because they didn't even acknowledge me.

Rix didn't even hesitate. "Go home."

The bolder one of the two, the one who'd stopped us, stepped forward. "We'd rather go home with you." She finally spared me a look. "Bet we'd be a lot more fun than her."

Rix's grip tightened on my hand. "I'm gonna say this once, so listen up. You stand around at parties, lookin' at every guy like you do, every one of 'em is gonna think you're a ho." He jerked his head toward me. "This right here, this is pure class. That ain't somethin' you can plaster on like all your fuckin' makeup and perfume. You can't put that on like your skanky-ass clothes or buy it like your fake tits. You got it or you don't. And you two, you don't. So go home. Close your legs. Find some goddamned self-respect."

I pressed my lips together to keep my jaw from dropping open. Had I heard him right? First, that was the most words I'd ever heard him speak. Second, he'd straight-out called them on their skankiness, and third, he'd complimented me in a big way.

His advice had actually been good advice. Actually, almost exactly what I would have wanted to tell those girls, in less blunt terms. Who would have thought that would come from Rix? Before now, I would have put my money on him taking them up on their offer. What guy wouldn't?

I watched him out of the corner of my eye, wondering if there was more to him than I'd thought.

The girls' pale shoulders slumped again, but they didn't say another word as we walked to my car. Honestly, what could they say?

"Keys, duchess." Rix held out the hand that wasn't laced with mine.

I jerked my head up to meet his gaze. "What?"

"Keys. I'm driving."

I looked from him to my Tesla. "But it's my car."

"And I'm not the kind of man who lets a woman drive me around."

A chunk of the points I'd just awarded him in my brain slid away. "Are you serious? That's ridiculous."

He walked me around to the passenger door before he responded.

"You ever take tactical driving lessons? You know evasive maneuvers and defensive driving techniques? The kind that keep people safe in fucked-up situations?"

The question stumped me. "Excuse me?"

"I'll take that as a no. Now, give me the keys and get in."

Safe. The word echoed in my brain.

He didn't even know me, but he was concerned about my safety. And with him, I felt safe, even though he scared the hell out of me. How was that even possible?

Because he's already defended you. Rescued you. And he might be a scary motherfucker, but apparently he's on your side.

I reached into my purse and pulled out the keys. "Okay. You can drive. Just . . . be nice to my car."

The door handles had already popped out when I'd gotten close with the key, and Rix pulled open the passenger side for me. As I climbed in, he said, "Like I'd hurt this car." With a ghost of a smile, he added, "Been dying to drive it."

"What—" He shut the door before I could finish, but when he climbed in the driver's side, I continued. "How much of your speech was true, and how much was you just wanting to drive because you like my car?"

Rix's expression turned serious again. "Every damn thing I've said to you is fucking true, but it doesn't mean you should ever trust me."

The man was bluntly honest, and I couldn't help but respect it. If I had to guess one thing about Rix, I'd be willing to put my money on always knowing where I stood with him, despite his warning. Not that I needed to know where I stood with him, because as soon as I knew Trinity was safe, I'd never see him again.

After I pointed out a few oddities of driving a Tesla, Rix was cruising along the streets of New Orleans toward Trinity's grandma's house. I'd texted her again, but still no answer. She'd better be home, asleep, or I was going to lose my ever-loving mind.

A yawn escaped my mouth, and I quickly reached up a hand to cover it.

"Long day?" Rix asked, glancing over at me.

"Aren't they all?"

"This shit with your girl's got you all off-balance."

His insightful comment surprised me. "Why do you say that?"

"Because I can't imagine you'd run out of the house with paint on your face for any other reason."

My hand flew to my cheek, and the crusty dust of paint met my fingers. *Well, hell.*

"Didn't figure you'd be the type to paint your own walls."

"I wasn't painting walls," I said, instantly wondering why I'd corrected him. My painting wasn't something I talked about. With anyone. Ever.

Rix's silver eyes lit with understanding, and I knew he put it together. "You've got that fancy gallery. You sell your own shit there too?"

"I don't sell my stuff at all. It's just a hobby. Something I do when I'm bored."

The explanation lay like dried paint on my tongue, hard to get out and bad-tasting. Painting for me wasn't just a hobby. There had been days when it was all that saved me from the darkness.

"Fancy woman, fancy hobby. No surprise there." Rix's eyes cut back to me when he slowed at a red light. "The surprise is that I'm finding I've got a strong taste for fancy these days."

Wait, did he mean . . . ? He wasn't interested in me, was he?

I didn't know how to reply, and the flashing red and blue lights ahead of us meant that I didn't have to.

"Oh my God."

The driver's side of a dark sedan had mostly been crushed inward by an older SUV, and a telephone pole had cracked in half and landed on the roof of both cars. Lights from police cruisers, fire trucks, and two ambulances lit up the dark night.

"Fuck," Rix bit out. He slowed the car to a complete stop and turned toward me. "I need you to hold it together."

My concern over the accident screamed toward panic, and my stomach dipped to the floor. "Wha—why? Is that—"

"The Impala is D-Rock's."

My nails bit into my clenched fists as I stared into Rix's silver eyes. "And the SUV?"

"All you need to know is this wasn't an accident."

I swallowed, my mouth already dry as tremors racked my body.

"Oh my God. Holy shit," I murmured, looking back at the mess of twisted metal. Grabbing the door handle, I yanked at it.

Locked, it's locked. Unlock it, and find Trinity. She's okay. She has to be okay.

"Valentina," Rix snapped, reaching across the car to wrap his hand around my jaw and turn me to face him. "Hold it together. You walk up there flipping the fuck out, it ain't gonna help your girl. We'll find her, make sure she's safe. The impact wasn't on her side. Now, open the door, pull it together, and go talk to whoever is on the scene who will give you answers."

I nodded, my head bobbing up and down. "Okay. Okay. Let me go."

Rix's grip tightened. "Calm. The fuck. Down."

I swallowed again, took another deep breath, and released it. "Okay. I'm good. I swear."

He nodded. "I'm taking your car. I'll be back in ten. Give me your phone so I can give you my number. You text me as soon as you find out anything, and if she's at the hospital, I'll get you there."

"Okay," I repeated.

"You walked up to me and gave me shit like no one else would dare. You can hold it together for your girl." When I nodded again, his thumb brushed over my cheek. "Good. Phone."

His hand dropped away, and the softness that had been in his eyes faded as I handed over my phone and he added his contact info. I was practically vibrating in my seat, holding back the urge to rip open the door, when he did something else and I heard a buzz from his pocket.

"I got your number now. I'll be in touch. Go find out what you can."

"Okay." When had my vocabulary shrunk to that single word?

He handed the phone back and I turned for the door. Rix's hand shot out and wrapped around the back of my head, pulling my face toward him as he leaned in. Before I understood his intent, his lips descended on mine for a hard, quick kiss. He pulled away abruptly.

"You got this."

All I could do was nod again because my vocabulary was nonexistent. *Rix kissed me. What kind of alternate universe am I living in?*

As soon as he released me, I was out of the car, practically running for the yellow police tape stretched across the road. When I made it there and an officer stopped me, I glanced back and Rix was already gone. My hands shook, and I could still feel the pressure of his lips on mine.

He kissed me. I gave myself a mental slap. *Forget about it, Valentina. Not important.* I pulled myself together and turned to the cop guarding the police line.

It took ten minutes of begging for information before he threatened to throw me in the back of a squad car, complete with handcuffs as accessories.

"You don't understand. Her grandmother is elderly, and I'm the only person out here looking for her. I know she was in that car."

"Ma'am, you need to leave before I make you leave."

Cops were quickly falling down my list of people who were useful in any way.

"Jones, give me a report." The familiar voice came from behind me. Both Officer Jones and I spun around to see Detective Hennessy slamming the door of a dark four-door sedan. He walked toward us.

"I don't think this is your—" the younger officer started.

"I have reason to believe this is connected to my ongoing investigation. Give me a report."

Jones looked at me and then at Hennessy, who had stopped next to me. "If you'll come over here, sir."

"Right here is fine."

Was Hennessy trying to help me again?

The young officer looked at me and then shrugged. "Two-car collision, only one victim on the scene when we got here— the driver of the Impala. He's been taken to a nearby hospital."

"What about the passenger in the Impala?" I demanded.

Jones didn't answer the question until Hennessy repeated it. With a huff, he replied, "Passenger door was open, purse on the ground. No sign of the passenger. We figure the female fled the scene."

"Did you get an ID from the purse?" Hennessy asked.

"Someone else did. I didn't see the name."

"Go get it, now." Hennessy's tone was authoritative, brooking no refusal.

Jones, looking pissed as hell, stomped off in the direction of the other uniformed officers at the scene. Hennessy took in my attire and looked around. His gaze landed on something, and I turned.

It was my car, parked across the street in a parking lot.

"You just happened to be out driving tonight and saw an accident, and thought it might be the girl you were looking for the other day?"

I cobbled together the best explanation I could under the circumstances, and because I was a terrible liar, I stuck with as much of the truth as I could.

"Trinity got in contact with me, but she was at a party and needed a ride home. I went to pick her up, but someone had already given her a ride." Pointing at the crushed car, I sucked in a ragged breath. "That was her ride home." The words came out on a sob.

"Jones said only the driver was on the scene, so she could've gotten scared and run."

I shook my head. "She wouldn't have left him. He's her boyfriend. She's eighteen and head over heels for the guy."

"D-Rock," Hennessy said, pulling the name from his memory.

"Yes."

"I don't even want to know about the party you went to get her at, do I?"

"No, probably not," I admitted.

Jones came back, holding up a license. "Trinity Frances Rodgers."

"Where is she?" I whispered, voice shaking.

"We'll find her," Hennessy said. "Jones, call all the hospitals to make sure some passerby didn't take her to one."

Once again, Jones looked less than pleased. "I'm on duty. I don't have time for that."

"While you're standing around, you can make phone calls. Let me know immediately if you get any leads." Hennessy turned his attention back to me. "You need to go home, Valentina. Wait for news. There's nothing you can do here."

His words were like jabs to the gut. "But—"

"Go home. I'll call you when we have something to tell you."

"She's a good kid. I swear. And she's really important to me."

"I'll do what I can to find her." He laid a hand on my shoulder. "You need to stand down. This isn't a joke. Let's go. I'll walk you to your car."

I blanked, thinking of Rix waiting in my car. Although I wasn't entirely sure if he was or not, but I wasn't going to take the chance and lead Hennessy right over to it. That would end in way too many questions I didn't have answers for.

"Thanks, but it's just across the street. I can make it there myself. And I know I need to be smart, but sometimes your own safety isn't as important as the person you're worried about. Trinity's a good kid. She just got herself caught up in the wrong crowd."

"She's not a kid, Valentina. She's eighteen years old. You can't protect her from her own decisions. How's she going to learn?"

I glanced toward my car again, wondering if Rix was inside and what he'd found out. "I'm not debating this with you." Turning my gaze back to Hennessy for a beat, I forced a smile. "Thank you for your help. If you hear anything . . ."

"I've got your number."

I nodded before turning and checking for traffic. I crossed the street to where my Tesla was parked, and the passenger side door popped open. That answered my question about Rix.

Before I climbed inside, I peeked over my shoulder to see if Hennessy was watching.

He was.

I hoped he realized it was none of his business who was driving my car, and that the tinted windows would prevent him from ever finding out.

When I climbed inside, Rix's expression was unreadable. I didn't wait for his prompt before I started rambling.

"They don't know where she is. Her purse was there, but she was gone when the first responders arrived. I don't even know what to think. They're going to call the other hospitals and make sure she wasn't picked up by some Good Samaritan and taken there. I need to check her house still, but I don't want to wake her grandmother this late."

Rix stayed quiet through all of this, but when I paused to take a breath, he held up a hand. Whatever else I was going to say fell away.

"I'm gonna give it to you straight, because I don't think you'd appreciate me dickin' you around on something this important."

My heart hammered against my chest in anticipation of whatever bad news he was about to relay. "What? What do you know?"

"Waiting on confirmation, but best we can figure, the FNDs wrecked on purpose, and when D-Rock was pinned too bad to get out, they grabbed your girl instead. I called a meet and issued a warning that the girl they took belongs to my crew, and is not to be touched."

"Oh my God." Cold chills ghosted over my skin. "Are you serious?"

I'd thought of dozens of disastrous things that could have befallen Trinity during those hours I couldn't find her and the police wouldn't take my missing person's report, but not a single one of the possibilities I'd considered were as scary as being kidnapped by some rival gang. Probably because I hadn't known gangs were something I needed to worry about.

I covered my face with both hands. *This isn't my life. How is this happening?*

"Is she okay?"

Rix pulled my shaking hands away from my face. "I'll get her back. No one is fucking stupid enough to hurt her now that I've laid claim."

I squeezed my eyes shut, wanting to block out the unreality of this moment. But blocking it out wasn't going to help. I opened my eyes and stared at him.

"I don't know what to do."

Rix squeezed my hands before releasing them, straightening in his seat and shifting the car into gear. "You're gonna go home, go to bed, and wait for word from me tomorrow morning. That's what you're gonna do."

"Tomorrow morning?" But I wanted him to go rush in and save her *tonight*.

"Meet is set for ten a.m. In the meantime, they won't touch her."

"How can you be sure?" I asked, not willing to leave Trinity's safety to chance.

Rix's answer was blunt. "Because they know they'll all be dead if they do."

His words didn't scare me. I didn't care that he'd threatened to kill people. I didn't care about anything except the fact that he was willing to do whatever was necessary to keep her safe.

"Then take me home so I can get on with the waiting. There's no way I'll sleep tonight."

He didn't respond as he drove to Saint Charles Avenue toward my house before slowing at my driveway. My gate opened automatically as my car approached it, and I hit the button for the garage door.

"How do you know where I live?" I asked.

"Told you it didn't take me long to get all the info on you. And your address is on your car registration."

When I shot him a sideways look for riffling through my glove box, he shrugged. "What? You talked to that cop forever."

"You can park it inside."

He pulled into the garage and turned off the car. "Nice digs."

"Thank you."

"Fancy as fuck, aren't you, duchess?"

How did I answer that? I was pretty sure *fancy as fuck* was a relative term.

"I don't know if fancy is the word. I inherited the house from my great-aunt. I spent a lot of time here as a kid, so it has a lot of great memories." I waited for some other judgment on my lifestyle, but none came.

He reached for the door handle and glanced over at me. "No point in you staying up the rest of the night. You need sleep."

Yeah, I'll get right on that, I thought as he climbed out of the car.

Gathering my purse from the floor, I reached for my own door handle, but the passenger door swung open before I could touch it.

He's opening my door for me? Who is this guy?

Rix offered a hand to pull me out of the low-slung car. "Come on. You need to get inside, and I've got a ride coming to get me."

I jerked my hand back in surprise. "You've got a ride

coming *here*?" Did I want more gang members knowing where I lived?

Rix's eyes narrowed, taking my meaning clearly. "Not here. A couple blocks toward the Quarter. Don't worry, duchess. I don't want anyone to know I'm fucking fascinated with you either."

My mouth fell open at the backhanded compliment, but Rix was done wasting time. He pulled me out of the car and led me to the side door of the garage that led into an enclosed portico connected to the house. The garage slid shut as I pressed the button on the wall, and Rix pushed open the door.

He was fascinated with me? How did I respond to that?

Apparently Rix wasn't waiting for a response, though, because he was already opening the door in the portico that led out front.

With one foot out, he turned and looked at me. "Get some sleep. I'll call or text if I hear anything." He shut the door and was gone.

I wandered from room to room, my house feeling more empty than it ever had before. I liked living alone, and normally enjoyed the solitude. When you lived alone, there was no one questioning why you were painting in the middle of the night, or working on financials on Friday at eight o'clock when everyone else was doing something fun to celebrate the weekend.

But tonight, I wasn't loving being alone. Worry for Trinity stalked me as I wandered, and the only thing I could do to stem the thoughts that spiraled out of control was go back to my studio, turn on my music, and start mixing my paints.

I painted furiously. Canvas after canvas, until my eyes

burned and my back ached. I blinked against the grittiness and looked out the window into the blinding orange and pink of the sunrise.

Crap. Didn't plan on that.

Instantly I was reminded that Rix had told me to sleep. I guess it was a good thing I didn't take my orders from him. Stretching my neck from side to side, I knew today would be hellishly long, and not even mostly because of the lack of sleep —no, because of the lack of Trinity.

No call or text from Rix had to mean he'd learned nothing. But he would bring her home safe. He had to.

When had I started trusting him? The question rolled through my brain as I cleaned my brushes and laid them out to dry.

He makes you feel safe. When has that ever happened before?

Never.

SIX

VALENTINA

I'd heard nothing from Rix all day. I sold paintings to customers and checked my phone every few minutes, just to make sure it hadn't mysteriously turned off or something. But no, it was functioning normally, and Rix still hadn't contacted me.

My finger hovered over the contact he'd added in my phone, but I didn't call. Calling was too intimate. A text, maybe? This was the debate I'd been having with myself for hours.

I couldn't take it any longer. I had to know something.

VALENTINA: *Any news? Please say you have news.*
VALENTINA: *This is Valentina, by the way. Hi.*

I fired off the messages without thinking, and then when I read them, I felt like a moron. *God*, it was probably a good thing I'd never, ever try sexting because I'd probably be the absolute worst at that too.

I stared at my phone for a full two minutes—based on the Salvador Dali melting clock ticking away on my desk—and got no response. Gritting my teeth, I tossed the phone down on the blotter and walked away.

Two feet. That's as far as I got before it buzzed.

I spun around and grabbed it like it might grow legs and walk away before I could read the response.

RIX: No.

VALENTINA: Give me something. Anything. Where is she?

RIX: I'm coming to you.

What? He was coming here? *Shit.*

I glanced at the clock again. It was too early for me to close up shop and go home, so he had to be coming here. But I didn't have time to think about anything further, or about what it might be like to have Rix in my gallery, because the repaired chime sounded and the man himself walked through the front door.

I had to do a double-take. Instead of worn jeans and a T-shirt, today he was wearing dark jeans and a pale blue button-down shirt. None of the ink on his arms was visible, and he looked like any customer that might walk into my gallery—and with his broad shoulders filling out the shirt to perfection, he looked better than most.

That's when it occurred to me why he looked familiar. The man could have been a double for Shemar Moore. I was standing there, silent and slack-jawed, most likely, as I came to this realization.

Rix raised his chin at me. "If it had taken you any longer to work up the guts to text me, you wouldn't have needed to."

Snapping back to reality, I demanded, "Is Trinity okay? Where is she?"

"I've been given assurances that she's fine. No one will touch her."

His response didn't allay my concern. "What do you mean, given assurances? Why didn't you get her back?"

Rix said nothing, but turned and walked toward the door.

"Don't leave, dammit. I'm not done with you." Once again, I'd forgotten who I was talking to.

He flipped the OPEN sign to CLOSED and locked the door before stalking toward me, his eyes never leaving mine. "Ain't going nowhere, duchess. Because it seems I gotta explain some shit to you." Even dressed as he was, Rix was still every bit as dangerous as he had appeared before.

I walked backward until my butt bumped into my desk. "Explain what?"

"That I don't take orders from you." He stopped a foot away from me.

What was he going to do? We were in full view of the windows on Royal Street. I derived a certain sense of safety in that fact, and kept pushing him.

"You said you were getting her back."

He gave me a nod. "And I am. But your timetable doesn't matter in my world. I do this my way."

"Last night you said—"

"That I'd get her back, and I will."

"What are you waiting for? A full moon? A solar eclipse? A sign from the heavens? There's no reason to wait." I realized I sounded ridiculous but I didn't care.

"You don't need to know why, you just need to wait."

"But they could be hurting her!" My patience was gone. Done. Out the window.

"They won't fucking touch her. And you're gonna go on

about your business, just like you normally would. Nothin' has changed in your world. You don't know a thing about this, and no one else knows about this."

"Are you crazy?"

Rix crossed his arms. "You're gonna do exactly what I told you, because anything else is gonna put your girl in more danger. You go to the cops and it's all over."

Talk about a leap of faith. "You're serious." I met his intense silver stare. "You really expect me to trust that you have it under control, and go on about my routine?"

"Yes."

"And pretend nothing is wrong?"

"Yes."

He was implacable. That was the only word for it.

"I can't."

"You don't have a choice."

"What about updates? Are you going to make me wait and wonder?"

"In person only. Anything else isn't a good idea."

Both my eyebrows shot up. "Paranoid much?"

"I call it smart."

"How long? At least tell me that. How long is it going to take?"

Rix's jaw tensed before he answered. "As long as it takes. I'm working it from more than one angle. She'll be fine. I give you my word."

The last words he spoke were so low and solemn that I knew he was deadly serious. Rix had just given his vow to return Trinity safely. In this situation, the only thing I could do was hope that his threats were scarier than the other guys. I didn't know how to navigate this world, but something told me that having Rix on my side was like having a ringer on your team.

"Fine."

He watched me, as if gauging the sincerity of my answer.

I squeezed my hands together to avoid fidgeting. For a moment, I wondered what it would take for Rix to lose a measure of that intensity, and laugh and smile easily.

None of my business, I reminded myself, but at the same time, his words from last night echoed through my brain. *"I don't want anyone to know that I'm fucking fascinated with you either."*

I needed to stop myself before I tumbled down the same rabbit hole. This man was dangerous. *And yet, strangely, I trust him.*

It didn't matter. All that mattered was getting Trinity back.

Rix, obviously not waging the same mental war I was, stepped back. "Take care, duchess. I'll be around." He strode toward the door without pausing to even look back.

"That's it?"

Rix stopped, steps from the door, and turned. "You want more from me?"

It was a loaded question. I must have looked like a deer caught in headlights.

Words, Valentina. You need words here. Say something. Anything.

"I, uh . . . I just . . ."

Oh hell, he's moving again. Toward me.

Rix stopped only inches away this time. "You think you can handle more, duchess?"

Handle more what? That was the question. More of him? God help me, but the idea was so much more tempting than it should have been.

He lifted his hand, moving it slowly toward my face, as if waiting for me to bolt. But I didn't bolt. I didn't *want* to bolt.

Because even though the air had shifted in the room from

all business to something decidedly not businesslike, I still felt safe. And that meant everything.

When his thumb finally smoothed across my cheekbone and his palm cupped the side of my face, he spoke. "I'm not gonna lie and say I don't want more. A fuck of a lot more. But you aren't ready yet. I know it, and you know it. But that don't mean I don't want it. I'll be back, duchess. We settle this business, and then we'll figure out the rest."

"Okay," I whispered.

A hint of a smile played around the corners of his mouth, but Rix didn't let it free. He dropped his hand, but only for as long as it took to pull me close and bury it in my hair. There was no hesitation, no asking for permission, before his lips took mine.

I gasped against his mouth and Rix shifted, his tongue sliding between my lips as he deepened the kiss. With his free hand, he palmed my ass and rocked his erection into me.

Heat flashed through me, violent and needy. My hands bunched in his shirt as my gasp turned to a quiet moan. My panties were soaked when he finally pulled away.

His silver eyes flashed with untamed desire, and he said only one word before heading for the door, unlocking it, and letting himself out.

"More."

SEVEN

VALENTINA

Trying to go about my life and pretend like nothing was wrong was nearly impossible. Actually, skip the nearly, it was impossible. Still, I attempted it.

After I flipped the OPEN sign to CLOSED again at the end of the day—and purposely avoided thinking about Rix doing the same thing earlier—I contemplated my choices. Go home and wander my empty house, worrying about Trinity, or go find a distraction.

A distraction in the form of good food won out.

I made it a point to go out to dinner alone often. Some might think it odd, but I was a single woman who loved all the amazing food New Orleans had to offer, and not just out of a take-out container. Tonight, I settled on oysters.

Slipping into Royal House, my favorite oyster bar in the city, which happened to be conveniently located near my gallery, I asked the maître d' for a table for one. There was no shame in it. I didn't care that most everyone else was paired off or in large groups. Okay, so I did have a tiny twinge of longing to be one half of a couple occasionally—especially, like tonight, when I needed a distraction.

As a hostess led me through the restaurant, I saw a familiar face at the next table over. *Detective Hennessy.*

I lowered myself into my chair and nodded at him.

"Ms. Noble," he said. "Fancy seeing you here."

"Detective." His presence didn't surprise me. He worked out of the precinct in the Quarter, and I'd seen him more than once on the street.

He gestured to the empty seat across from him. "Care to join me? Oysters would go down better across from a beautiful woman."

His compliment stunned me into an awkward silence, and I couldn't come up with an excuse quickly enough to decline gracefully. Although, did I really want to decline? Maybe he was the distraction I needed tonight.

"Um, sure, I guess. That'd be fine."

My even more awkward acceptance of his invitation hung between us as I stood and moved to his table. Things swirled further down the path of awkwardness when he rose to pull out my chair and seated me in it. How did I go from intending to eat oysters and distract myself to feeling like I was sort of on a date?

"You didn't call today and I haven't heard a thing about the wreck, so I'm assuming you found your employee?" he asked.

Crap. So much for forgetting for even a few minutes.

Rix's warning played through my mind. *No cops.* But I was also a terrible liar. Yet technically, the detective's question was whether I'd found Trinity, and I knew where she was now. It just wasn't where either she or I wanted her to be.

I decided to say as little as possible, and went with a nod.

Where was a server when I needed one to order a drink? I glanced over my shoulder, but didn't see one in the vicinity. Time to change the subject.

"So, is this one of your usual haunts?" I asked.

Hennessy smiled and leaned back in his chair, lifting his glass to his lips. He studied me for a moment before answering. "It's close, the food's damn good, and I like the atmosphere. Especially tonight."

"Why tonight?" I smiled back, relaxing into my own chair.

"Isn't it obvious, Valentina?"

My cheeks heated when I realized I'd walked right into that one. That's when it occurred to me what was different about tonight. He wasn't treating me like a victim. He wasn't handling me with kid gloves the way he had during every interview and subsequent meeting. Hennessy was treating me like a woman he was interested in.

The realization shifted everything in my head, and the distraction I'd so desperately needed presented itself. In a moment, I went from sitting across the table from a cop to ordering a drink with a man. A man who I could acknowledge was incredibly attractive. Around six feet tall, solidly built, with muscles that you couldn't get sitting behind a desk all day, and short, messy blondish-brown hair that used to be buzzed when I'd first met him. Before I would have said his most striking feature was his bright green eyes, but tonight I was shocked to see tattoos winding up his forearms and disappearing under his rolled-up shirtsleeves. How had I never noticed those before?

And when did I start seeing men as *men* again and not potential monsters?

I'd been hyperaware of Rix as well, and couldn't help comparing the men in my mind. Rix's skin was a few shades darker and also marked with ink, his eyes silver and intense, and then there was the fact that he'd given me his word that he'd get Trinity home safe.

Yanking myself away from the thoughts of Rix, I refocused on Hennessy across the table. He did make for a heck of a distraction. *And I still have no idea what his first name is.*

Grabbing my napkin and shaking it out, I waited for a break in our conversation about what type of oysters we planned to order.

"I feel stupid asking this question after so long, but what exactly is your first name? I can't believe I don't know it. I'm assuming it's not Detective."

Hennessy laughed, the sound deep and rich and . . . sexy, if I was being honest. When he finished, he smiled at me and answered, "Rhett. My mother has always been a junkie for the classics."

Rhett Hennessy. Yep, it was a good name.

"Do you have siblings?"

Rhett nodded and the ease in his features vanished. "Two brothers, one older and one younger. I had another brother, the oldest of all of us, but he was killed in the line of duty last year. He was on the force too."

"I'm so sorry. That's terrible," I said instantly, wishing I hadn't unknowingly brought up such a painful subject.

"It happens. We've got a lot of cops in the family, and we all knew the risks when we signed on for the job. My dad's retired from the NOPD. My mom had to deal with worrying about her husband on a daily basis for close to thirty years, and now she's still worrying about her sons."

I didn't know if I should offer more condolences or let him steer the conversation away from their tragedy, but I opted to go with the flow.

"Wow. Family tradition, huh?"

"You could say that. I just never wanted to be anything else. I always knew I'd wear a badge."

I picked up my water and sipped. "Both of your other brothers are cops too?"

He shook his head. "Just the older one, but he's living the cushy life on the force in Colorado at Vail. My younger brother decided to make his own way. He was military, and now no one has a clue what he does. He's down in Central America some-where, and he checks in every couple of months to let us know he's alive."

"Wow. That's gotta be . . . hard. Not knowing where he is and if he's okay."

Rhett shrugged and reached for his own drink. Whiskey, neat. "It is what it is. After he served in Afghanistan, he didn't have any desire to come back to the States and re-assimilate into civilian life. He's never gotten along with our dad, so the force wasn't for him. I don't ask questions when it comes to him because there are some things I don't need to know."

"I can't imagine what it's like to be so far away from family, though. My parents are less than a mile away, and while I acknowledge that sometimes it isn't far enough, I do love having them close. I'm an only child, so I can't imagine leaving New Orleans."

Rhett's smile eased again. "I've got no plans to leave this town either. It's home."

"So you like what you do?" I was always fascinated by the answer to that question.

He gave a short nod and turned the question around on me. "Do you? Running a gallery must be . . . interesting."

I laughed. There were plenty of people who weren't into art. I got it. I mean, I wasn't into a lot of things.

"It is, actually. Luckily there are plenty of people here who love the new artists I'm always trying to find, and I've devel-oped a reputation for the gallery as one that is constantly evolving and shifting with the cutting edge of the art world."

"I can't say I know a thing about that, but your eyes light up when you talk about it. Looks good on you."

"Are you flirting with me, Rhett Hennessy?" My tone was

also alarmingly flirtatious, and I wasn't sure what in the world I was doing.

Rhett's gaze turned serious. "I've wanted to flirt with you for years, Valentina, but you weren't ready. I think you're ready now."

Even I could feel my eyes widen at his words. How did I miss that? And what did I think about it?

"Years?"

His smile was wry. "Told you, you weren't ready. But I'm calling tonight our test-run date. Which means I'm buying you dinner and seeing you home."

His assertiveness, a quality I'd never really noticed before, surprised me. "You are?"

"Yeah. There's one thing I learned from losing my brother —life is too short not to take chances. I've waited long enough to take this one, and I'm not waiting any longer."

I didn't know how to respond to that. I wasn't prepared for this and was clueless about how to react. "Um. Okay?"

"Don't worry, we'll take it slow. Starting with dinner again later this week. I'll pick you up at your door, bring you flowers, and impress you with my ability to carry on a conversation and drive a stick. Maybe stage a flat tire so you can watch me change it with my shirt off and realize I might be useful in more ways than one to have around."

I couldn't help but laugh with a hint of embarrassment at his words and the attractive grin stretching across his face. This guy—Rhett Hennessy—was completely new to me. He was charming. And all man.

The rest of dinner passed in a blur of laughter, good conversation, and delicious food. When we left the restaurant, Rhett walked me back down the street to where I'd parked near the gallery, and followed me home in his car. He slammed his door as I climbed out of the Tesla.

"You're really taking this whole test-run date thing seriously, aren't you?" I said as I met him in front of my garage and the door slid closed.

Rhett reached for my hand and closed his around it before leading me up the walk to my front door. Normally I would have entered through the portico, but I wasn't going to contradict his gentlemanly gesture. I'd had few enough of those in my life to be completely charmed by the effort.

We paused at the front door, my keys in my hand, and I had that moment of wondering how seriously he was taking this test run. Was he going to try to kiss me? Did I want him to?

Rhett answered the question without me having to wonder for very long. "I'm not going to kiss you. Yet." But he moved in closer anyway, and my gaze locked with his. "Well, maybe that's a lie." And his lips lowered . . . to my forehead. Rhett stepped back and smiled, and I couldn't deny it—the man was incredibly attractive. "I wanted to make that kiss count, but I'm gonna let you get used to me first. I'll drop by the gallery, and we can work out our next date."

I couldn't help but smile back, and turned to my door as he headed toward his car. How in the world did this happen? A date . . . with the guy I was certain would never see me as anything but a victim?

Maybe things do change.

I slid my key into the lock and twisted, pushing the door open at the same time. Stepping into my darkened foyer, I pushed the door shut and locked it before deactivating the alarm and then setting it again immediately. I didn't take chances with my safety.

I flipped on the foyer light, but nothing happened. The bulb must have burned out. *Strange*.

I moved up the stairs, a niggle of apprehension stalking

each step. I flipped on every light as I went, but nothing hid in the shadows.

Working through my nightly routine, I stripped off my skirt and blouse and hung up what was still clean, tossing the rest in the laundry hamper. Making my way to the bathroom, I turned on the sink and reached for my face wash.

And then a shadow moved in my bedroom.

What the hell?

My heart kicked up as I pushed the door the rest of the way open. My gun was in my purse on my dresser. The shadow moved again. I reached for my phone on the counter, hands shaking as I punched in my pass code.

"I wouldn't do that if I were you." The deep voice was familiar.

I froze when he came into view, leaning against the footboard of my bed, arms crossed nonchalantly.

"What in the ever-loving *hell* are you doing in my house?" The words came out on heaved breaths. I slapped a hand over my chest. "You almost gave me a freaking heart attack."

I glanced down when my palm met skin and lunged for the door, intent on slamming it shut. Rix moved faster than I could, shoving a foot between the door and frame before it could close.

What is he doing? Fear clawed up inside me.

"Ain't polite to slam the door when we're having a conversation," he drawled, his gaze drinking me in from head to toe.

My lacy black bra and panties left just enough to the imagination to be sexy without being prudish. And Rix did not need to be seeing them. I reached up and yanked my robe off the back of the door, shoved my arms through the sleeves, and knotted the belt tighter than I'd ever knotted it before.

"What the hell are you doing here?"

Rix pressed a hand on the door to the bathroom, pushing it open all the way.

"I told you not to talk to the cops. So, what the hell was that?" He jerked his head to the front of the house.

"None of your business."

His silver eyes flashed molten. "I don't share."

My mouth dropped open at his ridiculous statement. "Excuse me? I don't even know how to respond to that. Oh, wait. How about *I'm not yours*. And how the hell did you get into my house? That's breaking and entering and illegal."

His chuckle was dark as he continued to stare at me, completely ignoring the most pertinent questions. "You are, you just don't realize it. And here I was trying to give you time to get used to the idea, and you're out on a date with a cop."

I backed up until I hit the glass block wall of my shower. "Get used to what idea?" My heart thundered anew, but this time, it wasn't fear causing the spike in my blood pressure.

Rix crossed into the bathroom, stalking me until he pressed his palms against the glass on either side of my head. And yet, I didn't feel trapped. I felt . . . alive.

"You walked into my world, totally clueless it even existed. You stood your ground, never giving up on finding your girl, even when you should've been hoppin' in your fancy car and runnin' away home."

I swallowed, unsure where he was going with this. "These are all things I know."

"But what you don't know is I've never met a woman like you. High class, but worrying about someone who isn't even yours to worry over. Fascinating as fuck. I'm guessing the cop sees the same thing I do. So I'm gonna say this once more so you understand. I don't share. There's something happenin' between us, and we're gonna see how it plays out. I was gonna wait, but you just pushed the timeline with your move."

I hadn't taken him seriously today when he'd told me that we were going to see what could happen between us.

"Don't I get a say?"

Rix shook his head slowly. "You're as rare as a Picasso at a fucking flea market, to put it in terms you understand. And when a man comes across something that rare, he ain't just gonna let it go without seeing what could come of it."

His words floored me. I'd never felt rare or precious or anything else like that. But still, was I going to let him dictate to me? Knowing that Rix was fascinated with me, my boldness grew. Instinctively, I knew he wouldn't hurt me, so I gave my tongue free rein.

"I hate to break it to you, but you've got no choice but to let it go if I say so."

His scowl darkened. "I don't take orders. I give them, duchess."

"Maybe in your world, but right now you're standing in mine." My gaze sharpened on him with that thought. He must have come here for a reason. "Why are you here? What's the update?"

His eyes stayed firmly fixed on mine. "The update is there's no change, but I did talk to her."

He talked to Trinity? And he's just now telling me?

"Don't you think you should have led with that? What did she say? Did she say she was scared? Hurt? Hungry? What?"

"Calm down, woman, and I'll tell you."

My hands trembled, and I barely restrained myself from grabbing his arm and shaking him. "Consider me as calm as I'm going to get." If he didn't spill what he knew *right now*, I was going to lose my grip on my emotions.

Rix nodded and pushed off the glass, and as he talked, he paced out of the bathroom into the bedroom. I followed, not willing to miss a single word.

"She's fine. Yeah, she's scared, but I told her not to be."

"I need to talk to her. Need to hear that from her myself. She has to be terrified."

"She ain't hurt or hungry. She's eating Cheetos and watching Netflix, and now that she knows someone's coming for her, she said she can hold it together."

I threaded my shaking hands together as I sat on the bed, bowing my head. Trinity was tough, but she shouldn't have to be. She should never know anything like this could happen. She should be sitting at home eating Cheetos and watching Netflix.

Gathering together the threads of my self-possession, I looked up at Rix. "Swear to me, on whatever you find holy, that she's okay." My voice was low, my words barely audible.

"I swear to you, she's fine." Rix's tone matched mine in seriousness.

"Thank God," I whispered.

Rix spun and stalked toward me. "It ain't God you should be thanking, duchess. I'm the one making this happen. And I don't use this much effort for anyone without a damn good reason."

Anger overwhelmed the fear that had gripped me. "She got into this because of one of your people!"

He stopped in front of me. "She made her own choice to get involved with him."

"That's bull. Besides, you have to get her back to cover your own ass."

"I don't have to do shit." Rix's chin lifted with the proclamation.

"So you're saying that I'm the only reason you're bothering to get her back?" I demanded.

He crouched down, a hand on the quilt on either side of my hips. "Glad you're finally catching on."

I didn't like that explanation. I wanted Rix invested on

every level. Glancing up at him, I met his gaze. "I don't even know what to say."

"You don't need to say anything except you're not gonna let that cop put his lips on you again."

"Don't tell me what to do." Palm shooting out, I slapped against his shoulder, and surprisingly, he stood and stepped back.

Rix crossed his arms. "You want your girl back? You do what I want."

My glare should have shriveled vital parts of his anatomy. "So it's going to be like that, then? You already gave me your word that you'd get her home safe. Doesn't that mean anything?"

His eyebrows drew together. "You don't question a man's word, duchess. That's dangerous territory."

"But you said—"

"You goin' out with the cop again, or not?"

I thought of Hennessy's promise to stop by the gallery and set up a date. Honesty won out. "Probably."

The muscle in Rix's jaw tightened and he dropped his arms, taking one step forward and leaning down. "Don't." The word came out on a growl, and yet I still felt no fear.

"I—" Whatever I was going to say died when Rix's head dipped toward me.

"I'm taking my shot, not asking for it," he murmured before his lips took mine. There was no warm-up, no coaxing. Just . . . conquering.

I went with it, opening my mouth to his tongue and letting him in. My hands had their own agenda, gripping his shoulders, pulling him closer, wanting more. How long had it been since I'd felt that *wanting*? That absolute need to feel someone's skin on mine?

Rix's fingers buried in my hair, tilting my head one way and then the other, changing angles, going deeper. I wanted more, needed more.

But he pulled back.

"Gotta stop or I won't. Got shit to do. I need to go." He pushed away from the wall and headed for the door.

"You have shit to do? You have to *go*? That's how you're going to leave it?" I asked, my tone incredulous.

The man had just kissed me like I'd never been kissed before, and he pulled away like I was a leper. Did I forget how to kiss? I knew it had been a while, but was I that bad? *Hell.*

"You get that you're mine?" he asked.

"I don't—"

"Yes or no, Valentina. It's not a hard question."

"I don't know," I yelled, pushing up off the bed and striding toward him. "You confuse the hell out of me, and even though you should scare me, you don't. And you make me think about wanting things I shouldn't—" I cut my rant off short as soon as I realized my filter had slipped, and I was so freaking confused, brutal honesty win out.

Rix inhaled sharply, alerting me to the fact that my hand was pressed against his chest and I'd backed him into a corner. Before I could move it, his wide palm covered mine and held it in place. My gaze clashed with his, and neither of us moved.

"You've got good instincts, duchess. I should scare the hell out of you, and you absolutely shouldn't want a goddamned thing to do with me. And you should definitely never trust me."

I choked out a surprised laugh. "That's your pitch? After telling me you want me, you tell me I should be scared and shouldn't want you or trust you?"

"Tell me to go right now."

My brain struggled to keep up with him. "You want me to tell you to go?"

"No, but you should. Because if you don't, I'm gonna be inside you tonight, and you're not ready for that."

Was he right? My body was dying for his touch, but he was absolutely not the guy I should be wanting. And as much as the devil on my shoulder urged me to take a risk and tell him to stay, I couldn't do it.

Why were the words so hard to say?

"Then go."

He nodded and turned away without another word. My staircase creaked as he hit certain steps. I listened for more sounds of his departure but heard nothing. The alarm didn't go off, but the house was silent.

What the hell was I going to do about him?

Just like the last night he'd left me at my house, the urge to paint flooded me. I should have been falling flat on my face in bed because I hadn't slept in a day, but instead I was hyper charged by the desire that Rix had ignited within me.

I stripped off the robe in favor of leggings and a T-shirt, and checked every room in the house to see if he was really gone. He was. I told myself I wasn't disappointed as I headed to my studio.

As soon as I flipped on the light, my stomach fell to the drop cloths covering the floor.

My easel was empty.

He didn't.

But who else?

The piece I'd done that I hadn't been willing to admit was Rix, except maybe in the deepest part of my mind, was gone.

But how?

And why?

My stomach churned as I looked around my studio at the remaining canvases. Part of my secret was I usually painted nudes. My fascination was with the human figure. The beauty of it, the differences, the imperfections. And the figure I usually painted because it was the one I saw naked most often? My own.

Did he take anything else?

Frantically, I sorted through them, mentally ticking off all the finished pieces as I saw them. It seemed that nothing else was missing, but that didn't calm my racing heart.

Rix took it. He frigging took it. My painting of him.

I wanted to whack my head against the wall for being so careless as to just leave it out. But this was my space, my home, and no one came in my studio but me. Ever. My cleaning lady knew to steer clear, and even then, I locked the door just to be safe. Martha didn't need to see my nudes spread out all over a room. *No one did.* Which was why I never showed anyone. Never told anyone. Never would.

Tomorrow. Tomorrow Rix and I would have words, and I would get it back and demand he stop screwing around and get Trinity back right the hell now.

EIGHT

HENNESSY

I wouldn't let this case go. There was too much at stake, including my reputation—what was left of it—and maybe my career.

Tossing the file down on my desk in frustration, I shoved my hand through my hair. It was strange not to have it buzzed short, but everyone needed a change now and then. Or so my last girlfriend had told me. That hadn't lasted long. She'd had a lot of things to say, and almost all of them involved changing me.

I was the last guy to claim to be perfect, and she was definitely searching for her version of happily-ever-after with the perfect guy who never wanted to watch the Saints, drink a beer, or fuck her in any position but missionary. Like I said, she hadn't lasted long.

"Hennessy, you make any headway with that interview?"

I'd finally tracked down one witness to a shooting after a drug deal gone bad, and he'd refused to give me anything useful.

"Not a single fucking thing," I replied, looking up at Mac Fortier. He was another detective on the drug case that I wasn't supposed to be working, but when budgets got cut, the department put me on it anyway.

In the end, it wouldn't matter. I wanted to close it more than anyone. My brother had been killed during one particular raid on this case that had turned into a clusterfuck, and during the internal investigation, evidence had surfaced that he was dirty.

I knew one thing to the core of my soul: my brother wasn't a dirty cop.

My father had retired within weeks of my brother's death, and I'd been bounced around the department because they weren't sure what to do with me anymore. I'd been the youngest detective on the force once upon a time, headed for the top of the food chain, and now they just wanted me out.

But no matter how badly they wanted to rid the department of Hennessys, I'd refused to leave. And they were insane if they thought I'd rest before I'd restored my brother's reputation.

"Well, that fucking sucks. Was the guy scared to talk?" Fortier asked.

"Yeah. Didn't even want to be seen coming or going from the station."

"So there goes that lead."

I grunted, because it didn't merit a response.

"We'll get 'em. I'll shake down my CIs and see if I can get any more names of anyone who might have been in the vicinity. There's gotta be someone we can get to talk. Enough people are on parole in that area that we just need to find the right one who has something to lose if they don't cooperate." He flashed me a smile. "It's their civic fucking duty."

Fortier was a bulldog when it came to chasing leads. He had a year or two on me in seniority, but he didn't delegate much. He seemed to actually enjoy still getting down in the trenches. Plenty of others didn't.

"You wanna grab some lunch, man?" Fortier asked. "I'm starving."

"Yeah, sure. You got a place in mind?"

"That little café down the street has a good po'boy, if it isn't packed with tourists."

That little café he was talking about was kitty-corner from Noble Art, which would give me an excuse to duck in and set up the date I'd promised Valentina I'd be taking her on. And I would be taking her on that date.

Once I'd realized what her issue was, I'd handled it. The fact that she thought I saw her only as a victim was ridiculous. Yes, I'd always remember that night. How could I forget it? But that didn't change the fact that she was a strong, beautiful woman.

We hustled through lunch, me eager to get on with asking Valentina out, and Fortier eager to start calling his CIs to meet and hopefully shake out some more leads.

When Fortier exited in the direction of the station, I said, "I'll catch up with you later. I've got a stop to make."

His eyebrow went up and he turned. "You realize I'm a detective too, right?"

"What's your point?"

"You've been staring at that place over there like a crack whore on the lookout for her pimp. Try to be more subtle when you finally get over there. Women don't go for nice guys. You're a cop. That's fuckin' dangerous. Don't act like a pussy and water that shit down. Own it. Use it. Get the girl."

Sage advice given, Fortier slapped my shoulder and strolled off.

Too bad my being a cop was the biggest hurdle I had to overcome with this particular woman.

NINE

RIX

How my life went from not knowing Valentina Noble existed to having her on my mind constantly, I didn't fucking know. It would probably help if I wasn't keeping tabs on her to make sure she was staying out of trouble. Regardless, I could see her sitting at her desk—a simple glass top with four black legs that hid nothing, including how her skirt rode up her legs when she crossed and uncrossed them.

A taste. I'd only had a taste of her, and it wasn't nearly enough. I knew it was a bad idea, but since when did I care? I'd had plenty. Somehow, I was still breathing. Against all odds and shit.

A customer walked into Noble Art and my little duchess rose from her seat, a smile spreading across her face. Not the forced and fake kind either. It was real, genuine, and I liked the way her eyes lit up with excitement. The mercenary side of me said it was because she was about to make some fat cash when she sold something to the poor fuck, but the other part wondered if she was really just that happy.

Happy. I didn't remember what that was like. I'd just been existing, day to day, wondering which bullet might end me. A rival gang's or a cop's. Didn't matter where the shot came from, because either would snatch me from this life and toss me into the next.

I needed to walk away from where I stood before I did something stupid, like go inside and drop some freshly laundered cash on a piece of art I didn't need, didn't want, and didn't fucking understand—all for the chance to see her light up like that. Would she smile at me? Nah. I'd probably get her glare. But at least that would be better than the fake smile. Fuck the fake smile.

I wanted real.

I wanted her.

Valentina smiled again at her customer as I pushed away from the door frame I was leaning against. Something caught her eye and she froze, her gaze locking on me.

I raised my chin in her direction before melting into the crowd without looking back. I had work to do.

TEN
VALENTINA

I couldn't stop thinking about it. The kiss. The one that had me on edge every moment of the day. I stuttered midsentence every time the memory would sneak into my head. How dare he? *I bet he'd dare more*, my subconscious would purr. Calling myself distracted would be the understatement of the century. Every time the door opened, I practically jumped out of my skin, expecting to see Rix walking in.

What would I do if I saw him? I had no idea. But if I didn't see him, I knew I had no choice but to march myself right up to his doorstep and demand an update on Trinity, and get my painting back.

The door opened again, and I tensed before spinning around. Not Rix. No, it was the other man taking up space in my thoughts—Rhett Hennessy.

His grin was quick, and I was reminded how much I'd enjoyed dinner with him last night. There had been camaraderie I hadn't felt in a long time, and yet I had no idea what to do about it. Or anything else going on in my life.

It was official. I was clueless about this adulting thing when it came to my personal life. And since when did I even *have* a personal life? I'd been the original *all work and no play* girl for the last decade. That's how I'd managed to keep my gallery from hovering in the red long enough to drain my trust fund and instead fought tooth and nail to make it a success. I did not give up. And . . . that still gave me no clue as to how to deal with my present situation. Which was standing and looking at me, waiting for me to respond.

Crap. Had he said hello while I was buried in my thoughts?

"Am I interrupting?" Rhett asked.

I shook my head, telling myself to get back in the game, and rose from my desk. "Not at all. I was just running through my schedule for this afternoon."

"Busy day?"

"Busy enough, but I like it that way. The alternative would be too boring."

"Understandable. I didn't decide to go the cop route because I thought it'd be boring either."

His comment about his brother being killed in the line of duty came back to me from our conversation the night before. "Definitely not boring, I'd assume."

Rhett ditched the small talk almost as soon as he started with it. "You know why I'm here?"

For flash of a moment, I wondered if he was here because of last night—the part where he'd dropped me off at my house and there had been a known gang member waiting for me inside.

But he didn't know anything about that. Right?

No, Valentina, of course he doesn't.

"That date you said you were taking me on?"

Hennessy nodded. "Yes, ma'am. I'm taking you out on a proper date, one that ends with my lips somewhere other than your forehead."

My eyes widened as, obviously, all the possibilities of where his lips could end up flipped through my brain.

Rhett must have read my surprise because his eyebrow went up before a smile slid over his face. A moment of silence hung between us.

"Where exactly were you picturing my lips just now?"

I hadn't expected him to go the bold route, but I couldn't lie about my body reacting to it. It did. The heat reflected in his gaze filled me, but something held me back from responding in kind. *Something?* Try *someone*.

"I'm not that kind of girl, Detective Hennessy. Especially not on a first real date."

The heat stayed firmly in his gaze, not dimming at all. "I guess we'll see where the night takes us. You can show me exactly what kind of woman you are, because you're definitely no girl, Valentina. Seven o'clock. Tomorrow night. I'll pick you up at your house."

Swallowing and still trying to keep up with this different version of Rhett Hennessy than I was used to, I nodded. "Okay."

"Have a great afternoon, Valentina."

He turned and walked out of my gallery, leaving me standing in the middle of the room, not sure why I couldn't come up with a more coherent answer than *okay*.

ELEVEN
VALENTINA

A cop, a gang leader, and the daughter of a judge. It sounded like the punch line of a joke should come next, but instead it was my life.

I had a date with a cop tomorrow night, I was waiting to hear from a gang leader, and my father, the judge, had invited me over for a family dinner tonight.

I hadn't heard from Rix and hadn't caught another glimpse of him on the street, despite keeping a close eye on it all day. I wanted my update about Trinity. I wanted to demand he get her back right now and quit screwing around. I didn't care what his reasons were, and I didn't understand why he hadn't already done it.

When I let myself into my house, I turned on all the lights and checked every room. No sign of him.

Was I hoping he would be here? I'd never admit that, even to myself.

In my studio, my most recent paintings were all still in place. I thought about moving them out of sight, but dinner with the parents meant I couldn't be late. I quickly changed out of my gallery skirt and blouse and into a white knit dress and gold sandals.

I walked to my parents' house, rather than driving, because it was only six blocks away, and that meant I could drink a few glasses of whatever excellent red my father decided to choose for tonight. Because tonight I needed something to take the edge off or I'd lose my mind.

Trinity had been scheduled to work today, and knowing she was being held somewhere by some gangbangers had gutted me every time I'd looked around the room and expected to see her cheery smile and pink streak in her hair. But there was nothing I could do myself to get her back, and that helplessness ate at me. Hence the wine I'd be drinking tonight.

When I opened the front door of my parents' house with my key, their dog greeted me first, as usual. Chaney was a ridiculously friendly golden doodle that could barely manage to keep his front paws on the ground because of his ridiculous friendliness.

"Hey, pup. Where's your ball?"

He froze for a split second before running off in the direction of wherever his ball was hiding. Probably under the couch.

"Is that the sound of my baby girl?" my mother called from the kitchen. She bustled out, still drying her hands on a dish towel. "You're here! I'm so glad! I haven't seen you all week." She didn't slow until I was caught up in her arms for the kind of hug only my mother could give. Like it had been five years since she'd seen me rather than five days.

"I know, I know. I've been busy trying to keep up with the gallery. Lots of new business lately." I wasn't lying; that was the truth. But my mother didn't need to know about the other things keeping me busy.

"You're working so hard lately. You really need to take some time and enjoy yourself."

"You know she won't, Jo." My father came out of the kitchen, wearing an apron that read KISS THE MASTER GRILLER. "She's too much like her old man. All work and no play. At least until he met his better half."

My parents hadn't gotten married until their early thirties and had me a couple of years later. My father loved to talk about the years he spent chained to his desk as a lowly assistant district attorney before the magnificence that was my mother opened his eyes to everything he was missing in life.

It was adorable. Until he dragged her away to kiss her in a way that would "scandalize the child." Just like I'd developed a decent case of envy when it came to Yve banishing her demons and allowing herself to be swept off her feet by Lucas Titan, I had always been envious of what my parents shared. It was real. Solid. Permanent. If you tried to tell my dad that the sun rose and set anywhere other than directly over my mother, he'd probably give you a stern lecture on how not to be a moron.

Love. It was a thing that other people experienced, and I was wondering if I ever would. I'd had zero prospect of it on the horizon, and now, against my better judgment, I seemed to be drawn in two separate directions.

I'm fucking fascinated with you, Rix had said. But you could be fascinated with a duck-billed platypus.

I've wanted to flirt with you for years, Valentina, but you weren't ready. I think you're ready now. Rhett was right; I was ready. Ready to start living again.

"See, she's probably spacing out right now thinking of something she forgot to do before she left the gallery."

My dad's voice pierced through my swirling thoughts. Thoughts better left alone.

"Sorry," I said, just in time for Chaney to come running back with her ball. "It has been a crazy few days."

"That's why you need to make time for things other than

work," my mother said.

I knew she wanted to say *Go on a date, have fun*, but given the circumstances, she never would, and I couldn't miss the flash of pain on her face when she held back the words. I hated that they both still saw me as their daughter who'd been raped. I wasn't a victim anymore, but the sympathetic looks hadn't changed in ten years. How would I ever get them to see me as I was today rather than their baby girl who'd been violated?

Her pained look tightened the corners of her mouth, and there wasn't much I wouldn't say to erase it. And that was why I opened my big fat mouth.

"I am making time for things other than work. I sorta went on a date last night. And I have another tomorrow."

Both my parents stilled and looked at me. "A date? Really?"

It was proof of how little I told them about that aspect of my life and how little I dated. There had been guys here and there I'd seen casually, but no one I would have ever mentioned to my parents. For them, this news was almost groundbreaking. And maybe it would finally help me shed the victim image in their eyes.

"Who's the lucky man?" The question came from my father.

Well, crap. Of course they'd want details.

"He's a cop. NOPD."

This grabbed my father's attention even more. He knew *lots* of cops. "Does he have a name?"

"Rhett Hennessy. Detective Rhett Hennessy."

Both my parents, but especially my father, had been very involved in my case, and I knew he'd recognize the name. I didn't know what kind of reaction I'd get, however.

"Good man. I've always liked him. He's young, but that works in his favor. He's got drive. Great cop. Not a bad choice."

My mother glanced at my father before faux whispering,

"And he's handsome in that rough, primal sort of way. Good choice, for sure."

My father raised an eyebrow at my mother. "I'll show you handsome in a rough, primal sort of way." He growled and stepped toward her.

"Do you want me to grab my steak off the grill and take it to go? I can leave you two . . . alone."

My parents both laughed, and my father stepped back. "No, we'll save this for later."

"Okay. Ewww. Just ewww. I don't want to hear it."

My mother leaned in and hugged me again, and Chaney wiggled between us. "It's good to see you smile. Now, let's go throw together a salad and eat."

Dinner was filled with my father telling stories about some of the crazy happenings at the courthouse. The family that attempted to stage a protest on the steps before they realized their son had agreed to a plea bargain. The defendant who had head-butted the bailiff and tried to make a run for it, but tripped over his own feet and sprained an ankle before he could get out of the courtroom. I swear, it was stuff that I would have never believed if I hadn't been raised around a dinner table hearing stories like that.

My mother added anecdotes from her docent position at the New Orleans Museum of Art. Her influence and spending so much time at the museum as a kid had begun my love of art and ultimately determined my career choice. I hadn't wanted art to sit in a museum, though, so people could only see it when they visited. I wanted more accessible art—the kind you could take home and enjoy every day.

By the time I'd filled my belly with steak, veggies, and

homemade raspberry pie, I'd also drunk several glasses of wine.

"It's a good thing I'm walking home," I said as I stood to clear the table. "I wouldn't want to end up in front of one of daddy's colleagues."

My dad laughed. "You're too smart to ever do anything that stupid."

My insides squirmed a little when I thought about Rix, and the night Trinity was taken. My father would tell me I was being incredibly stupid. And I probably was. But as much as I wanted to spill all of the details and beg my dad for help, I couldn't risk her safety. He'd tell me to leave the matter to the police, which was exactly what Rix had told me not to do.

Since when was I listening to Rix over my father? It was a sobering realization.

When I headed for the door, after giving hugs to both of them, my father stopped me.

"You better not be leaving without letting your old man walk you home."

I paused with my hand on the doorknob. "It's only a few blocks."

"And you're still my baby girl." Turning, he called to my mother, "I'll be back in fifteen minutes, Jo."

"I'll be waiting!" she yelled back.

Chaney came bounding up as if on cue, with a look in her doggy eyes that said *You're not trying to leave without me, are you? Why would you do such a thing?*

My father, used to that look, grabbed a leash off the hook by the door and clipped it to her collar. "I'm taking the dog too."

"Okay, honey."

The exchange was so routine and so domestic, but it knocked something loose in me. I wanted that. The routine. Walking the dog. Cooking dinner. Being part of a couple instead of always being solo.

Is Rhett the guy to give me that?

I couldn't even consider the other man who'd barged into my life. Rix was not an option. At all. The very fact that I couldn't tell my parents about him spoke volumes. My father would be more likely to use his connections to have him arrested than invite him to a family dinner. He was like any father, wanting what was best for his little girl, and I was pretty sure he wouldn't say Rix was that man.

As we carefully picked our way along the broken sidewalk, my father wasted no time. "So, Detective Hennessy? He's not a guy I would've guessed, but I think he's a good choice."

Lifting my gaze from Chaney as she tugged at the leash and sniffed everything within reach, I looked at my father. "So he's got the Harold Noble stamp of approval?"

My dad smiled. "As my daughter, whoever you pick with your superior good sense and taste will always have my stamp of approval."

His words were pretty bold, considering he had no idea what I'd gotten myself into.

"Thanks for the vote of confidence."

"Of course." He reached down and gripped my hand. "We just want you to be happy. That's all we've ever wanted for you."

"I know. I'm working on it. Gallery sales are finally holding their own and growing every month, so I'm hoping to be able to hire a full-time employee and not put in quite so many hours as I have been."

I'd worked nonstop for years, it seemed, and without Trinity, I was spending even more time at the gallery. My other part-time employee was on vacation and due to return tomorrow. I supposed all the time at work was good for distraction purposes.

"I know when you're young, you're focused on attaining

every goal, but you're prone to tunnel vision, Valentina. There's a lot of life out there to be lived, and you need to take advantage."

"I'm working on it. I really am."

If my dad had any clue my tunnel vision had been blown wide open and I'd stepped into a world not my own, he'd have a much different opinion. But I also didn't want him taking it upon himself to try to set me up, so telling them about Hennessy hadn't been a bad choice. I didn't know if my father knew, but I was well aware that he'd strongly suggested that Lucas Titan take me out several times. Given how happy Yve was, I was thoroughly glad that he hadn't caved to the pressure.

"Good. Your mother worries."

And clearly, so did my father. We'd arrived at my house, and Chaney instantly tugged at her leash. Not expecting the strong pull, I dropped the leash and she ran for my house, pushing through my broken gate.

"Crap. I'll get her," I said, taking off after the dog. Her barks came fast and close together, all focused on the window to my dining room. "Chaney, hush. That's enough."

That's when I saw the curtain flutter. I froze, my hand on Chaney's collar.

There was someone inside.

My first thought was Rix, but what if it wasn't?

It had to be. No one else would be breaking into my house. *Right?*

"I wonder what's got her dander up?" my father said as he came toward me. "She doesn't usually bark at nothing."

I turned away from the window, grabbed the end of the leash, and walked Chaney back toward my father.

"No idea. I guess she thought she saw something."

"Have you been setting your security system?"

"Of course." But my brain added silently, *Not that it stops everyone*.

"Do you want me to go inside and take a look around?" His offer was that of a man concerned for his daughter's safety. His daughter who was going to lie and pretend she wasn't freaking out more than a little about who might be waiting inside.

"It's fine, Dad. My alarm would have every cop in a five-mile radius here if someone were to try to get inside."

Lies. All lies. And it hurt to tell them to the one man I trusted implicitly.

"You sure?"

"Yes. Positive."

"Okay. I'll be getting back to your mother then." He leaned in and pressed a kiss to my forehead, like he had so many times. "Love you, baby girl."

"Love you too. Be safe walking home," I told him.

"Always. And you make sure you use that revolver I know you're carrying if you even here a single noise in that house that you question. We believe strongly in self-defense in the state of Louisiana."

"Okay. I will."

My dad strode back toward the street with Chaney leading the way, and I pulled my keys from my purse. My hand shook, and I missed the lock twice before the key slid home.

It was Rix inside. It had to be.

I twisted the handle and pushed the portico door open. One more door to go before I knew the truth.

Except I didn't have time to open it before it swung inward, and a figure stood in the shadow-darkened doorway.

"You didn't tell him I was inside. Why's that, duchess?"

I ignored Rix's question. "Stop breaking into my house."

He didn't move from the shadows. "I guess you don't want an update on your girl, then."

Trinity. She was the only reason I should even be speaking to Rix. She was all that mattered.

"What? Tell me." I hated the thought of her spending another night in some place with those drug-dealing gang-bangers.

Rix finally stepped out of the shadows. "I think you're forgetting who you're dealing with. You don't make demands here."

The menace was back in his tone, and tendrils of fear curled up my spine. I think I'd just made the mistake of treating a tiger like a house cat. But I didn't care. I forged ahead, secure in my certainty that Rix wouldn't hurt me.

"What are you gonna do about it? Not help her?"

"Nah, but I just upped my price."

I crossed my arms over my chest, my narrowed gaze colliding with his. "Your price? What price?"

"I don't do anything for nothing."

"You never said you wanted to get paid to get her back. How much?" It truly didn't matter, because I would pay it. I wasn't broke.

A predatory smile slid across Rix's face. "Ah, duchess. So fuckin' innocent."

I knew then what he wanted as his price. My cheeks heated, and it wasn't anger causing the flush.

Rix's eyes never left my face. "Maybe not so innocent then."

"That's extortion," I whispered.

He lowered his head and spoke low in my ear, his breath sending shivers skating across my skin. "Is it really extortion when you're hot to pay the price?"

Was I? I couldn't deny that he fascinated me too, and last night when he'd kissed me I hadn't been ready to stop. But more? Images of him tossing me over his shoulder, carrying me upstairs, and throwing me down on my bed before he stripped me naked played through my head. *All alpha*. And good grief, that was hot.

Swallowing against the mouthwatering thoughts, I searched for something to say.

"I'm not hearing a protest," he taunted.

"If I agree to your *price*, then what? You'll get her back quicker?"

Rix lifted his head, but his lips were still achingly close to mine when he spoke. "I'm going to do exactly what I'm doing now."

"Then why—"

He gripped my hips with both hands, thumbs coasting up and down my belly over the material of my dress.

"Because you need a reason, and I'm giving you one."

I didn't follow. "A reason for what?" I whispered.

"For me to be in your bed."

He lowered his mouth, and his teeth closed over my bottom lip and tugged. I sucked in a shallow breath. When he released it, his tongue slid out and lashed the spot he'd nipped.

"So fucking sweet. And I want it all. That's my payment, and I can't wait to collect." He pulled back a few inches, want and need burned into his features.

I'd done that?

"When?" I asked quietly.

"Whenever I decide."

He wasn't waiting for a yes or no answer from me. He'd simply decreed it was happening. Heat licked at my insides, and if he'd told me he'd decided right now, on the rug in my foyer, I might not have protested.

Time for a change in subject. I had to stop thinking this way or I'd be throwing myself at him as shamelessly as those girls the night of the party.

I slipped sideways, stepping out of his hold. I wasn't

kidding myself that he could have kept me where he wanted me, but he let me go.

I glanced down. Oh, great, my overactive nipples had decided to join the party—and the dip in Rix's gaze told me he hadn't missed that fact. I crossed my arms over my chest and lifted my chin.

"Update, then?"

Rix crossed his arms, mimicking my posture. "She's fine."

The heat running through my body morphed into frustration. "Then why haven't you gotten her back? This is ridiculous. You act like you're the king of the damn jungle, but you're dragging this out for no reason." I dropped my arms and stalked toward him. "You can break in here and get around my alarm and scare the hell out of me, but you can't break into some gang house and grab one girl?" Somehow, by the end of my speech I was jabbing my finger into his chest for emphasis.

Rix's hand was quick, wrapping around mine before I could snatch it back. "Don't push me, duchess."

"But this makes no damn sense!" I tugged at his hold, but he didn't release me.

"Because blood running in the streets isn't something that's ever gonna make sense in your world."

"What are you talking about?" Blood running in the streets didn't sound good to me.

"All you need to know is that if I run a smash-and-grab, we're looking at more dead bodies, and I'm trying to keep that from happening."

"I don't understand." My voice was shaky. The last thing I wanted was for Trinity to get caught in some gang crossfire.

"You don't need to understand. Your girl is a pawn right now. She's safe, but even in my world, there's a thing called diplomacy. I'll work that angle until I can't. You may not realize it, but I don't particularly like blood on my hands. Got too much already, and I don't go out of my way looking for more."

"But—"

His silver eyes flashed, irritation obvious by the ticking muscle of his jaw. I got the impression that Rix didn't explain himself to anyone very often, but I didn't care. I'd have my explanation. This was too important.

"You want her back all in one piece, or are you not too particular about it?"

"That's a ridiculous question," I shot back.

"Then we do this my way."

"Your way is taking too damn long."

Dropping his arms, Rix backed me into the wall again. "My way is smarter than some snatch-and-grab that could end with her having holes in her body where there were none before."

"I don't believe you. I'm pretty sure you're capable."

"You're right. I am. I could have had her home in hours that first night."

My mouth dropped open, but no sound came out at first. "What?" I yelled, my tone edging into the territory of a screech. Both of my hands shot out and I shoved at his chest. It was completely solid, and Rix didn't move. "Why? How could you just leave her there?"

Rix's expression hardened further. "I'm trying to keep this from becoming a war. Innocent blood gets spilled when that shit gets unleashed, and it ain't what we need right now."

"A gang war?"

He gave me a short nod before continuing, and I wondered if he'd said more than he'd intended. "I can't agree to their demands without losing power and position. So I'm working the angles. Takes a little more time, but I'm gonna get her back without looking weak or starting a fucking bloodbath."

The reasoning made some sort of strange sense. But I still

didn't like it.

"Work faster. She has to be terrified. I don't care what you have to do, but you need to get her out, and *quick*. God only knows what they've done to her." My stomach, which had been tied into knots since Trinity had disappeared, twisted violently.

Rix laid a hand on either side of my face and tilted my head so I was staring directly into his unusual eyes. "You have my word that they haven't touched her. They don't want a war any more than I do. And I swear to you, I'll get her back as soon as I can. But we're doing it my way. This ain't your world, duchess, so you're not callin' the shots here."

What could I do, short of calling the police and forcing them to launch a full-scale recovery operation? Rhett would almost certainly believe me when I told him. Maybe. But I believed what Rix said, and I didn't want to put Trinity at risk.

The cops were not a safe option.

Against all odds, the man in front of me continued to be my best choice.

"Okay, but please hurry."

Rix's expression softened a fraction. "You're lucky I like you, duchess, otherwise those orders wouldn't fly." His gaze dropped to my lips. "Fuck. I gotta taste you again."

I didn't have time to think or protest before his lips landed on mine. This kiss was slower than the first, almost as if Rix was savoring it. Savoring me.

With a soft moan, I pushed up onto my toes and leaned into him, my arms rising of their own accord to loop around his neck. It was my turn to savor.

I had no idea how long we stood in my foyer, tasting each other with long, lazy strokes, before Rix pulled away again, this time stepping back and letting me go.

"I'm gonna collect sooner rather than later. That's a promise."

TWELVE
VALENTINA

I *'m gonna collect sooner rather than later. That's a promise.*

Rix's words haunted me, and I was caught between lying to myself and admitting what I really wanted. This fascination wasn't healthy, and it absolutely wasn't normal to hope that someone would break into your house and be waiting for you at night. And yet here I was fascinated and hoping.

Because I want updates about Trinity. That's why. That's it. It was at least part of the truth.

Thankfully, today had been a constant stream of buying customers, which might have kept me busy, but didn't stop me from thinking about Trinity constantly. I was failing at keeping her safe. Should I have gone to the cops? Would this all be a bad memory already?

I faced that decision head-on when Rhett walked in the door of Noble Art. He smiled and nodded at the older woman leaving with a small watercolor by a local artist.

"In the market for some art?" I asked, keeping my tone intentionally light.

"More in the market for the proprietor." His gaze was direct and intense, just like his words.

I fumbled for a reply. "The proprietor appreciates your interest."

"That's a good thing because I'm taking her out tonight. Just wanted to make sure plans hadn't changed."

His green eyes were sharp, taking in my every expression. It would be so easy to open my mouth and spill everything. *But at what cost?*

I'd lost the thread of conversation for a moment. "Nope, plans haven't changed."

"Good. I'll pick you up at seven."

"I'll be ready. Text me or call if something comes up." I was assuming the cop life meant he had a schedule that he couldn't always control.

Rhett nodded. "That means you have to give me your number."

I blinked. I knew he had it already. "But you have it."

Another slow nod and serious stare. "And I'm not going to use it to call you personally until you give it to me somewhere other than your case file."

A shard of pain panged my heart at the reminder. There was no way to erase that part of our past. Rhett and I would always be connected by what had happened to me that night.

I forced a smile and turned to my desk to grab a pad of paper and pen. After I'd jotted down my number, I tore off the top sheet and handed it to him. We were starting a new chapter, and what had happened in the past was irrelevant.

"Here you go. Personally from me to you."

Rhett looked down at the paper, and I wondered if he already had my number memorized before he slipped it into the breast pocket of his suit jacket.

"I'll be sure to use it."

I had nothing to add, so I just smiled. I wasn't prepared for his next question.

"No employee today either? Did you fire her?"

My heart thudded against my chest. *Dammit.* The man was a detective, so it wasn't surprising that he was curious, but I also was terrible at lying. This was my opportunity. My opening. I could tell him everything and ask for help.

Before I could open my mouth, the door opened again and two familiar and welcome faces strolled in. Yve and Lucas Titan.

"Detective Hennessy, you really are everywhere," Lucas drawled. He extended his arm and the men shook hands.

"How are you, Titan? Mrs. Titan?"

Yve smiled as her eyebrow arched. "I still have a first name, Detective."

"I recall. I'm glad to see you survived your belated bachelorette party."

Lucas's deep laugh filled my gallery. "I sure won't be forgetting that night anytime soon."

Yve shot a pointed look at her husband but the chuckle didn't stop; Lucas's wry smile only deepened. Rolling her eyes, Yve turned her attention back to me. "I suppose if I invite you to a girls' night, you might have second thoughts this time."

I considered for a beat for responding. The alternative was waiting around my empty house at night for an update on Trinity from the man who would break in.

"Not at all. I'm in. Just tell me when and where."

Yve's grin was quick and looked lovely on her. She'd been through so much more hell than I had, and I loved seeing her happy. "Good. I'll text you the details. Now, I'm starving and this guy promised to feed me."

"I promised to feed you *after* we picked out a piece to go above the fireplace. I'm making you spend money today, and you're not going to get out of it by pretending to be hungry now."

The grin morphed into a playful glare. "I'm not pretending. I'm always hungry."

I interjected. "By all means, Lucas, please spend some money. I'm happy to take it off your hands."

Yve's smile came back. "I guess if I'm going to spend his money anywhere, it might as well be with friends." She rubbed her hands together. "Okay, let's do this."

She strode toward the walls of artwork and began perusing them with an eye toward lightening Lucas's wallet, which made me one happy gallery owner.

"You've got to have more than one fireplace, Lucas. I'm sure you need more than one piece."

"That's all up to her. It's impossible to get her to buy anything for herself, so I have to resort to extreme measures."

"I'm sure we don't need to know what those are," I replied.

"No, you really don't," Yve added from across the room, right before she gasped. "This one. This is the one. It's beautiful."

I walked toward where Yve was crouching by a painting leaning against the wall. My confusion mounted as her body blocked it. I didn't lean pieces against the wall; they were all carefully displayed for maximum impact.

I racked my brain for what could have happened. Remy Burton, my other gallery employee, had returned from vacation and been working this morning, but he wasn't careless either. I'd been so sidetracked I hadn't even noticed.

Jeez, Valentina, get it together.

Yve stood and lifted the canvas, bringing it into view.

What. The. Hell.

I stutter-stepped in midstride.

That canvas wasn't supposed to be here. It was supposed to be in my studio at home, behind another stack of canvases.

And there was only one explanation for how it had gotten here. I was going to kill him.

"Isn't she gorgeous?" Yve whispered, holding the painting up for all of us to see.

A woman reclined on a divan with colorful swaths of silk covering her strategically. Her dark hair hung in long curls, mixing with the vivid colors. I'd painted it months ago and never looked at it again.

Lucas met Yve and paused. "It's beautiful." Turning his gaze to me, he said, "We'll take it."

"Wha—what?" I stammered.

His eyes narrowed on me before flicking down to the painting and back. "There's no artist signature. Whose work is it?"

I cursed Rix silently for landing me in this situation. "The author prefers to remain anonymous, so I can't share that information."

Glancing down at the canvas again, Lucas lifted it from Yve's hands and turned it over. "No price either."

I'd never considered selling my artwork, and therefore I had never thought to put a price on it. I fought the urge to wring my hands, and instead adopted my cool businesswoman mien and turned for my desk.

"Let me check my catalog. I'm afraid I haven't committed that one to memory."

"Do you have any other pieces by the same artist?" Lucas asked.

Shaking my head, I reached with trembling hands for the three-ring binder on my desk containing the details of all the pieces in my studio. "No. The artist provided only the one piece."

"Well, ask the artist to provide more. The vivid colors and bold technique are exactly what I'd envisioned for the living room, and we'd love to see more."

"It sure is impressive."

This comment came from Hennessy, and I kicked myself for momentarily forgetting about his presence.

I flipped through the plastic sheets in my binder, my brain racing for something to say. They wanted to buy *my* art. Over everything else in my gallery. Stunned didn't even begin to cover how I was feeling.

Think, brain, think.

I stopped on a page and stared down at the picture. It was a piece of art by a relatively new artist with little exposure and few sales. I was selling her pieces for substantially less than the others in my gallery, and reasoned therefore mine should be about the same.

I tossed out a price to Lucas and Yve, and all the heads in the gallery snapped in my direction.

"You're underpricing that piece by several thousand dollars, in my opinion," Lucas replied.

"That's a steal," Rhett agreed. "And I don't know jack shit about art."

"Well, that's the price. So I guess you're getting a bargain."

With any other piece, my shrewd business instincts would be cringing because I was leaving money on the table. But for my own work? I couldn't be objective. I wasn't a real artist. My work wasn't in this gallery for the very reason that it wasn't the same caliber as what I normally sold.

Lucas came toward me, canvas in hand. "Then you'll have to disagree when I say I'm paying you based on the perceived value and not your sticker price, which I think is ludicrous."

"That's not how you're going to keep those billions, Titan."

"Deal with it." He handed the canvas to me and pulled out a

money clip. Peeling off bills, he laid a stack on my desk. "Tell the artist we want to see more."

Lucas lifted the canvas from my hands and waited for Yve to join him.

"Thank you so much! You made this way less painful than I thought it would be. Normally we end up arguing over every goddamned thing, but this we agreed on. Shocking."

"Would you like me to wrap it up for you?" I asked, still stunned that Lucas and Yve had bought my painting.

"No need. It'll go in the car where it can't be damaged. Thank you again, Valentina. I'm sure we'll be seeing you soon."

And then they were gone, leaving the sound of the chime fading away and me alone with Rhett and a stack of cash on my desk. Part of me wanted Rhett to leave so I could count it and find out how much Lucas Titan had deemed as the perceived value. The other part wanted to beg him to stay and tell him everything.

"Sounds like you're going to have one happy new artist on your hands."

"She'll be very surprised."

Rhett studied me closely, and again I was reminded that I was facing a detective. He couldn't know I'd painted it. There was no way he could know.

"Well, I'd best get on my way and back to work. My cases aren't going to solve themselves."

Do I add another case to it? Rix's words came back to me. Should I even trust him to get her back?

I'll give him another day, I decided. *Then all bets are off.*

I smiled at Rhett and wondered if I looked as conflicted as I felt. "Thank you for stopping by. I'll see you later."

He continued his study of me for several moments, and I wondered if he'd push. He didn't. "You certainly will."

The door whooshed open and two more customers walked in. Rhett nodded and headed out.

What was I doing with him? And how in the world had Rix gotten a painting from my house to the gallery? And why?

After a steady stream of customer until closing, I finally had a chance to sit down at my desk and pull up my security footage from last night. It showed me leaving and locking up, and then nothing for hours. I was near the point of dozing off when all of the security feeds went black.

"What the hell?"
I skipped back and let it replay. Again, black. For six minutes. And then the picture reappeared and there wasn't a soul in the gallery.

I knew he could disable my home alarm system, so how much of a stretch was it really that he could disable my security cameras?

Shoving up from my desk, I grabbed my purse and stalked to the door. I flipped the OPEN sign to CLOSED and set the alarm —gritting my teeth because I knew it couldn't keep one particular person out.

And that one particular person had some explaining to do.

THIRTEEN
VALENTINA

It was hard to believe I was once again parking my Tesla across the street from Rix's house. This was a neighborhood I never should have set foot in to begin with, and here I was making it a regular stop.

Again wondering if my car would be there when I returned, I locked the door and crossed the street. The metal gate opened soundlessly on well-oiled hinges, and I picked my way over the cracked path and up the porch steps before hammering on the door.

I could have done this via text or phone call, but I wanted to see Rix's face when he tried to explain why he did it—and I was going to use the opportunity to press him about Trinity again.

There was no answer.

I remembered that the doorbell didn't work, so I ignored it and kept up with my pounding on the door.

Still nothing.

In my hurry to get here, it hadn't occurred to me that he might not be home for me to unleash my tirade on. I pulled out my phone and found his contact.

VALENTINA: Where the hell are you?

I wasn't in the mood to be nice, and yes, once again, I'd decided any rules about Rix being scary didn't apply to me.

At least this time, his response was almost instant.

RIX: Busy.

Busy? What the hell? He wasn't allowed to be busy. No, he was not.

VALENTINA: Get unbusy. I"m on your doorstep.
RIX: WTF, duchess? Go home. Now.
VALENTINA: No.
RIX: Stubborn woman. Be there in 5. Wait inside. It's unlocked.

I stared down at my phone. *He leaves his house unlocked? In this neighborhood?*

Maybe when you're the leader of one of the most notorious gangs in New Orleans, you're not worried about someone breaking in.

I chanced a look over my shoulder before I tucked my phone away and reached for the door handle. Sure enough, there were at least two men watching my every move. One had a phone in hand, and his thumbs were moving furiously. So maybe Rix didn't need to lock his house if he had people watching it. The man texting looked up at me and gave me a nod.

It didn't take a genius to guess who he was texting with. Apparently I'd been given the official go-ahead.

Twisting the handle, I pushed open the door and stepped inside the house. It was quiet and still, and I felt like I was trespassing, even though I had permission to be inside. Then I decided that feeling was ridiculous because Rix clearly hadn't felt the same way when he'd broken into my house multiple times and now my place of business too. *And* he'd snooped and stolen from me.

Now it's my turn.

Because I was a rebel, I left my shoes on—after wiping them carefully on the rug—and started my survey of Rix's domain. It was clearly a bachelor pad, and minimalist at best. There was a comfy couch in the living room, and a giant brown leather recliner that showed more wear than the rest. Apparently Rix liked his creature comforts.

The glass coffee table was empty except for some discarded mail. My curiosity ramped up when I realized his full name had to be on the mail. Crossing the worn wooden floor, I picked up an envelope. *Rix Jones*.

Well, that was boring, and it sounded fake. I couldn't help but wonder if it was. Given that he was involved in less-than-legal activities, would he really use his real name?

Replacing the mail on the table, I surveyed the living room more closely. A giant flat-screen television hung on the wall, but not a single picture. Actually, the entire room was devoid of knickknacks. I was headed out of the living room when the front door opened and the man himself stepped into the entryway.

I wasted no time.

"Why? It was one thing to take the picture I painted and keep it for yourself, but why the hell would you take one and put it in my gallery where someone could mistake it as a piece for sale?"

Rix didn't deny anything. "Because your pictures should be hanging on the walls of that gallery. I just gave you a push. Bet someone already bought it, didn't they?" He came toward me. "Is that what's got you all fired up?"

I propped my hands on my hips, refusing to back down. "You broke into my house—again—and stole from me—again—and then you broke into my business. That's what I'm fired up about! You can't just do whatever you want. There are rules."

"I make my own rules."

"I've heard that before, and guess what? It's bullshit. Did it ever occur to you that my work wasn't in my own gallery because I made the decision that it shouldn't be?"

Rix took another step toward me. "Did it ever occur to you that you're wrong? Your shit deserves to be on those fancy walls you own just as much as anything else. Now tell me, duchess, how fast did it sell?"

Gritting my teeth, I refused to give him the answer he wanted to hear. "That's not the point."

"I'd say it's a really fucking important point." One step closer and we stood toe-to-toe. "How fast?"

"My friends bought it, so it doesn't count," I said in a rush of breath.

One side of Rix's mouth lifted. "Did you tell them it was yours?"

"No," I admitted.

"Then it fucking counts." He lifted a hand, caught a lock of my hair, and held it between his thumb and index finger. "How much did you sell it for?"

I glared at him and snapped, "Shouldn't you have priced it too? I mean, since you went to the trouble of making sure it ended up for sale?"

"How much?"

"Several times more than the price I asked."

That's when Rix started laughing. A full-bodied, deep laugh. The kind that came from the gut. "Figures. Guess you should be thanking me."

Glaring, I crossed my arms. "You can't just break in whenever you want and take whatever you want. You have to stop."

His laugh quieted and he shook his head. "I haven't taken nearly everything I want. But it's about time I do."

He stepped forward, and I barely had time to breathe before his lips covered mine. His kiss was raw, unapologetic, and *honest*. The heat that had been growing in my belly while we argued seemed to burst into flames, licking up my body and burning away all my inhibitions.

Rix slid his hands under my ass and lifted me up to wind my legs around his waist. My arms twined around his neck and before I knew what was happening, we were moving. I didn't care because I kept my lips on his, the kiss sustaining me, urging me on, wanting to be closer. The heat from his body burned through my clothes, and I wanted to touch that skin that I'd painted.

Doubt and warnings battered my brain, but in my mind, I'd thrown up a barricade against reality, wanting only to live in this moment. Wanting this man. Having this man.

Was this why I'd wanted to come and deliver my reprimand in person? Because I wanted this to happen?

I couldn't answer my own question, and no other thoughts processed until Rix started moving. He tilted me down and my back pressed against something soft. Blinking my eyes open, dark jade walls and dark, heavy wood furniture came into view.

Rix's bedroom. Rix's bed.

I hadn't made it that far in my self-guided tour of his house, but I knew that was where we were without question. It should have been the wake-up call I needed to snap out of this haze, but my barricade against reality kept out the thoughts that should have been screaming *What the hell do you think you're doing? Stop! Now! Before it's too late.*

I knew one thing for sure—it was already too late to stop this. I wanted Rix. And for once, since that night that changed my life irrevocably, I was going to leap without looking. I was going to take what I wanted. I wasn't a victim anymore; I was a woman. And I could have what I wanted.

Rix didn't hesitate, didn't second-guess. He just kept his mouth on me as his hands roamed my body.

God, the feel of his hands on my body. Big, strong, kneading, coaxing, *perfect*.

I reached out to touch him, my palms meeting the hard planes and curves of muscle of his chest and shoulders. This was what all men should feel like. Strong. Capable. *Amazing*.

He finally lifted his head away, both our breaths coming in gasps and pants.

"Want you naked. Now."

Nodding, I didn't waste the oxygen or brainpower it would take to make words.

"God, you're fucking beautiful, duchess."

"Hurry up." They were the only words I could even think to speak at that moment. Everything he was saying was everything I wanted. And I wanted it right now.

His mouth curved in satisfaction as he reached for the back of his T-shirt and yanked it up and over his head, revealing all of the muscles my hands had explored through the soft cotton. And let me tell you, holy hell, they were even better to see. The man's body was art carved from bone and sinew. Smooth, sleek muscles built into the most aesthetically pleasing form I'd ever seen.

I'd never thought much about the differences in men's bodies, but after seeing this man's body, I wasn't sure I'd ever be able to look at another's the same. In that moment, my standards of male beauty jumped up a notch, and God help me, but I didn't ever want to lower those standards again. And I wanted to touch him, naked.

"You like what you see."

It wasn't a question. And God, why would it be? The man should have the ultimate confidence looking like that under his clothes.

"I want to see more," I said. "All of it. Hurry."

One side of his mouth quirked higher and I wanted to kiss the smirk off his face, but I wanted him to be naked even more.

I reached for the zipper that held my blouse together instead of buttons, and slowly lowered it inch by inch.

"Ah, woman, I didn't think I could get any harder, but when you tease me like that . . ."

"Hurry." I swear, my vocabulary had shrunk to that single word. I wanted more. I wanted him. I wanted it now.

Rix reached for his heavy silver belt buckle, which actually looked like brass knuckles, and unhooked it. When he unbuttoned and unzipped his pants, he let them fall, the weight of the belt buckle taking them to the floor.

My sexy, slow unzipping motion froze when I realized he was wearing nothing beneath his worn jeans. Not a stitch. To the boxers or briefs question, Rix's answer was neither.

And I completely approved.

Long and thick, his cock bobbed once it was free, and steadily rose toward his belly button.

The condoms I used to stuff in my purse before that infamous night that everything had changed would never have fit him. He was the myth, the legend, the *magnum*.

My mouth practically watered at the thought of getting that thick, dark, and beautiful cock between my lips.

Wait, what? Since when had I ever been that excited to suck a dick? I mean, yes, I loved the innate power I felt when I was able to bring a man to his knees that way, but I never actually desperately wanted to do it. That was something other women claimed to love to do, and secretly I thought they were all spewing loads of bullshit, because *hello*, sucking dick was kind of awkward.

But when I saw Rix's perfect cock, it was like my instinctive feminine desire to please him bubbled up out of the primitive part of my brain. When had that happened before? Never.

Thinking too much, Valentina.

And all of a sudden, thinking was no longer a problem because Rix wrapped his hand around his perfect cock and squeezed and stroked, pre-cum already wetting the head.

"You want this, duchess?"

Nodding was all I could offer in response. My thoughts were short-circuiting at the sight.

"Good, because you're going to take it all."

A rush of slickness hit my panties, because I didn't go commando like Rix, and the remnants of my patience melted.

"Now. Please."

I spread my legs, and realized I wasn't even close to naked. My blouse was halfway unzipped, my skirt was still intact, and my panties were in place.

"You don't look ready to take me, duchess. And besides, I'm going to taste that perfect little pussy before I fuck it."

I was still trying to kick-start my brain to decide what exactly I should do to move this process along and get to the part where Rix's body was touching mine, when he dropped to his knees and spread my legs wide, shoving my skirt up to my waist.

Today I'd gone bare-legged, with only a thong under my skirt. A rumble from Rix clued me into the fact that he approved. A lot.

"Red. Wasn't the color I was expecting, but fuck if I don't love it."

Those were the only words he spoke before he tugged my panties to the side. He lowered his face and paused.

"Fuck, you're dripping, duchess. You want me, and I fucking love that I can see it. Soaked from only a kiss. I haven't even had my mouth on those tits of yours."

Actually, he hadn't even seen my tits, but I wasn't about to point that out either. I just wanted him to get to what he was about to do.

I didn't have to wait another five seconds before he buried his face between my legs and began lapping at my pussy, licking up all the slickness his kiss and his words had caused.

The thought brought a giggle to my lips, and Rix stopped and looked up.

"No. Don't stop," I ordered, my hands going to his completely buzzed head, and uselessly trying to push it back down between my legs. Rude? I didn't care. I cared about his mouth being on my pussy, and that was it.

"I'll get right back to eating this pussy as soon as you tell me what the giggle was for."

Fuck it. I didn't care. Whatever would get him back to what he was doing most expediently was all that mattered. I had no shame when it came to this. My orgasm was going to come fast and hard, and I wanted it *right now*.

"I was thinking it was your mess, so it was only right you cleaned it up. You got me wet. There you go. Back to what you were doing. Please."

The words were a mess of awkward, embarrassing, and jumbled, but I was beyond caring. If he decided he didn't like it and wanted to stop, I was pretty sure I could develop some crazy upper-body strength to get his head back down to where it belonged.

"I like that. Now hold on, baby, because I'm not stopping until you come all over my mouth."

"Good."

Rix buried his face back where it belonged and didn't waste a moment before delving between my pussy lips and finding my clit. My hips bucked against his mouth, and then bucked harder when one blunt, thick fingertip circled my entrance and teased.

Oh Jesus. Sometimes you forget the old *the size of the hands and feet* being good predictors of cock size, and for Rix, that would have been a dead giveaway. His hands were enormous, and if he tried to slide two fingers inside me, I wasn't sure they'd fit.

But the one finger slipped inside effortlessly, made easier by the slickness he'd caused, and whatever he did with that finger in combination with what he was doing with his mouth on my clit caused near-immediate detonation.

I didn't even realize I was making noises until the words "Please, now, oh God" echoed off the walls of his room. And then the scream ripped from my lungs with the orgasm that hit me in a wall of pleasure.

My hands dropped to his shoulders, gripping and clinging as his name fell from my lips over and over while the orgasm kept rolling through my body. My hips bucked of their own accord, seeking more and then backing away. It was almost too much, but I couldn't help but want more and more and more.

Wherever this man had learned this particular skill, they needed to bestow some kind of honorary doctorate on him, because he was a master. A maestro even. My brain ran a million miles an hour, and all of those thoughts centered on—*if he's this good at oral, how good is he at everything else?*

Rix lifted his head and stared down at me before taking a step to the side and pulling open a drawer on the nightstand, retrieving a condom packet. When he lifted it to his teeth, the enormity of what I was about to do hit me.

He'd told me he wanted this as payment for returning Trinity safe and sound, and she still wasn't. I hadn't even demanded an update yet. Not to mention I had a date with another man tonight. What the hell was I doing?

I couldn't. Hands shaking, I pushed up to a sitting position on the bed and smoothed my skirt down. My movements clearly telegraphed my intentions, and Rix paused in his task.

"What the fuck?" His voice was deep and rough. "You get yours and then decide that's all you want?"

His silver gaze drilled into mine, and I had to look away before I spoke. "I—I can't do this."

"This ain't a matter of *can't*. It's a matter of *don't want to*."

I shoved a hand in my tangled hair and attempted to smooth it into place. "I'm sorry. I . . . I really can't. This isn't me. I don't do this."

Rix tossed the condom packet on the nightstand and reached for his pants. He pulled them on roughly before speaking. "I don't think you have a clue who you are, but it's your loss, duchess."

I wasn't going to make excuses. I was going to get the hell out of there and back home so I could shower and forget this had ever happened. Already, a small part of me—probably my lady bits—were screaming at me to lie back down and get this show back on track. But it wasn't right. I couldn't do this.

Rix stared at me for another beat before turning on his heel and striding out of the bedroom, shirtless.

My body screamed at me to rewind, but I shoved the thought down and hopped off the bed. Gathering my pride with both metaphorical hands, I held my spine straight and tall as I walked toward the door. It was closed and Rix leaned against it.

I paused a few feet away from him.

"You thought I'd make this easy for you?"

"What do you want me to say? I changed my mind. And I have a date tonight."

As soon as the words were out of my mouth, I knew they were a huge mistake. Rix pushed off the door and closed the gap between us. My chest touched his as he stared down at me. The muscle ticked in his jaw, and I read caged rage in his eyes.

"With the cop?" The question was gritted out from between clenched teeth.

I should have kept my mouth shut, but it was too late now. "Yes."

"I can't tell if you're brave or stupid. I tell you you're mine, tell you to stay away from the cop, tell you I'll get your girl back, tell me you're gonna pay with this hot little body, and you're still goin' with him." He lifted his hand to my hair and brushed it over my shoulder. It was almost as if he couldn't help touching me. "So, which is it?"

Brave or stupid? I didn't have any idea. The only thing I was sure of down to my bones was that Rix wasn't going to hurt me. I'd just inflicted some wicked blue balls on the man, and he was pissed, but he wasn't going to hurt me. I didn't think he would let Trinity suffer either. I didn't know how to answer his question, though. When it came to Rix, I was probably a little of both.

"Most likely brave and stupid."

He threaded his fingers through my hair and cupped the back of my head possessively.

"You're right. So listen up, duchess. I'll say this one more

117

time. You're mine. You let that cop have a taste of this sweetness and you're gonna be tipping toward the stupid side of the scale. Nothing changes. You get that?"

"And because you decreed it, it must be so?"

"Damn right."

"I guess we'll see," I whispered.

"Guess we will."

Rix lowered his head and took my lips. No asking, no easy kiss. A kiss of possession, as if he were trying to imprint himself on me so I'd be remembering it all night. Which I would be. There was nothing about this afternoon I'd forget.

And that was the problem.

Rix pulled away just as abruptly and spun, yanking open the door. "I'll be in touch."

"And Trinity?"

"I'm working on it."

"If you're dragging this out to keep me coming back, I promise it's going to backfire."

Rix reached out and gripped my chin. "I gave my word. No one questions my word." He must have read the frustration in my eyes at his response because he added, "Keep it together, duchess. Just a little longer."

He released me, and I gave him a nod but said nothing as I walked out on legs that I refused to admit wobbled slightly. How could this man affect me so much?

He didn't close the door until I was pulling away from the curb. Even three blocks away, I could still feel his eyes on me.

FOURTEEN

VALENTINA

R hett picked me up in his Jeep and took me to a little place not far from my house. Dick & Jenny's was a cute little cottage that had great creole and seafood. I'd driven by it a million times, but only eaten there once. It was funky and fun and completely perfect.

The entire time I was getting ready, I consciously ignored the languid ache in my body left by the orgasm Rix had given me and the promise of more to come. No matter how hard I scrubbed, all I could feel was his touch on my skin.

"So, what else do you do for fun besides sell art?" Rhett asked.

I realized I'd let the conversation fall into a semi-awkward lull after the server took our drink orders. I opened my mouth and shut it again immediately. I'd almost told him that my favorite thing to do was paint. But I didn't tell anyone that. Apparently Rix's insistence that my work was good, and Yve and Lucas's purchase of my piece, was emboldening me.

Instead, I went with my canned answer. "I enjoy volunteering, improving my green thumb, and target shooting."

Rhett's smile was quick. "I suspected you were a hell of a woman, and now I'm sure of it."

I laughed. "It's the green thumb, right? Don't get your hopes up, because when I say improving, I mean it's a work in process. I can't cook, I'm a terrible housekeeper, and I'm absentminded when I'm tied up in business stuff. So you should probably reassess your opinion until you land on something more realistic."

"And you're legitimately modest," he added.

My cheeks heated with my blush. "I'm aware of my faults and shortcomings. I consider that one of my strengths. Although, I'd rather spend time improving my strengths than working on my weaknesses. It seems to be a better investment of my time."

"I'm going to add unique to the list."

The server returned with my glass of wine and Hennessy's two fingers of bourbon before I could respond, and asked for our orders. I opted for the bouillabaisse and Rhett chose the duck.

After the server collected our menus, I turned the questions back on Rhett. "What do you like to do? Besides fight crime and keep the city safe?"

He smiled and sipped his bourbon. "Spend time with my folks, watch football, hunt, fish, and take out beautiful women."

My eyebrows went up. "Women as in plural?"

"I try to keep them to one at a time. I don't often find myself in my current predicament."

"What's that?" I asked.

"Being more interested in her than she is in me."

Wow. He was just going to lay it all out like that, was he?

"Excuse me?"

Rhett leaned back in his seat and crossed his arms. "There's something going on with you, and I know you don't want me to know what it is. But I am a detective, and that means I know when something's not right. Why don't you save us this song and dance and just tell me what's happening? If I can help, I will. If you're in trouble, I can get you out."

I dropped my gaze to my wine and took a drink. A really, really big drink.

"Guess that's all the answer I need then." He set his glass down on the table. "So cut the shit, Valentina, and tell me what it is."

I sucked back the rest of my wine, not meeting his eyes until I lowered my glass.

"I'm not in trouble. I'm fine."

"I don't believe you."

I had to give him something. He wasn't going to leave it alone. And I sucked at lying. "You said you've taken out multiple women. Well, I'm seeing someone else too. And no, I'm not telling you who he is."

Hennessy reached for his bourbon and knocked back the rest. "Guess I was right, then. I'm definitely more into you than you're into me."

I smiled weakly. "I . . . This wasn't exactly planned." To myself I added, *And "seeing" isn't even accurate because I don't have a clue what I'm really doing with him.*

"Some of the best things aren't planned."

The server stopped by our table to deliver another round of drinks, and both Rhett and I reached for them immediately.

"So, I totally understand if you just want to take me home and forget I exist," I said after another gulp of liquid courage.

Rhett shook his head. "Nah. I'm not out of this race yet. I'm sitting across from you, not him. That means I've still got a shot."

I was an idiot. It took me until just that moment to recognize that I'd found myself caught between two men who were the rare and mystical alpha breed. And I'd just made this a competition. Neither Rix nor Rhett were the kind of guy to turn down a challenge.

"Well . . . um . . ." *Come on, Valentina, think of something to say.*

I was rescued once again by the server who asked if we were interested in dessert or needed boxes. I took that moment to excuse myself and headed to the ladies' room.

Once inside, I locked the door and stared at my reflection in the mirror. "What the hell am I doing?"

I pulled my phone from my bag and saw I had missed a text message from Rix. It was a single word.

RIX: MINE.

Woulds he be inside my house waiting when I got home tonight? What if Rhett kissed me at the door? Would Rix come storming out and . . . God, what would he do? My anxiety jumped several notches.

What the hell was I going to do about this mess? Rhett was the better choice. The safer choice. I didn't even know what to categorize Rix as other than *not a realistic option*. Did I want him to be an option? My ongoing fascination with him, not to mention me being flat on my back in his bed this afternoon, said I did.

After washing my hands in cold water and giving myself another pep talk, I ignored Rix's text and walked back to the table. Rhett was gone.

I turned in a circle, surveying the restaurant. Had he changed his mind and left? Was I wrong about the competition? I had a hard time believing that, but there was no sign of him.

The server hurried over. "Your boyfriend had to step out to take a call. He'll be right back. He ordered you a latte and the chocolate torte. I'll have both out in a second."

I opened my mouth to protest the boyfriend label, but decided the server didn't care. At least the mystery was solved. I took my seat, and she came back with the most divine chocolate confection I'd ever seen. I was scraping the remnants from the plate and trying to talk myself out of licking it clean when Rhett came back inside.

"Sorry about that, Valentina. I need to cut this short and get you home." He gave me a rueful smile. "Work. Never stops."

Being a cop was ingrained in every aspect of Rhett's life, and seemed to rule it too. I wondered if the other ladies in his life had found it to be trying, but I was more curious about what had come up. Thoughts of Trinity were never far from my mind.

"Is everything okay?" I asked.

"Not usually. Let's get you home, and I'll get back to fighting crime and keeping the city safe."

I stood, and as we left the restaurant, his hand rested on the small of my back. It was a clear sign that he wasn't giving up on this yet, and I needed to figure out exactly what I thought about it.

My mind raced with the same thoughts I'd had in the bathroom as Rhett walked me up the sidewalk to my front door. Was Rix inside? Was Rhett going to kiss me? What did I want?

I was saved from having to answer that question when his phone rang again. He pulled it from his pocket and apologized.

"I gotta take this. I'll make it up to you. I'll stop by the gallery tomorrow." He stepped toward me and pressed a quick kiss to my lips. "And that'll have to tide me over until I get another chance to make it a better one. Sleep well, Valentina."

And then he was gone.

My hand was steady as I let myself in the house, but my heart pounded. I turned on the light as soon as I stepped inside. The foyer was empty. Wherever Rix was, it wasn't here.

I closed and locked the door behind me and set the alarm. Pulling my phone from my purse, I read the single word of his text again.

MINE.

Where was he? I hadn't realized I was expecting to see him again tonight until that moment. Walking through my empty house gave me far too much time to think. I'd always loved my space and my time alone, but now it didn't seem to be enough.

Things were changing. I was changing. I needed to decide what I wanted, and then figure out if it was even realistic.

I wandered into my studio and selected a fresh canvas and set up a mirror. It was time for an introspective, and what better way to do that than a self-portrait?

FIFTEEN
HENNESSY

"What the hell is your problem, man? I told you I was coming," I said as soon as I was back in my car. "This better be a fucking emergency."

"Shit's going down tonight. A big deal. My CI just called me, and we need to get there and see who's doing the buying and selling," Fortier replied.

"Where am I meeting you? I'm in my Jeep."

He relayed an address, and a quick search of my mental map told me I was heading into the hood. Worked for me as long as it got us another step closer to bringing down the head of a drug ring. Cartels getting their claws into my city pissed me the fuck off.

"I'll see you in ten. And you owe me a night without this bullshit because you hijacked my date," I said, not waiting for a response before I ended the call.

My mind was on Valentina as I backed out of her driveway. She'd been acting strangely all day, both earlier at the gallery and then tonight.

The fact that she'd admitted she was seeing another guy

surprised me. That could be what was causing her off behavior, but I wasn't entirely sure yet.

I'd find out, though. She was the first woman to grab my attention like this in a long time. Before she'd been off-limits, and now . . . now I'd decided that those limits weren't relevant anymore. Life was short. You had to take chances to get what you wanted or you'd miss your shot.

I could handle a little healthy competition. Hell, I thrived on competition. I just had to find out who my competition was.

SIXTEEN

RIX

She didn't respond. I didn't expect her to, but like a little bitch, I kept my phone close all night. Buying. Selling. Another day in my shadows.

How in the fuck had this woman become the shaft of light that showed me exactly how dark my world was? And now that I knew it, what was I supposed to do about it?

I wanted her in my bed, but I couldn't take her out in this city like the cop she was with tonight—and that burned. I lived in the shadows and she was the light. We couldn't coexist peacefully, and yet I couldn't just leave her alone. Not yet. I wasn't ready.

The image of her face as she rode out her orgasm rose in my memory. Hottest fucking thing I'd ever seen. Life-changing even.

And she was dating a cop.

That had to end. I would make it end. I didn't share, and I wasn't going to start now.

"Yo, Rix. You comin' or what?"

Eight-Ball waited for me on the far side of the warehouse. Product was supposed to change hands tonight, but Eight had gotten a tip that the cops were on the move, and called it off before even talking to me. Healthy fear of going back to prison made him quick on the trigger with decisions like that, but also made him a good second-in-command.

"Right behind you."

I surveyed the empty warehouse once again. The cops wouldn't find a damn thing here thanks to Eight's quick thinking. When I shut and locked the door behind me, I caught sight of a Jeep across the street, tucked between an abandoned building and a burned-out van. I would have missed it, but since the van was destroyed, I could see through it in sections.

Well, there they are. Hello, Five-0. Nothing to see here tonight.

I climbed into the passenger seat of Eight's Yukon and watched the Jeep from the side mirror until we turned the corner.

SEVENTEEN
VALENTINA

Girls' night was one of those things that women who had a bunch of other female friends did. I'd been a loner for so long that I barely understood how this kind of thing worked, and I felt even more guilty about going because Trinity was still locked up somewhere and I was helpless to get her out. Distraction. This was all a distraction.

While I waited in my portico for the car to pick me up, my thumbs hovered over the screen of my phone. No update from Rix, and no sign of one coming.

Screw it. I needed to know what was going on. I didn't give myself time to think as I fired off a text.

VALENTINA: Update?

I waited semi-patiently for five minutes. No reply. The car pulled up and Elle threw open the door. I hurried outside, about to shove my phone in my purse when it vibrated.

Rix: You let him touch you?

"Hey, girl!" Yve called from inside the car.

Elle was waving like Miss America before she switched to motioning to the open door like Vanna White. "Your carriage awaits."

Smiling despite my urge to strangle Rix, I slid inside.

Yve and Elle's excitement could be explained by the bottle of Fireball in Yve's hand. "We're meeting the others at the restaurant, and then after we're going to a jazz club for a little atmosphere."

"Okay."

Yve handed over the Fireball. "We're doing a little pre-gaming, old-school style."

Elle laughed. "More like I grabbed the fifth that was on the counter right before you rolled up in this fancy car, and you decided it was a great idea."

My phone buzzed again and I pulled it out.

Rix: Still waiting on that answer.

I was thinking the Fireball sounded like a great idea as well. Rix was playing games with me, and my patience was shot.

"Feel free to pass the bottle this way."

Both Elle and Yve looked at me, smiling in approval.

"Tonight's going to be fun," Elle said as she grabbed the bottle from Yve and passed it over.

I swigged and handed it back, rather proud of myself that I didn't cough. Other than the shots at the bachelorette party, drinking straight liquor wasn't exactly normal for me in the last ten years.

The shot of liquid courage had me pulling out my phone to respond to Rix.

VALENTINA: None of your damn business. I want an update.

His response was almost instant.

RIX: I'll get my answer one was or another.

He wouldn't be getting an answer out of me tonight, that was for damn sure, especially if I wasn't getting an update. All I could hope was that Rix wasn't going to renege on his promise and would keep Trinity safe.

Surprisingly, it didn't take but one more shot of Fireball for me to get comfortable with the idea. Rix might not live on the right side of the law, but I couldn't be this fascinated with him if he was truly a bad person, right? And Trinity was innocent in all of this. He wouldn't let her suffer for the consequences of D-Rock's actions. I hoped I was right, because I was betting Trinity's safety on it, which terrified me.

But what could I do about it tonight? Yve passed the Fireball around again, and the only answer to my question seemed to be another drink.

It was safe to say that having our own private room at the restaurant was in everyone's best interest. Creative cocktails were flowing, and food was eaten defensively to try to soak up some of the alcohol.

"Are we really going to the jazz club next?" Vanessa asked. "Because I'm already hammered. Con's going to have to carry me home at this rate."

"I'd let that blond Viking carry me anywhere," JP, one of Yve's employees said.

I'd seen him carry Vanessa before, and I couldn't help but think she didn't mind it.

"I thought you were crushing on Bishop?" Vanessa asked.

As the newest addition to the group, I didn't know who Bishop was, and I'd just met the cute, tattooed JP tonight.

"Who's Bishop?"

JP sighed. "A bearded, man-bunned, tatted-up gift to womankind. And he's also capable of tattooing me and pretending I don't exist. Apparently I'm too young for him."

Yve narrowed her gaze on JP. "What did you do?"

JP grabbed her drink and chugged. When she lowered the glass to the table, she replied, "Maybe surprised him with a little naked JP. I've never seen a guy look so horrified or throw my clothes at me so quickly. Embarrassing. I can never go back to Voodoo Ink. Which sucks, because who's going to finish my sleeve now?"

The table went silent before laughter broke out.

"You didn't!"

"Seriously?"

"Oh my God, that's epic."

"Stop!" JP said. "This is my pride we're talking about. Maybe if my tits and ass were bigger, he'd be into me?"

"Or maybe he's not into girls," I tossed out.

Once again, silence fell.

"Oh, he is definitely not gay," Vanessa finally offered. "He's lumbersexual to the extreme, and definitely not gay."

"I don't know what any of this means. Someone please explain."

For the rest of dinner and dessert, I was introduced to an entire culture I'd never heard of. Apparently men took beards very seriously these days. I was all for male grooming, so more power to them, but I couldn't help but be thankful that Rix leaned toward clean-shaven or the occasional stubbly look.

Wait, what?

I couldn't think about him. I *wouldn't* think about him. There was nothing between us. And I was sort of dating a guy who would arrest him in a heartbeat. Who I also appreciated leaning toward the stubble more than the beard.

My life was officially a hot mess.

Pushing it all out of my mind, I followed the women as we piled into the car that Elle and Yve had picked me up in, and we headed for the jazz club.

When Elle called for shots, I didn't argue. Not thinking was exactly what I wanted to do.

EIGHTEEN
VALENTINA

"Y‌ou sure you're good, girl?" Yve asked as she walked me up to my door.

"I'm fine. No worries. I think I drank about a gallon of water before we left."

"That explains your seventeen trips to the bathroom."

I giggled, because she didn't know that I was also learning how to drunk text. I had a very distinct feeling that this would be something I regretted in the morning, but tonight, I was altogether too entertained to stop.

I pulled out my key and shoved it in the lock of the portico door. "Thank you for inviting me. I'll see you soon, okay?"

Yve hugged me. "Take care. And make sure you get on that artist to put some more work in the gallery. We love the painting and definitely want a few more of the same style. You better not sell them to anyone before you let us see them. I'm calling dibs."

"Mmm, okay. I'll let you know," I mumbled, pulling the door open. "Soon."

If she hadn't walked away at that very moment, I might have spilled my secret. I was feeling altogether too chatty right now, so inside my house I went. Shutting the door behind me, I unlocked the door that led into the house, slipped inside, and punched in the code to my alarm. I didn't even notice the figure sitting on my staircase until I nearly tripped over him.

Slamming my hand against the light switch, my heart in my throat, my scream died when Rix stood and covered my mouth with his hand.

"Should be getting used to me waiting for you, duchess."

I wavered on unsteady heels, and he dropped his hand to wrap an arm around me.

"Didn't expect to see you."

"After those texts? You've gotta be joking."

Oh God. "What texts?" I decided that playing dumb was an excellent choice.

"The ones that said you were thinking about me. That you wanted to—"

This time it was my hand covering his mouth. "Stop. I don't want to remember. I need to go to bed."

His lips moved beneath my palm, and I couldn't tell if he was pressing a kiss or whether he was smiling. He peeled my hand off and spoke. "I'll get you to bed."

"No, you need to go to your bed."

"I like yours better."

"Too bad."

But apparently my protests were going to go unheeded, because Rix ducked and swung me up into his arms.

I struggled for a moment, but once he was climbing the stairs, I stilled. *Alpha,* my brain whispered.

I curled my hands around the soft cotton of his shirt and sniffed. "You smell good. You always smell good."

"Glad you think so." He lowered me onto my bed, but I didn't let go. "Tempting as fuck."

"Tired too."

Rix pried my hands off his shoulders and stepped back. "You need anything, or are you gonna pass out?"

I could think of one thing I needed, but I wouldn't give voice to that particular thought. "Shoes off. Skirt and blouse too."

Rix came back into view, a smile tugging at the corner of his mouth. "I think I can handle that."

He slid off my heels and rolled me partially to the side so he could unzip the skirt and tug it down and off. I'd worn a black thong under my skirt to combat the panty-line issue.

"More than tempting." Rix bowed his head, his lips close to my hip. I waited for the contact . . . but got nothing. He moved up my body and in a low voice said, "Arms up."

My shirt was off and gone in a matter of seconds.

"Bra too," I whispered, and Rix squeezed his eyes shut.

"Trying to see if you can break me?"

Break him?

I didn't know what he meant, and I was drunk enough to say it out loud. "I don't understand."

Rix reached behind me to unclasp my bra and drew it down my arms. With a growl, he tugged the duvet free from behind me before pulling it up over my body.

When he deemed me suitably covered, he met my gaze again. Liquid silver. That's what his eyes looked like in my drunken state.

"You confuse the fuck out of me. I want you, made that shit clear. You want me, but you can't seem to wrap your head around it. I don't like it when a woman changes her mind when I'm rolling a condom down my cock, but I ain't ever not gonna listen. I've put it out there every way I know how, but you're a different breed, duchess. You're gonna have to ask for it. Beg for it, even, before we get that far again."

"I don't beg," I said. "For anything."

"Then I guess we've reached a brick wall."

My glare should have communicated everything I felt, but instead, Rix laughed softly.

"How can you look so fucking beautiful even when you want to tell me to go to hell?"

I blinked against his intense stare, and murmured, "I've been to hell. I don't think you want me to tell you to go there."

"I hate that for you. I'd kill anyone who hurt you."

I yawned. "Too late. He's already dead."

"I know, and I'm sorry I can't kill him again."

My eyes snapped open at the pity in his tone. Reaching up, I grabbed his arm. "Don't. Don't even think about treating me differently because of it."

His eyes widened slightly before they softened. "You got a deal." Lowering toward me, he pressed a kiss to my temple. "Sleep, duchess."

NINETEEN
VALENTINA

A low pounding reverberated in my head, and my tongue stuck to the roof of my mouth when I swallowed.

Opening my eyes seemed like the next logical step, but I wasn't sure I was brave enough to do it. Two hangovers in a week was a new record for me.

I groaned and rolled over—into the warm body of another person. My eyes snapped open, and I registered the weight of an arm low on my hips.

What the hell?

Rix woke as soon as I moved. "You okay, duchess? Or you feel like you're gonna die?"

"Why are you in my bed?"

"Don't remember last night?"

I searched my memory and, sure enough, I remembered every single thing. I hadn't drank that much. "No, I do."

"Then why are you asking me why I'm here?"

"Because I guess I thought you'd leave after you'd done your good deed of getting the drunk chick in bed."

Rix's lips twitched before he gave me a half smile. "I don't do good deeds because that means I'm not getting anything in return."

"Of course you don't," I drawled, and then slapped a hand over my mouth at the horrible taste. I shot out of bed. Not the smartest thing I've ever done. My head swam, but evened out so I could walk calmly toward the bathroom.

I shut the door behind me and took care of my morning routine. Once my mouth no longer tasted like roadkill, I slipped on the robe on the back of my door, a short and silky one Rix had seen the first night he'd broken in. I ventured back into the bedroom and Rix was where I'd left him—sprawled out in my bed, shirtless, and from the look of the tent under the sheet, pantsless.

"Better?" he asked.

I ignored his question and asked one of my own. "Are you naked in my bed?"

A single short nod was his only response.

"Why?"

"Because I sleep naked."

"Which begs the question why you were sleeping in my bed?"

"Because you didn't answer my texts last night."

"Sure, I did."

He shook his head slowly. "Not with the answer I wanted."

"You were just worried that I was out with the cop again," I said, delivering the challenge before I could think better of it.

A harsh laugh came from Rix. "Reminding me of that while I'm naked in your bed might not be your best bet."

"Why, what are you going to do?"

My taunt was more than ill advised. Rix sprang out of bed and wrapped a hand around my wrist, dragging me back to the mattress and pinning me down. Beneath him, I struggled, but there was no way I could move over two hundred pounds of man unless he wanted me to.

Note to self: Beware of people with lightning-fast reflexes.

"I'm gonna keep you here until I have answers to my questions," he said. "Starting with, did you see him again last night?"

"No, I didn't. Not that it's any of your business."

"You're my business, duchess, so I'm gonna have to disagree with that one."

"Whatever."

His face came closer to mine. "Do whatever I want to you? Is that what you mean?"

I struggled under his hold. "Of course it's not. Now, let me up."

He shook his head. "Don't think so. I want answers. You seeing him again?"

"I don't know," I said, protest ringing from my words, and my struggles increasing.

"Easy, you know I'm not gonna hurt you."

"Why should I make it easy for you?"

"When have you ever?" He lowered his lips almost to mine. "And for some reason it just makes me want you more."

Heat surged within me and I tugged my hands free. Not to get away, but to pull him closer.

He wanted me? Well, I wanted him. The clear light of the morning was all the illumination I needed—along with the realization that I liked waking up and finding him next to me. It was dangerous. Forbidden. But this morning I would take it.

"Kiss me," I said.

"You begging yet?"

"Shut up and kiss me."

Rix hesitated a few more beats before our lips connected.

Kissing him was a full-body experience. Zings of energy ripped from my head to my toes, bouncing off all the important places in between.

How could a single kiss unleash so many sensations? I didn't know, but I strongly suspected that whatever it was made Rix even more dangerous to me.

He took, seizing control, and the kiss went on for long minutes before he pulled away and sat up.

"Can't stay in this bed without wantin' inside you, and you're not beggin' for it yet."

"Wha—"

My protest died on my lips as I caught sight of the curve of his naked ass. I'd seen it before, but I couldn't get over it. The man's ass was perfection. He turned and reached for his jeans, giving me a side view of his erection and the muscles bunching in the rest of his body.

I want to paint him. Naked.

My brain not functioning completely quite yet, I blurted it out.

Rix turned and stared at me. "You want to do what?"

"Paint you. Naked."

"That's what I thought you said."

"Will you let me?" I was already mentally mixing the colors. I'd already done it once before, and I was eager to do it again with him in front of me.

Rix didn't answer, just watched me as I sat up and belted my robe more tightly.

"Why?"

"Because."

"You gonna sell it? In your gallery?"

I shrugged. "I don't know. I guess that would be up to you."

"The only way I'll let you paint me is if you put another painting of yours—any painting—in your gallery."

The request made no sense. "Why do you care so much?"

He shook his head. "Because you need a push."

"And you decided you're the one who should be pushing me?"

"Whatever it takes, I guess." He shrugged. "Let's do this."

TWENTY
VALENTINA

I'd never painted a live subject before other than myself. And when the live subject was Rix . . . it seemed that all bets were off on my ability to concentrate. It took me forever to mix my paints. I agonized over how much and which shades, and could feel his stare resting on me like a heavy weight.

"Nervous, duchess?"

I dropped another tube of paint. Was that four times so far? "What gave it away?"

"You've got nothing to prove. Just chill and do your thing."

Something about the sound of his voice and his words calmed my shaking hands. "Keep talking."

"'Bout what?"

"Whatever you want," I said, repositioning the canvas on my easel. I was ready to start. "Anything, actually."

"I don't like you seeing that cop."

I stopped before my brush touched the canvas. "That's what you want to talk about?"

"You said anything. I'm going with that."

Rolling my eyes, I began to paint. "That's not really your decision."

"Pisses me off, though. Knowing he can take you out to dinner, in public, and I can't. It fuckin' bothers me."

I bit my lip because I didn't know how to reply. I decided to go with the question that was really on my mind. "Why do you do what you do?"

Glancing up at Rix, I watched the interplay of his muscles as he shrugged. For now, he had his pants on, because I knew he'd be too distracting to paint without them at first.

"This is what I know. It's what I'm good at. You wouldn't understand, duchess. My life isn't something that will ever make sense to someone like you."

"Are you ever going to stop doing what you do?" My question hung between us, and I knew the impact his answer would have.

Even though it seemed utterly impossible, I was fascinated with him. If there was a chance he would leave this life behind, then maybe there was some sliver of a possibility that we could have a future where he wasn't breaking into my house.

Since when do I want a future with Rix? Since I woke up with him in my bed, apparently. I liked it way too much and wanted it to happen again.

Rix flexed his hand, curling it into a fist and releasing it. "It ain't that easy. This isn't something I can just walk away from any time I want." Curling his hand back into a fist, he added, "And while I'm in this life, I can't take you out and let people see me doing it—even if you'd let me. It's not safe. You don't get to where I am without collecting a hell of a lot of enemies, and those enemies are always looking for weaknesses."

I paused as I dabbed my brush in the paint. "Am I a weakness?"

Rix's nod was short. "Yeah. Because if someone took you, I'd tear this town apart to find you."

The vehemence behind his words should have been scary, but it wasn't. It was actually comforting. He felt something for me, and whatever it was, he felt it strongly.

"So you think someone would target me to get to you if they knew?"

"That I'm hung up on you? I'm not taking the chance. That's why you won't ever find me knocking on your front door. That's why I won't be picking you up and taking you out. That's why I need to stop fuckin' thinkin' about you, but I can't." He looked at me, the muscle in his jaw clenching.

"I—I don't know what to say."

Rix shook his head. "You don't need to say anything. I don't have family, don't have friends outside my crew. Because it's too dangerous. I can't afford to have weaknesses, and once you get your girl back, you should never see me again."

His words hit me with the force of a blow. "You—what? You're going to just disappear?"

"I said *should.* Guess we'll see what happens." He met my gaze over the canvas. "You want me gone anyway."

I replied with the truth. "If I wanted you gone, you would've been in jail the first time you broke into my house."

His expression changed, the silver burning brightly. "That so?"

Nodding, I knew I had to change the subject. "Drop your pants. I'm ready to do your lower half."

Rix threw his head back and laughed. "Didn't even offer to buy me dinner first."

"I'd offer to make you dinner, but you might not survive. I'm a terrible cook."

Rix reached for the button on his jeans and unhooked it before shoving them down.

Three.

That was how many times I'd officially seen him naked, and every single one of them was going to be burned into my brain for the rest of my life. One man shouldn't be allowed to have such a beautiful body. I'd also never been so thankful to have a paintbrush in my hand.

"You can sit back down, if you want." I nodded to the chaise behind him.

"How do you want me?" he asked, the double entendre clear in his tone.

"Sit, lay back. Throw your arm over the back of the chaise. Just . . . get comfortable."

Rix complied silently.

"You can keep talking."

"You want me to keep spilling secrets?"

I shrugged. "I want you to keep my mind off the fact that I'm staring at you naked, and the silence is making it awkward."

"Long as you see something you like, we're good."

"I think it's pretty clear I like what I see."

"Seems like you should be naked too," Rix said, a mischievous smile on his face. "Only fair."

I'd thrown on a pair of leggings and an old, paint-covered tank top. Without a bra, there was no way he could miss the press of my hard nipples against the thin cotton.

"I think you're getting mixed up about how this works." Heat curled between my legs, and I felt myself grow wet.

"Nah, I'm just saying that if you're going to study every detail of me, I should have the same opportunity. Watching you sleep wasn't quite the same."

I paused. "You watched me sleep?"

Another shrug from Rix. "Maybe." He shifted on the chaise.

"I struck a deal for your girl. Should have her back to you before the end of the week."

"Really?" Hope filled me, because that was the best news I'd gotten in a long, long time. "You could've maybe led with that, you know."

"I was gonna tell you before I left either way."

I kept painting, and we lapsed into silence. I concentrated on the canvas, and when my gaze flicked back to him, I froze. His hand was wrapped around his cock and he was stroking it, his eyes burning into me.

My thighs squeezed together. "Wha—what are you doing?"

"Think that's obvious."

"You . . . have to stop." I swallowed, unable to tear my eyes away from the sight.

He didn't. Stroke after stroke, I stared as he grew even bigger and harder. I wanted him in my mouth. Right now.

Rix wanted the same thing. "Put your brush down, duchess. I want you on your knees."

Unmoving, I continued to stare.

"Come here."

I lowered my brush to the tray beside me and wiped my hands on a rag. Standing slowly, I crossed toward him. He nodded to his hand, which was still wrapped around his cock.

I pressed a knee to the chaise, and then the other, finding space between his spread legs. Licking my lips, I lowered my head.

At the sound of the doorbell ringing, we both froze.

"No fucking way. Do not move."

My phone buzzed on the side table with a text, and I bit my lip. "What if—"

Rix growled. "Go. I'll keep myself entertained."

"It'll just take me a second. Stay here."

"I don't take orders, duchess."

"I know, but it could be my parents. Or one of my neighbors." I headed for the door.

"How is someone getting to your door anyway? You've got a gated yard."

"I know, but the pedestrian gate isn't locked. It broke a couple weeks ago, and I haven't gotten it fixed."

"Jesus, here I've been jumping the fence, and all along you've got a broken latch? You need to get that shit fixed ASAP."

"How about I worry about that later," I said, my gaze once again dropping to his cock, which had softened only slightly, before I stepped back and headed out of the studio.

When I reached the front door, I peeked out the sidelight and recognized my visitor immediately.

Rhett. What was he doing here? And what would Rix do when he realized who it was?

I felt like I was sitting on top of a powder keg, box of matches in hand.

Rhett's eyebrows shot up when I opened the door. I shouldn't have been in such a rush to answer it. No makeup, paint on my hands and arms, and from the way his gaze rested on my face, I'd probably smeared some on there too.

I pushed back my hair, wondering if I looked like I'd been doing what I'd just been doing. My cheeks were hot, and I quickly crossed my arms over my still hard nipples.

"Now, what exactly were you doing?"

"Uh . . . painting?" I bit my lip and lifted a hand to my face to cover what I was sure were even redder cheeks than I'd started with. That's when his gaze dropped to my nipples.

Something lit in his green eyes. "Fuck, I want you."

He didn't even give me time to react before he wrapped a hand around my waist and yanked me against his body, his lips finding mine and his tongue sliding inside.

Oh my God. Oh my God. This is not happening. Rix is going to go to prison for killing a cop.

And yet the kiss was *good*. Delicious, actually. Rhett had serious skills, but the heat that roared through me when Rix kissed me was missing.

Finally, Rhett released me. "I probably shouldn't have done that, but I couldn't help it. You can't answer the door like that."

"Um. Uh. Okay. Sorry?"

I was babbling words that made no sense. The kiss had thrown me completely off-balance, but Rhett just smiled. A little smugly, in my opinion.

"Was there something you needed?" I asked, grasping onto the fact that I needed him gone as quickly as possible because I didn't want to clean blood off the floor in my foyer.

"Besides another taste of you? I thought I could take you to coffee to make up for cutting our date short early the other night. It's been a hectic few days and I had a couple hours free, so I stopped by."

Oh shit. I looked down, desperately thinking of something to say. I caught sight of the paint and my nipples pressing against my shirt.

"I'm a mess," I blurted. "I'm really not in any condition to be leaving the house." I looked up as he reached out and caught a tangle of my wild hair.

"But you look beautiful. I hope you were thinking about me before you answered the door."

My mind immediately went to Rix and the memory of him stroking his cock. Heat flushed my cheeks again.

"Well . . . I, uh . . ." *Get it together, Valentina*, I scolded myself. "I guess a lady should have some secrets. But thank you. I appreciate the invite."

"That's too bad. How about tomorrow?"

149

Tomorrow. Tomorrow. I bit my lip, trying to remember what was going on tomorrow. *The opening*.

"Work," I said. "I have a work thing. Maybe another time?"

"Thursday night."

Thursday. Crap. What was Thursday? I was beginning to think my brain was fried from man-overload.

"Um," I mumbled. "I don't think I have anything going on." As soon as the words were out, I kicked myself. I wasn't supposed to be seeing him again.

"Then Thursday it is. Enjoy your Sunday." He leaned in and stole another kiss. "This is a good look on you."

I smiled and shakily closed the door and locked it. I jumped when I felt the heat of a body behind me. A really big, really hot body.

"You let him touch you," Rix growled in my ear.

"I didn't ask him to."

"Don't care. No one touches what's mine."

I spun to face him. "You just told me that you couldn't really have someone because it was too dangerous. So explain to me how that makes me yours?"

Rix's growl deepened. "Don't throw that back at me. So long as no one knows about us, you're safe."

"I don't even know what that means."

"Guess I'll have to show you." Rix cupped my jaw and lowered his mouth to mine. "No lips but mine kiss you. I don't fucking care whether you like it or not. Mine." His other hand smoothed the hair out of my face. "No hands but mine touch you."

"So you want me to tell him no?"

His grip on my face tightened slightly. "You're gonna tell him no. Whatever he thinks you're doing on Thursday night, you're not. You're gonna be with me. I'll have your girl back, and we'll figure out how this is gonna move forward. You got that?"

Finally. God, the relief of having a defined date was palpable. That was the best news I'd heard all day, and in exchange for that, I'd agree to just about anything, including canceling a date with Rhett.

After that kiss, I knew I didn't want him the way I wanted Rix. Rhett was an honest, good guy, and I couldn't keep jerking him around. This *juggling two men* business was exhausting, and I was ready to be done.

But even having made that decision, I knew that I wouldn't necessarily get to keep Rix when this was all over. He'd made that clear. His life didn't allow for attachments, and I needed to find a way to unattach myself before I was in too deep and set myself up for a fall.

Who would have ever thought I'd be worried about falling for him?

"You get me, duchess? That's how it's goin' down."

I slid my hand around the back of his head and raised up on my toes to press a kiss to his lips. "I think I get you."

TWENTY-ONE
VALENTINA

Because I was still a novice when it came to girl posses, I didn't realize having one meant that they'd show up uninvited at your exclusive gallery openings. But halfway into the evening, Yve, Elle, and Vanessa came through the door of Noble Art.

"I need something for the lake house," Vanessa said. "And I saw the flyer for Burton Ridgeway's work, and I fell in love."

"That's only because you didn't see the painting I snagged by Valentina's anonymous artist friend," Yve countered. She turned to look at me. "Did you get more yet?"

I shook my head. "No, sorry."

"Let me know. I called dibs."

"I'm here for the champagne," Elle added. She shrugged. "I mean, let's be honest. Someone's going to pawn some of this stuff eventually, and I'll get it for a song."

Elle was a nut. But she was probably right. People pawned all sorts of things at Chains, where she worked with her boyfriend, Lord.

"Well, thank you so much for coming. Feel free to look around. Champagne is on the table in the corner."

"Good looking out, girl." Elle looped her arm through Vanessa's took off in the direction of the champagne.

I was turning back to Yve when I caught sight of a man across the street in a black T-shirt with a build like Rix's. Was he watching me tonight?

"You aren't listening to a word I've said, are you?" Yve drawled.

I jerked around to face her as she studied me. "Sorry. I thought I saw someone out there."

"Is there something going on with you? You've been acting different lately."

I wondered if she was referring to me actually going out and having fun, but I couldn't be sure. "Things have been a little hectic lately. I'm . . . distracted."

Elle and Vanessa came back with champagne and caught the last bit of my explanation.

"Distracted? I'm calling bullshit. You look like you've got man problems."

Oh shit. I didn't want to discuss this. Not right now. I scanned the rest of the gallery, looking for a customer who needed assistance, but Burton was speaking with one small group and Remy was chatting with another couple.

When I didn't immediately answer Elle, she kept going. "Mm-hmm. Man problems, for sure. You find yourself an alpha to keep you busy at night?"

I thought of the man I'd woken up next to yesterday morning—who'd stroked himself while I painted. My cheeks flushed with color every time I thought of it. And then the one who was insisting on taking me to dinner on Thursday. What a mess.

"I'll take that as a yes." Elle laughed. "Tell us about him."

"Which one?" I said, not thinking before I spoke.

153

"Whoa, girl. You got two on the hook? You work fast." Yve sounded incredulous.

"It's a mess. I . . . I don't know what to do. I'm trying to figure out how to let one of them down easy, but he just won't take the hint. He knows there's someone else, and I think he gets off on the competition."

"They all do," Vanessa said. "It's an alpha thing."

"Who are they?" Elle asked.

I froze because I couldn't tell them about Rix, which told me once again that I was insane for even thinking that we could possibly have something. And did I really want to tell them about Rhett?

"I'd rather not say just yet."

"Cagey. I like it." Elle raised her glass to me and sipped.

"How do I get the one to stand down?"

"Hmm . . ." Yve tapped the side of her glass. "You could tell him you require a better-equipped man. Generally, insults about dick size work really well."

"Oh no, don't do that. You'll damage the poor guy for life," Vanessa said. "Just tell him you don't feel the same way about him, and that if the other guy ever screws up, you'll keep him in mind. Lets him down easy without breaking his heart completely."

That could actually work. "I'll give it a try and see what happens."

In the back of my mind, I couldn't stop myself from thinking, *Maybe when this thing with Rix blows up in my face . . .*

I would let him down easy, and this would be over.

TWENTY-TWO
VALENTINA

I was not on a date. I swore I wasn't. And yet, here I was sitting across the table again from Rhett Hennessy. Table ambush. Let's call it that. Much like the first night we had dinner together, this one wasn't intentional, and I hadn't been able to come up with a polite excuse as to why he couldn't join me.

To celebrate the success of our Monday-night opening and all the hard work Remy had been putting in without Trinity there to help, I'd taken him out to dinner after we closed the gallery. Burton Ridgeway had sold well over half of the pieces we'd been showing.

But Remy's roommate had texted a few minutes after we'd been seated and she'd lost her key. Being the nice guy that he was, Remy ditched a free dinner to help a friend.

Which left me sitting at an empty table in the window when Rhett Hennessy had been walking by. Sometimes, New Orleans really was the smallest town on the planet.

"I could've sworn you'd said you were busy tonight," Rhett had commented as soon as he helped himself to the seat across from me without asking for an invitation.

"The opening was a success, and I came to celebrate with one of my employees. But he had something come up unexpectedly."

"Then I guess it's my lucky night."

Rhett was persistent; I could give him that. And he was a nice guy. But all I could think about while I was sitting there was the promise I'd made to Rix, and the plan to let him down easily the girl posse had helped me concoct. The words formed on my tongue dozens of times, but I hadn't been able to find the right moment to get them out.

My conversational skills were decidedly subpar as the server brought food, which also coincided with Rhett's phone receiving a barrage of text messages.

Pulling it from his pocket, he frowned.

"Something wrong?" I asked.

He didn't reply until after he tapped out a response. "A neighbor of mine called in a prowler around my house. Local units are headed that way."

A prowler? That sounded bad. "Shouldn't you go and check it out?"

"You trying to get rid of me? You pick the other guy?"

His direct questions threw me off, and I choked on the sip of water I was currently taking. "Excuse me?"

"You said you were dating someone else. I want to know if I'm fighting a losing battle."

This was my opening. "Well—"

His phone went off with another text. "Fuck." His tone was low and disbelieving. When he looked up, his expression was hard. "I gotta go." He rose, pulled his wallet out, and tossed some bills on the table before he cupped my chin.

I met his piercing green eyes.

"Losing battle or not, you're worth the fight. I'm not giving up." He leaned down and pressed a hard kiss to my lips.

The intensity flowing from Rhett was impossible to ignore. He released his hold on my chin and I opened my mouth to respond, but he was already heading for the door.

Are you serious right now? How can I not break up with this guy that I'm not even trying to date? This was becoming ridiculous.

I finished my dinner alone, wishing the man I was trying to choose was able to sit across from me. But that wasn't going to happen. The impossibility of the situation killed my appetite for dessert.

TWENTY-THREE
RIX

"You got balls the size of fucking boulders to break into my house," the cop yelled as he slammed the door and walked into his living room.

"Worried someone's going to think you're a dirty cop like your brother was accused of being?" I asked.

"Fuck you, Rix."

"That ain't why I'm here. I'm here to deliver a message, one I thought might get lost in translation." I shoved up out of Hennessy's recliner and stalked toward him. "Valentina Noble is off-limits."

Hennessy's expression twisted with shock. "Are you fucking kidding me? You're staking a claim on her? She's so far out of your league, you must be trippin' on whatever shit's runnin' the streets lately."

I stopped a foot from him, and even though we were evenly matched in size and weight, I could take him. I had rage on my side. And a little duchess who had questions to answer.

"She's off the menu. Find someone else."

Hennessy shook his head. "No. Fucking. Way. I'm not bowing out of this when we both know you can't have her."

His vehemence pissed me right the fuck off. She was already mine.

"You still want help proving your brother wasn't dirty, or not?"

Hennessy stilled. "So it's like that."

"Take it or leave it. I got nothing to gain by helping you on this one, so a little extra motivation is in order."

And when it came to Detective Hennessy, I knew there wasn't much he wouldn't give up to prove that his brother wasn't a dirty cop. His reputation had been blackened by the suspicions, and his pops had retired because of it. The whole family of die-hard cops had suffered a serious blow the day the older Hennessy brother had been killed when a bust went bad.

When Hennessy didn't respond at first, I wondered if I'd miscalculated how deep his fascination with Valentina ran. Didn't fucking matter. She was mine. He might be the better man, but I didn't care. I'd laid my claim, and I wouldn't give her up for anything or anyone. Not even a cop who could sit across from her at a restaurant in a window where my guy saw him and reported back to me.

Valentina had some explaining to do, after I took it out on her luscious ass. I could see my rules hadn't quite sunk in as well as I'd thought they had. But she would learn. I didn't share.

"Yes or no, Detective," I prompted. "I ain't got all night. I got another stop to make."

Hennessy glared at me. "You're fucking her, aren't you?"

I smirked. "A gentleman doesn't kiss and tell."

"Fuck you, Rix. You've never been a gentleman."

"Yeah, well, neither have you. Now, make your call, and know that if you pick her, you're choosing the losing side on every front. Then you'll have no help proving your brother's innocence, and you're not getting the girl." When he still didn't answer, I shook my head and backed up the way I'd come in. "Don't be stupid. You know how to find me when you've made your choice."

I had my hand on the doorknob, and still he didn't speak. The house was silent as I slipped out into the night.

I had another stop to make.

TWENTY-FOUR
VALENTINA

F ace washed, lotion slathered, and eyes drooping, I climbed into my bed. I'd wondered if Rix would be waiting at my house tonight, and had tried to ignore the shaft of disappointment when he wasn't.

I'd decided. I'd made my choice. But was it really even a choice? Could I even have Rix? I was ready to lay it out and see what our options were. Maybe he could get out of this life and have a fresh start somewhere?

And you're an idealistic and naive idiot because he's a criminal.

I also needed to shed the guilt that was weighing me down. Rationally, I knew it wasn't my fault that Rhett had decided to join me. It wasn't like I could be rude and tell him no, right? I had a feeling that excuse wasn't going to fly.

I lay awake for long minutes, watching the numbers of my bedside clock change before I finally drifted off.

Hands.

Decadent hands.
Clever fingers.
Everywhere.
Teasing, touching.
And the lips . . . tasting, sucking, kissing.

The sensations were too real to be a dream. My body heated and my eyes fluttered open. There was no fear when I realized I was no longer alone in bed. There was nothing but *need*.

Rix knelt over me, hands pressing my legs apart as his mouth lowered to my center.

"Oh God, yes. Please."

His head lifted and his gaze shot up to mine, flashing in the dim light of the room. "You're gonna have to do better than that, duchess, if you want my mouth on this pretty cunt."

"What?" The word came out on a breath, and my inner muscles clenched at the possession in his eyes.

"You've left me hanging twice, and if you want yours this time, you're gonna beg."

"Beg?"

He nodded slowly, lowering his mouth to hover over my clit.

"Please, just . . . please."

"What are you gonna do for me? Gonna leave me stroking my own cock, thinking of you, while you're letting another man put his mouth on you?"

"No. I'm going to tell him. I swear." I lifted my hips, trying to reach him, but Rix's hands clamped over my thighs and held me down.

"I feel like we keep having the same conversation over and over again. This is the last time."

"Okay. Now, *please*."

"Please, what?"

"Please make me come."

His eyes flashed again, and his lips curled into a satisfied smile before he lowered his mouth to my pussy.

My palms found their way to his buzzed head, and it took all of my self-control not to shove his face between my legs. A plea left my lips and he began to devour me. Like with everything else, Rix followed no one's rules when it came to the bedroom. He licked and tongued and sucked at my clit until I was arching up and writhing against him. And when one finger slid inside me, I knew I couldn't wait long before he filled me.

I needed. I wanted. And I might combust if I didn't get it.

An orgasm slammed into me when his teeth closed around my clit and tugged. Or maybe it was the finger pressing against the entrance no one had ever breached.

Either way, I lost my grip on reality as pleasure rolled through me.

"Please. I need—"

Rix lifted his head and stared down at me. "Me, duchess. You need me. I'm the only man eating this pussy. I'm the only man sliding inside you. I'm the only man you're ever gonna feel this way for. Get me?"

"Yes."

"I see you again with that cop, and I'm going to tie you up and tease you until you're about to come—over and over—but not let you, even when you're dying for it. And then I'll spank that ass of yours red. My woman. I don't share. You need a lesson. I'm here to deliver it."

Caveman.

Realization sank in. He knew about me having dinner with Rhett again? Was he having me watched?

But as much as I wanted to protest that I was not the kind of woman who would ever allow herself to be spanked, all I could do was nod, because his thumb pressed to my clit and another orgasm broke free. My fingers curled into the sheets of the bed as I bucked and rode it out. How he could play my body so easily, I didn't know, and I didn't actually care. I just wanted more. Everything else could wait.

Rix was rolling a condom down his cock, and that was exactly the *more* I wanted. Needed.

He pressed the head to my entrance but went no further.

"Wha—"

One hand shot out and Rix grasped my nipple between his thumb and index finger, increasing the pressure with every passing second. Shards of pleasure-laced pain clawed through me. My eyes cut to his, another question on my lips.

"You want to know what? You remember last time we got this far and you decided you'd had enough?"

A tendril of fear twisted around the pleasure and pain as he rolled my nipple, his silver gaze burning with intensity.

I nodded.

"Good. Because that shit don't fly with me. You're gonna beg for this—" He nudged his cock against me, making my inner muscles clench with need. "Before I give it to you."

Beg? A frown tugged my lips downward, but Rix increased the pressure on my nipples and gave me another teasing push with his cock.

God, I want him. Now. I was already begging in my head, and the words would soon be on my lips.

Rix raised an eyebrow. "You want this?" He thrust an inch before pulling out completely, never letting go of his hold on my nipple.

"Yes. Please. I need it," I whispered. "Please—"

A slow smile spread over his face. "Then say it, duchess."

I shook my head, confused about anything beyond the pleasure he was withholding from me. I'd begged. What else did he want from me?

He pressed his cock to my entrance once more and I raised my hips, trying to take more. Shaking his head, Rix tsk-tsked.

"Not until you say it. Or I walk."

"Say what?" I demanded, frustration edging my words. I needed him inside me. Now.

"You're mine."

He spoke the words like a vow, and I could do nothing but give the words back to him. Because they were the truth.

"I'm yours."

He slammed home with one thrust and I arched into his lean, muscled body. It was beautiful. A perfect blend of pain and pleasure, and I wanted both from this man.

"Fucking perfect. Everything I knew you would be." The words were a low growl. He gripped my calves and lifted my legs until they rested on his shoulders. "Gonna take everything I need from you, but you'll get what you need too."

And that was the last he spoke before he began to pound into me. Over and over. Readjusting the angle and my position so he could get deeper and, *oh Jesus*, he found my G-spot.

My vision blurred as he worked his hips and never slowed his pace. An orgasm like I'd never experienced before gathered inside me, building with every thrust until I teetered on the edge, detonation imminent.

Rix never stopped. He pushed me over the edge mercilessly, sliding his hand between my legs and pressing his thumb over my clit.

My scream might have woken the neighbors, but I didn't care.

It. Was. Glorious.

I rode out the orgasm as Rix continued to take me with decadent intensity. His own roar sounded as his hips stilled and his cock pulsed inside me.

Sweat dripped from his face, and my own skin was slick. I didn't know if it had come from him or me, but it didn't matter.

I think I can check "fuck of a lifetime" off my bucket list.

A small giggle escaped from my lips and Rix's gaze snapped to mine. "Now is not the time to be laughing, duchess."

I covered my mouth, my smile growing larger. "I can't help it. I think my brain quit working. I'm blaming you."

His lips curved upward into a genuine smile, and the expression on his face relaxed. "Guess I can handle that."

He squeezed my hip before he lowered my legs and slid out from between them. The loss of his fullness wasn't welcome. I wasn't ready to let him go. But instead of saying those ridiculous things out loud, I watched as he crossed to the bathroom and disappeared inside.

I pulled the sheet up around my cooling body and curled onto my side, facing the bathroom.

I can't believe that just happened.

Being woken from a dead sleep on the brink of the best orgasms of my life was a new experience for me. And I was happy to repeat it anytime.

Rix came back into view within moments, his attention skimming over my body as he moved toward the bed.

He didn't speak as he lifted the sheet and slid under it. He also didn't speak as he rolled me over and pulled me back into his big, warm body. His arm wrapped around me, pinning me against him, and I didn't protest. I'd never really spooned with anyone before, and he would have been the last person I would have expected it from. But I couldn't stop myself from snuggling back into him, soaking up his warmth.

His lips found my ear, and the words he growled into it left no doubt as to how much had truly changed in the space of the last hour.

"You sleep in my arms. Come on my cock. Reach for me in the night. That's how it's gonna go from here on out, duchess. That's just the beginning of being mine."

I didn't know how to respond. A simple *okay* seemed weak. But I didn't have any declarations of my own to add to it. I was completely okay with everything he said, but I also wondered what followed *just the beginning of being mine*.

"Now, turn your head and kiss your man. Because I'm beat, and we need to catch some sleep."

I twisted my head to meet his eyes. "I guess this means you're mine too, right?"

Rix gave me a sharp nod. "Damn right."

"I can work with that." I pressed my lips to his and turned to get comfortable again.

I felt his lips on my hair, and as I drifted off, I thought I heard him say, "Yeah, you'll work with that."

TWENTY-FIVE
VALENTINA

I woke alone, and if not for the messy bed and the definite soreness between my legs, I would have thought I'd dreamed the whole thing. But it had happened. I replayed every memory as I let the hot water of my shower cascade over me.

Give your man a kiss.

My man was a criminal. My father was a judge. And very soon, I had to tell the cop who said he wasn't giving up the fight that he'd already lost.

How had my quiet life become this unrecognizable tangle of craziness?

Toweling dry my hair, I stared at the rumpled sheets of the bed. How had I not woken up when he'd left? Probably because I'd slept better than I had in recent memory while in his arms. Not something I expected in the least.

You sleep in my arms.

Did that mean he was planning on sleeping here every night? Was I even okay with that? The memories kept replaying on a constant loop as I brushed my teeth, put on makeup, and blow-dried my hair.

Apparently getting lost in the thoughts of amazing sex from the night before wasn't good for my punctuality, because I arrived at the gallery five minutes after I should have been open. But it wasn't like there was a line of customers out the door, so no one would ever know.

As I walked inside, a wave of frustration and helplessness washed over me. Trinity should be here today. She should be working with me, and arguing about how to rearrange at least one wall. Instead, I was trusting in Rix that she was safe and he was getting her back. Even though it seemed to be taking a ridiculous amount of time. That's the funny thing with faith, you don't get to question if you were going to believe. And if I was believing Rix, I'd have her back soon.

I did. I believed him. I had faith.

And then the front window of my gallery shattered.

Dropping to my knees, I crouched on the floor, covering my face and waiting for the sound of gunshots or screams. But when none came, I blinked open my eyes slowly and turned my head toward the front window. Broken glass covered the old wood floor, and in the middle of it was a brick.

Once I'd pushed up to my feet, I walked on unsteady legs toward it. A piece of paper was wrapped around it, but the writing wasn't visible. I wanted to touch it, but thoughts of all the cop shows I'd seen over the years stopped me before I reached for it.

Fingerprints. Maybe there were some. I needed a cop.

Obviously, Rhett was the first one to come to mind. The saying *kill two birds with one stone* came to mind, but it seemed less than ideal considering the brick I was staring at.

The shattered front window mocked me as I walked to my desk and pulled my phone out of my purse. I had two calls to make, one to Rhett and the other to the man I could always count on.

My daddy.

Two crime scene technicians collected evidence while one of Rhett Hennessy's colleagues questioned me about the events of the morning. Was I usually late for work? Did I see anything before the brick came through the window? Did anyone yell anything? Did I hear a car? Could it have been someone on foot? Did I have any enemies or possible motives for someone to vandalize my gallery?

I answered all of his questions patiently, and stumbled over a *not that I can think of* in response to the last question. The fact that Trinity was still missing and I wasn't able to report it to the cops definitely was at the forefront of my mind. It wasn't a stretch to think it could be related. Or maybe it was just some random crime. I had no idea.

Rhett had asked his colleague to interview me, and I couldn't help but wonder if he was avoiding a conflict of interest by not doing it himself. I had to tell him. I had to find my lady balls and woman up, and tell him that nothing was going to happen between us.

But I wasn't doing it in front of this audience.

A crime scene tech unwrapped the paper from the brick just as my father walked through the front door.

"What the hell happened? Are you okay, baby girl?"

When he rushed toward me, for some reason tears burned in my eyes, and I blinked them away. He was the picture of *dad to the rescue*.

Ignoring everyone else in the room, he pulled me into a hug and squeezed. "You scared the hell out of me. I haven't told your mother yet because I want to know what's going on so I can answer her questions."

Typical Dad, protecting his ladies from anything he could.

I quickly relayed what I knew, which wasn't much, and my father looked to Detective Fortier.

"So, what do you think?"

The good detective shook my father's hand. "We're just starting our investigation, but have no doubt we'll figure out what happened. Probably just random vandalism. Someone who got started partying a little too early and found a brick to play with."

"Sir, I don't think that's the case," the crime scene tech said. She was in her mid to late twenties, and had blondish-brown hair and blue eyes.

Detective Fortier crossed his arms. "What do you mean?"

Rhett joined the powwow and looked at the paper she was carefully holding with her latex-covered fingertips. On the paper was a grainy picture with a red slash through it. I didn't get a clear view of the image until the crime scene tech held it up in front of me.

"Do you know this girl, ma'am?"

My stomach dropped to the floor. *Trinity*. Her hair was a ratty mess—not something she'd ever allow on purpose—and she had a forlorn expression on her face.

Oh my God. I needed to call Rix.

"Isn't that the girl who works here? The one you've been mentoring for years now?" my father asked.

Rhett's sharp green gaze drilled into mine. "The one that was missing but you said was no longer missing."

All three men and the two crime scene techs looked at me.

In that moment, I had a choice. I could lay it all out for the cops and put Trinity's safety in their hands, or I could keep my mouth shut and trust that Rix would get her back. Like right now.

My mouth opened and closed again without words coming

out. Finally, I said, "I think this has to be some big misunderstanding. I don't know why someone would do this."

Detective Fortier studied me carefully. "If there's something you know or something you're afraid of, it's in your best interest to tell us right now, Ms. Noble."

My father frowned. "Valentina, what's going on?"

I opened my mouth to lie to all of them, but both Rhett and his partner's phones started ringing. Sirens filled the air outside, and my father's phone started ringing as well. And so did the crime scene techs'.

What in the world?

The people on their phones looked at each other, and everyone froze for a moment before asking rapid-fire questions to whoever was on the other end.

From what I could hear, there was a bomb threat called in on all government buildings in the parish. Police stations, city hall, courthouses, and the like.

Suddenly my little broken window was no longer important.

My father turned to me first. "I've already got someone on his way to board up the window, and then I want you to get home. It isn't safe to be out and about right now. I'm going to get your mother. She'll to want you to come to the house, but you decide what you want to do."

"I'm fine, Dad. Go do what you need to do. I'm sure whoever you sent will be here in a minute. This is no big deal compared to whatever else is going on out there."

"Okay, baby. Call me if he isn't here in five minutes."

I hugged my dad. "Fifteen minutes. It's going to be a madhouse of traffic out there."

Sirens wailed from streets all over the Quarter.

My dad nodded and turned to go. "Call me when you get home too."

"I will."

The crime scene techs reached for their gear bags and packed up the evidence. Before it was gone, I snapped a picture of the piece of paper that had been wrapped around the brick. You'd better believe Rix was going to be explaining what the hell was going on.

Rhett and Fortier were wrapping up their calls, and I watched them out of the corner of my eye as I reached for my phone to text Rix.

But there was already a text from him.

RIX: *I just heard about your window. Sending someone to fix it. Don't leave until I come for you.*

How had he heard?

VALENTINA: *Waiting for the repair guy now. My dad send someone too.*

His response was instant.

RIX: *Be these in 10. Get your company moving out.*

So he knew the cops were here too? How did he know that? Seriously, the things Rix knew were creepy. Had he called in the bomb threat to get the cops out of the gallery?

And you've officially picked him over the cops.

I'd made my decision. That much was clear. I had a side, and that side wasn't the right side of the law.

Rix came in the front door, glass crunching under his feet from the pieces I'd missed with my broom. He didn't stop to look at the window. He didn't look at anything but me.

"You okay, duchess?" His hand cupped my face as he stared down at me, his silver eyes soft but his jaw muscle clenched.

I nodded. "Just shaken up, I guess. That was a first for me."

"My guys are just behind me. We'll get the window boarded up, and get you out of here."

"Is that going to be secure enough? Or do I need to move the artwork?"

Rix's thumb skimmed along my jaw. "No one will touch this place. I'll have people on it 24/7. No one targets you."

He dropped his hand and I reached for my phone, the picture of the note on the screen. "What the hell is going on?"

Rix's gaze dropped to the screen, but before I got an answer as to why her picture was with the brick, two young black men walked up carrying large pieces of plywood.

"Later. I gotta go. Shit's unfolding and I need to be on top of it. I'll meet you back at your place in a few hours."

He turned, and I reached out a hand to grab his arm. "That's it? You're not going to tell me anything?"

Rix met my concerned gaze. "There ain't nothin' you can do right now to help your girl. I'm the one who's got a lock on that. Get home. Set your alarm. When I've got news, you'll hear it from me in person."

I cocked a hip, not altogether sold on Rix's non-informative decree. "And what if I'm not okay with that?"

One move. That's all it took for Rix to reach out and yank me against him. "Thought we were on the same page, duchess."

I pressed both hands to his chest. "I'm starting to wonder if we're in the same story."

His silver gaze was determined. Unyielding. Possessive. "There's only one story. The one where you're mine, and you chose me. You didn't say jack shit to the cops, and you cemented that choice. I'm gonna protect you and your girl, but I'll do it my way."

In my peripheral vision, I could see the men working on the window. Rix must not care about our audience because he didn't release me.

"We clear now, duchess?"

I wasn't used to this level of caveman behavior in any man of my acquaintance, but Rix had been different from the beginning. He didn't ask permission. I wasn't even clear on whether he asked forgiveness. He wrote his own rules, and instead of being completely put off by that, I was drawn to it like metal to a magnet. Something in me responded to his constant display of confidence.

How a man could be that sure of everything all the time, I didn't know. But not having to have all the answers and be expected to make all the decisions . . . it freed a part of me. Yet that didn't mean I didn't want to have some say, and it surely didn't change the fact that I wanted to be kept informed.

I broke the stare with Rix and flicked a glance over his shoulder to the men who were already almost finished boarding up the window.

"We've got an audience."

"Don't care. Just waiting for one word from you, and we'll be on our way."

"Okay. I get it." His grip on my arms loosened, and I added,

"But I want you to fill me in on everything when you get to my house."

His fingers flexed, and I could tell he was frustrated with me.

Rix leaned in close, his breath brushing my ear. "You make me want to turn that ass of yours red, duchess."

A shiver worked down my spine as he pulled away, pressed a hard kiss to my lips, and released me.

Turning, he nodded toward his guys who were packing up their tools. "Let's go."

TWENTY-SIX

VALENTINA

The doorbell ringing threw me off completely. I'd been expecting Rix to magically show up—despite my active alarm—and find me in my studio where I was covered in more paint than I probably should be. But I'd thrown myself into my work so I could try to stop worrying about whatever might be happening with Rix and Trinity. It wasn't working.

It wouldn't be my parents. They'd called to invite me to stay in their guest room, and when I'd declined, my father had tried to tell me I needed a bodyguard. That hadn't gone far, and not only because I couldn't have a bodyguard because said bodyguard would find out about Rix. And then there was the fact that I didn't need a bodyguard because I had Rix.

So, who in the world was ringing my doorbell—I glanced at the clock on the wall—after ten o'clock at night? I cleaned my brush, killing time and hoping whoever it was would give up and go away. But they didn't. The doorbell rang again.

I need to get that gate latch fixed. And maybe electrify it. Would that be bad? With my luck, I'd zap some Girl Scout selling cookies, and she'd have curly hair for the rest of her life.

With that random train of thought winding through my head, I paused at the kitchen counter where I'd laid my purse to pull my gun out and stuff it in the back waistband of my yoga pants. After the events of today, I wasn't taking a chance with my safety. I knew all too well what could happen if I wasn't careful.

Not thinking about that. I've moved on.

And I had. The last week held the longest stretches I'd gone without thinking about that night. I took that as a huge win.

The doorbell rang again and a strong, steady knock followed.

I peeked through the sidelight. *Crap. Rhett.*

He'd had way too many questions in his eyes when he'd stood in the gallery earlier today. He knew that Trinity had been missing, and then I'd dodged answering when he'd asked if I'd found her. Tack on a picture of her wrapped around a brick, and anyone would be suspicious.

I unlocked the dead bolt and pulled open the door.

"A little late to be stopping by to invite me for coffee," I said, shooting for breezy and carefree.

He didn't smile. His gaze dropped to the paint on my hands and clothes—and probably on my face.

"How many of the paintings in your gallery are your work?"

Of all the secrets I had, that one used to be my most closely guarded. Oh, how my life had changed recently.

"None."

"But there was. The anonymous artist. That was you."

It didn't seem worth the effort to lie about that anymore. "Yes, but no one knows."

"Why were you so surprised to see it there? Hell, you were straight shocked."

Dammit, his perceptiveness was really starting to become a pain in my rear.

"Because I didn't know it was there. Someone decided to push me into showing a piece to prove a point."

"Who?" His gaze narrowed.

"Does it matter?" I countered. "Because that can't be why you're here."

"Are you going to invite me in?"

I glanced out the front door to see his Jeep parked on the opposite side of the street. Would Rix notice? Or would he sneak in unaware?

My heart thumped in my chest at the thought of Rhett and Rix coming face-to-face in my house. In my head, Desi Arnaz's voice said *Lucy, you got some 'splaining to do.* I really didn't want to do any 'splaining tonight, but what choice did I have?

"It's pretty late, Rhett."

"I'll make it quick." His expression stayed blank. This was not a social call, or at least not a lighthearted one.

I opened the door wider and stepped back. "Then come on in."

I made espresso, in part to keep my hands busy, and partly because I wasn't planning on falling asleep before Rix showed up. Rhett didn't start talking until I turned around with two espresso cups in hand.

I set one on the counter where he leaned, opting not to take a seat on a bar stool.

"Are you going to tell me why you're here, or are you going to make me guess?" At this point, I decided playing dumb was probably my best bet.

"I'm pretty sure you know why."

"Stop being a cop for thirty seconds and cut the crap, Rhett."

That finally got a hint of a smile out of him. "I like the fire when you stop keeping it banked."

I said nothing and sipped my espresso. I was still gathering the words to let him down easy when Rhett tipped his double shot back and downed it in a single gulp. His smile faded and he cut right to the point.

"Where's Trinity?"

Lie or don't lie. *What the hell do I do?*

The back stairs that led into the kitchen creaked, and I froze.

Oh. Fuck. I didn't use the F-word very often, even in my head, but using it right now made a hell of a lot of sense.

I didn't turn to look. Maybe Rix would see Rhett and duck back up the stairs. And how the hell did he get upstairs? He had to have used the front stairs in the foyer.

Rhett's eyes went wide with shock.

Oh shit. Oh fuck. I bit my lip, which was a good move considering the voice I heard next.

"I'm right here."

I spun around, shock and relief coursing through me. My eyes searched every inch of Trinity for evidence of injury or mistreatment. Sweeter relief followed when my inspection revealed a well-rested, well-fed, unmarked girl. She'd never looked more lovely to my eyes. Her hair wasn't in its usual intricate style, but it looked like she'd recently showered.

My gaze darted to the stairs for a moment. Rix had to be up there. He'd gotten my girl back, and I couldn't wait to deliver on what I owed him, even though technically I already had. Mostly, I just wanted to throw myself at him and climb him like a tree.

My chaotic thoughts and emotions ran together as Trinity came toward me and stopped beside me, leaning slightly against my side. I wrapped an arm around her and hugged her tight.

"As you can see, we're having a bit of a slumber party tonight."

Rhett's eyes were every bit as assessing as mine had been on Trinity. "You just happened to be upstairs?" Skepticism edged his words like blades.

She nodded. "It's almost time for me to go to bed, so yeah." A ring of attitude came through loud and clear. She was still my feisty little trooper. And thank God for that.

"Where've you been the past few days?" Rhett asked. "I stopped by to talk to your grandmother today, and she's been worried about you. She said she hasn't seen you in over a week."

Trinity stiffened, and I thought for sure the gig was up. We were screwed.

I opened my mouth to interject something, anything, but Trinity beat me to it. "I was staying with my boyfriend. Gran just didn't want to admit it to you because she doesn't approve of *pre-marital relations*. But I'm eighteen and I'm not committing a crime."

Rhett's gaze sharpened on both of us. "So, why aren't you with your boyfriend tonight?"

Trinity trembled beside me. "We got into a fight today and we broke up. When I asked Valentina if I could crash here, she said yes. I'll go home to Gran soon, but I'm not ready yet. She's just going to tell me she told me so, and then I'll get a lecture about *why would he buy the cow when he's getting the milk for free*. I couldn't handle it tonight."

Rhett nodded, and I wondered if he was buying it. If I couldn't feel Trinity's shivering against me, I might have bought the whole story too.

"I'm glad you're all right then. You should definitely keep

the people around you informed of your whereabouts. They worry. Especially your boss."

"Thank you for your concern, but I'm all good," Trinity replied.

Rhett looked to me. "So, how does that explain the brick?"

Again, Trinity came to the rescue. "It's my fault. I told my boyfriend I was breaking up with him to spend more time on my art, and that was how he decided to show me how he felt about it. Dick." She looked to me. "You're right to avoid men. They're all assholes."

Trinity's comment showed just how out of the loop she'd been since she'd been gone. I hoped Hennessy would assume that I didn't share my personal life with her.

He laughed. "Yeah, we are dicks, but some of us are worth it." He turned to me, and all I could see was the mocking skepticism in his eyes. "Valentina, I'll see you soon. I can show myself out then. I'm sorry for disturbing you so late, ladies. Thanks for the coffee."

I followed Rhett as he strode toward the door, my gaze darting up the front stairs. Was Rix up there watching and waiting?

Rhett paused, hand on the doorknob, and looked at me. "I know there's more going on here than you're ever going to admit, which means you don't trust me. I hope to fuck you know what you're doing, and you know who you're trusting. Just . . . be careful."

For some eerie reason, I had the distinct impression that Rhett didn't need any late-night confessions from me because he already knew everything. But that couldn't be right. And did I really know Rix? Maybe not, but I knew I could trust him with the life of someone I loved. And I really needed to hug the crap out of Trinity, so Rhett needed to get a move on right now.

"There's nothing to worry about other than the jerk

boyfriend of Trinity's who tossed a brick through my window—"

Rhett interrupted me. "Save it, Valentina. You don't need to keep lying to me. But I'm willing to listen if and when you change your mind." He glanced over my shoulder to where Trinity stood. "My door is open to either of you. Anytime."

With that, he stepped outside and pulled the door shut behind him. I threw the dead bolt and spun, running to Trinity. She met me in the middle of the foyer and threw her arms around me. Tears soaked the shoulder of my shirt.

"I'm so sorry. So sorry," she said as she sobbed.

I smoothed her hair and squeezed her tight. "Oh, baby. You've got nothing to be sorry for. None of this is your fault."

Her words were broken by shaking breaths. "I dragged you into all of this. I'm so sorry."

"Shhh. It's okay. Everything's okay now that you're safe. That's all that matters, honey. It's okay."

The stairway creaked again, and this time it was Rix coming down. He stopped a few feet from where Trinity and I were hugging it out.

"You take care of your girl. I'll be back later. Got some more shit to do."

Tears welling in my own eyes, I nodded, even though I wanted to argue with him and demand the entire story. Trinity's head lifted from my shoulder at the sound of his voice. She turned toward him in my arms, her voice a little shaky.

"Thank you. For everything. I'm sorry about . . . everything too."

I didn't know what she was apologizing to Rix for, but I'd get the details from her soon enough.

"You thank me by doing what I asked of you. Got that?"

Her nod was quick and short.

"Good. Be back soon as I can, duchess."

He turned for the portico, and that's when I noticed the dark stain on the side of his dark gray T-shirt.

What the hell?

My eyes followed Rix as he walked toward the door. His movements were a fraction slower and more careful than normal.

"Wait, Rix. Are you okay?"

My eyes flicked to Trinity, who stared directly at the floor.

Clearly, I missed something big.

"Don't worry about it. I'll be back when I can."

I started toward him, not willing to accept that non-explanation. He reached out to fend me off, but I was quicker. Yanking up his T-shirt, I saw a large gauze pad taped over his side, and my stomach twisted. My gaze cut to his flashing silver one.

"What the hell happened tonight?"

"You can wait to hear it until I'm back."

"But you're hurt!"

"Ain't the first time and won't be the last. Settle down, duchess. Your man ain't exactly fragile."

"No, but he sure is stubborn."

Rix tugged the shirt out of my grip and let it fall over the bandage. Grabbing my hand, he pulled me closer. "Glad to see we're finally on the same page." He pressed a hard kiss to my lips before releasing me and spinning toward the door.

He was gone before I could think of another thing to say.

Trinity's awestruck voice came from behind me. "He's your man? Damn, I missed out on a lot."

It had been a week since I'd last seen Trinity, and the magnitude of the changes in my life in such a short span of time was ridiculous.

Crossing the foyer to her, I hugged her again, squeezing her tight in my arms. "I'm so glad you're safe." Trinity shook again and after another round of tears, I finally pulled away and asked, "What in the world happened?"

Her expression shuttered immediately. "You're gonna have to ask Rix, because he told me I couldn't tell you anything."

Excuse me? He did what*?*

"I don't care what he told you. This is between you and me."

Trinity shook her head. "I can't. He's Rix."

I knew who he was, and I didn't see how that registered as important.

Trinity and I were only a few inches apart in height, so looking down into her dark brown eyes was no difficult task. "You know you can tell me anything. I've been worried to death about you. Rix promised he'd get you home safely, and said there was no guarantee that the police could do the same. That's the only reason I didn't send a SWAT team after you the first night."

Trinity's smile wobbled. "I know that. I talked to him the day after they grabbed me. He told me he'd kill them if they hurt me, and they knew it too." With a hiccupping sob, she continued. "He also told me you were losing your shit being worried about me, and I was going to have to be on my best behavior for the rest of my natural-born life to make it up to you." Her tears dried up when she added, "He's really protective of you. I don't know what kind of voodoo you worked on that man, but I'd say he's gone for you, girl. Maybe even in *love* with you."

And that's when I knew my eighteen-year-old Trinity was back without lasting harm, because even though her boyfriend had gotten her kidnapped, she was still a hopeless romantic.

Which reminded me, I'd never once asked for an update on D-Rock. Subconsciously, I probably feared I might murder him myself. I also wasn't about to bring him up now to her, especially if her story about them breaking up was true.

"Are you hungry? I can fix you something."

Her giggle was quick, assuring me once again that all was going to be just fine. "How about I fix something, because I don't think I'll ever get the smell of burned grits washed from my nose after that one time."

My glare was playful. "I'm still blaming a malfunctioning timer. My cooking skills aren't *that* bad."

Trinity laid a hand on my shoulder, her expression mocksober. "If you want to keep Rix, whatever you do, don't cook for him. Your skills aren't gonna catch any man."

"Impertinent child." I shook my head, crossed to the counter, and made myself comfortable on a bar stool. "Your punishment is cooking for both of us."

"And your man. But don't even try to claim it was you. You'll never live up to my skills in the kitchen."

"Brat."

Trinity's laughter was the best sound I'd heard in weeks.

She still wouldn't give up any details. I'd pushed and prodded throughout the late-night snack she'd prepared, but Trinity had stonewalled me. With a sigh of exasperation, I'd settled her in the downstairs guest room that she preferred and retreated to my own bed, which was empty.

Lying awake for another hour, I wondered if Rix was indeed coming back. When I drifted off sometime in the dark of the night, I was still alone.

TWENTY-SEVEN
RIX

"You gonna get that looked at?"

The familiar voice stopped me in my tracks as I reached for the door handle of my Escalade two blocks away from Valentina's. I turned to see good ole Detective Hennessy leaning against his Jeep, which was parked a few cars down from mine.

Fuck, pain is killing my mojo. No one got the drop on me, but then again, I didn't usually roll alone after a bullet wound.

"The fuck you want, Hennessy?"

"The truth. I know you were in her house. I know you made sure the girl was there. Valentina Noble might think I'm stupid, but we both know that isn't the case. I see through both your bullshit."

"Not sure why you're even worried about it. The girl is home safe."

"And I can close my case really fucking quick if it was really D-Rock who tossed that brick through the window." Hennessy pushed off the Jeep and walked toward me.

"You're a detective. It shouldn't be that difficult to figure it out."

"It wasn't D-Rock. It was the FNDs, wasn't it? I don't buy the *breaking up with the boyfriend* story, even though the girl would be better off it that were true."

The good detective knew exactly who my biggest rival was, so it wasn't much of a leap. He nodded down at the wound that had soaked through both the bandage and my shirt and the blood that dripped down onto my jeans.

"You start a war?" he asked.

"I don't start anything. I'm more of a finisher."

"Bullshit. You've started your fair share these last few years. Isn't it getting old yet, Rix? Or is it really that good to be king?"

"Maybe you should give it a try. Walk on the dark side and see how it feels."

"I'm not built that way, and we both know it."

"You never know until you try."

"Cut the shit. You know you've got no shot at something real with Valentina. You're gonna end up hurting her."

The laugh that escaped sounded rusty, even to my ears. "That's what you really tracked me down to say, isn't it? To appeal to the noble side I don't have? To get me to walk away from her by telling me it's better for her?"

Hennessy crossed his arms over his chest. "You know I'm right. And we both know whatever noble side you might have isn't missing completely, just buried deep."

"I'm not walking away. No way in hell."

"So you're gonna drag her into the shitstorm you call a life?"

I glared at him. "If she's willing. God knows I can protect her."

Hennessy dropped his arms, hands clenching into fists, and I wondered if he was going to swing at me.

"Hope you're sure about that."

"I'd bet my life on it." I stepped up to him, so our chests were only inches apart. "So you can drop your fascination with her right now. She's under my protection, and if it comes down to her or me, I'll lay down to keep her safe. You get that?" I touched my hand to my side and lifted my blood-covered palm. "I bled to save her girl, but I'd die for her."

Hennessy stepped back. "You love her."

His words hit me like another bullet to the body. But this was a welcome blow. My brain might not have gotten to the word first, but that's exactly what I felt for her.

"Goddamned right I do."

"Then I guess I really was fighting a losing battle."

I shrugged off the comment as a surge of energy roared through me. What did that mean? My future was a dark and winding road, and the exits off the path I'd taken were few and far between. But I would make it work. I would find a way to have her in my life and keep her safe.

"I'd say I'm sorry, but we both know I'm not."

Hennessy shrugged, but I could tell losing his shot at Valentina bothered the hell out of him. He didn't dwell on it, though.

"You got any information for me? On my brother?"

"You bowing out gracefully?"

"Depends on what you've got."

Did I want to tell him what I'd learned? I was already bleeding from one hole in my body tonight.

"Look, man. I think you should drop this one. Let the dicks in Internal Affairs figure out what happened. You don't want to go digging here."

Green eyes drilled into mine. "You know something, and you're gonna fucking tell me."

"Nothing but the word of a tweaker who'd been hanging around the warehouse before the bust went down."

"So fucking tell me what he said."

"You don't want to hear it."

Hennessy's entire body tensed as if he was bracing for a blow. "Just fucking tell me."

"He said he heard someone answer to the name Hennessy in that same warehouse the day before it went down. Had heard the name on the street a few days before too. It's not looking good."

"I don't fucking believe it."

I cleared my throat. "He had a wire, man. He says he recorded it."

Hennessy surged forward and grabbed a handful of my T-shirt. "Where the fuck is it? I want it right the fuck now."

The only reason I didn't put him on his ass for touching me was the pained expression on his face. Finding out your blood was dirty was no picnic.

"Don't have it. But I can try to track it down for you. Chances are, the recording's already in someone's case file somewhere. You might have a way faster time finding it than me. Then again, if you find it and it's what I think it is, you've got exactly the proof you don't want."

"Fuck off. He wasn't dirty. I don't believe it."

I untwisted his hand from my shirt and stepped back. "Then find the tape. Someone in the cop shop has to have it."

We stared at each other for long moments before Hennessy backed away toward his Jeep.

"This isn't over, Rix. Not by a long shot."

"I didn't figure it was."

"Keep looking."

"Stop sniffing around my woman."

"Keep her safe and happy then."

"Don't fucking need to tell me that."

"Later, Rix."

"Detective."

TWENTY-EIGHT

RIX

The graze on my side kept bleeding, and I wasn't about to bring the blood that colored my world into Valentina's bed. A visit to an old friend, a retired ER doc in a subdivision near Lake Pontchartrain, fixed me up.

He raised his eyebrows plenty, but he didn't ask questions. We'd met when his kid had gotten tangled up in the wrong crowd—my kind of crowd—and he'd been desperate to get him back on the straight and narrow. I'd run my own version of *Scared Straight* and the kid had nearly pissed himself. This life was hard, and some middle-class kid who had plenty of other options for his future and parents who gave a shit didn't have any business getting involved.

We'd capped off his experience with a trip to the morgue, and a few looks at the unfortunate sons of bitches who'd been on the wrong side of a drive-by bullet had him puking up his lunch in a trash can.

That was the best way I could explain this life. *If you want to live until you're old and rocking on your front porch, your white-haired woman beside you, then don't get in it.*

But what did that mean for me? Fuck, I'd never intended to

fall in love. Didn't even see that shit coming. But I also couldn't deny it. Couldn't stop it. Didn't want to change it. My path was filled with land mines. I couldn't bring her down it. I couldn't do that to anyone I gave a damn about.

So that left me with two options: find a new path or let her go.

Hennessy would be fucking waiting with open arms if I did it. Might be better for her, but I wasn't about to give her up. No one's future was final. I had plenty of power, and just maybe I could find a way to have it all. I liked that idea. Having it all.

As I made my way through the darkened yards of the Garden District to get into Valentina's the back way, I moved slower than normal because of the pain in my side. Didn't want to tear the good doctor's stitches out. Maybe the first thing on my list of having it all would be a key to her place.

As I slipped through her back gate and up to the door I used routinely to break in, I laughed to myself. A guy like me didn't need a key because you couldn't keep me out anyway. I also needed to upgrade Valentina's security system. It wasn't much of a challenge anymore.

Making my way quietly through the house because I knew Trinity was sleeping somewhere, I headed for the stairs.

The girl's voice stopped me. "Did you get an update on Derrick?"

Trinity had asked me more than once. All three times I'd forced the FNDs to let me talk to her to assure her safety, and then again after shit had gone down and we'd gotten out of there. I wasn't the only one to catch a bullet, but my guy's wounds had been superficial compared to the FNDs. We'd left two bodies behind when shit had gone south. Trinity didn't know that either. She'd been a good kid and run when I'd told her to run.

But D-Rock. *Fuck.* I'd kept telling her he was recovering

from the car wreck, which was true, but he was also recovering five states away and had been banned from coming back to NOLA because he'd pissed me the fuck off. She didn't need him screwing up her life again. Because of the respect I had for Valentina, I'd keep D-Rock as far away from the girl as I possibly could.

"Not tonight."

Her face fell.

"Shouldn't you be in bed, girl?"

Shuffling her feet, she shrugged. "Yeah, but I wanted to talk to you first."

"Okay. Talk." My patience was running thin after the clusterfuck of a night, especially now that I was only steps away from Valentina's bed.

"You're going to tell her what happened, right? Because I didn't tell her anything."

Well, that was good at least.

"I'll tell her."

The girl finally met my eyes, and concern lined her face. "She's good people. Please make sure you know what you're doing with her. I don't want to see her get hurt. She doesn't know that I know, but she's been through some tough stuff. She deserves her happily-ever-after."

Getting warned off from another source wasn't doing anything to improve my mood. But these two shared a bond that I didn't quite understand, so I wasn't going to question it.

"You've got my word."

Trinity's face lit up. "You're going to make sure she gets that happily-ever-after, right? She needs it. She won't ever admit it, but she wants to get married and have babies, and I know she'll be the best mom ever."

I held up a hand. "Whoa. Slow down, girl. One step at a time."

Trinity's smile didn't fade. "You might not realize it, Rix, but you're a knight, whether your armor is shiny or not. You saved me, and I know you'll protect her. Sometimes the dragon is a better choice for the princess than a prince."

Now the girl was talking in so many mixed fairy-tale metaphors, I didn't even know how to respond.

"Go to bed, kid. Get back to your life, and keep an eye on Valentina when I can't."

"Done."

She gave me another brilliant smile and spun before heading down the hallway toward the guest room.

I wanted nothing more than to go climb in bed with Valentina upstairs, but the studio drew me in. It was like a window into her thoughts and feelings, and one I knew I was never supposed to see.

The piece on the easel wasn't finished, but seeing it rocked me all the same.

This one wasn't of a person, it was two partial people, walking down a tree-lined path, holding hands. One tanned the color of my skin, and the other pale like Valentina's.

Trinity's words rolled through my brain. *Happily ever after. Babies.* Those things had never existed as a possibility in my world. Could they?

Something about the woman sleeping upstairs made me refuse to rule them out.

I crept up the creaky old staircase, avoiding the noisy treads. It was telling that I knew what steps to avoid when I wanted to be silent.

As much as I wanted to slide inside Valentina while she was still half-asleep, I didn't wake her tonight as I climbed between her pristine white sheets. There was a kid in the house, and when I took Valentina again, I wanted her screaming my name.

TWENTY-NINE
VALENTINA

The sun shining brightly through the bay window in my bedroom woke me gradually until I registered the heat against my back and the arm wrapped around me. My eyes snapped open.

He was here.

And he hadn't woken me.

I turned in his arms and found him wide awake. "How long have you been here?"

"A while."

"How long have you been awake?"

"A while."

I flipped the sheet back so I could get a look at his side. A clean bandage covered it. My hair fell into my face as my gaze darted back up to his and I asked, "Are you okay?"

Rix nodded and reached up to tuck my hair behind my ear. "I'm fine. Your girl's fine. So I'd say life is pretty good."

"You got hurt getting her out, though. Tell me what happened."

The soft smile on Rix's face faded a few degrees. "You

don't need to know anything except that she's back and she's fine. No harm to her."

I gritted my teeth. The man was ridiculously stubborn. "I need to know."

Rix shook his head. "No, you don't. It's better for everyone if you don't ask questions."

I pushed up on one elbow and propped my other hand on my hip. "I'm asking questions, dammit. And I want answers. Trinity wouldn't tell me anything because you ordered her not to, and you said you'd fill me in."

"I just did."

I was going to scream. "You didn't fill me in on a damn thing. Nothing. I know *nothing*."

Rix tugged my propped arm, and I fell toward him. Before I could untangle myself, he had me pinned beneath him, both arms over my head, rendering me helpless.

"What are you doing?"

He pressed a hard kiss to my mouth to silence me. When he lifted his face, his expression brooked no argument. "I'm explaining how things work."

"I'm not going to like how things work, am I?"

He didn't respond, just waited, eyebrow raised, as if expecting me to keep protesting.

I didn't, instead opting to wait for whatever he was about to decree.

"Maybe, maybe not. But either way it doesn't change a thing. The less you know, the better. So that means you're gonna know as little as possible about what goes on in my world. There's nothing good there, and you don't need to be any part of it."

I bristled at his pronouncement, but not because of the reason he would expect. "You're in your world, so there has to be something good."

Rix's expression was almost pained. "Trust me when I say I'm not good either. And if you want to call this off right now because you can't handle what I've got to offer, then do it. Tell me to go. You got your girl back. That's what you needed from me, so if there was ever a time to drop my ass, it's now. Do it before this goes any further."

He caught me off guard completely. "Drop your ass? You think the reason I haven't called the cops when you continually break into my house and sneak into my bed is because I only wanted Trinity back? Are you insane?" I struggled beneath him, trying to break free. It didn't work. "If I recall correctly, you laid out some asinine requirement that I sleep with you for payback, and I'm pretty sure I'm not the only one who can follow the chain of events here because that happened *before*. You didn't have to extort anything from me because I gave it to you freely. Does that make it sound like I want to drop you now that she's safe?"

I'd finally made my decision. And now he was throwing it back in my face? *Oh. Hell. No.* That's not how this was going to work.

Rix hadn't said anything yet, and I was ready to drag the words out of him.

"Let me up," I demanded.

He shook his head. "No. I'm still deciding what to do with you."

"You don't get to decide what to do with me. I do. And I'm ready to shake some sense into you."

His chest shook until a deep laugh echoed through my room.

"You're one of a kind." He lowered his forehead so it rested on mine. "I don't deserve you. Shouldn't be here. But I'm not goin' anywhere. You're stuck with me, duchess. You had your out. I'm keepin' you."

I strained upward and pressed my lips to his. "Good thing I'd already decided I was keeping you."

"Fuck, I wish I was inside you right now."

"Why aren't you?" My body was molded to his, and more than ready.

He pressed up on his elbows. "Because there's a kid in the house, and I don't roll that way. But I gotta get out of this bed or I'm gonna forget I have a problem with it."

Trinity. Crap. I forgot.

How could I forget?

I rolled out from under Rix, only because he let me this time.

"I need to make sure she's still okay. And get her some breakfast. And—"

Rix snagged my hand. "Chill out. It's okay. She's fine."

I might have growled at him, but I'd never admit it.

Rix laughed again and dropped my hand. "Or don't chill out. Do what you need to do. I'm gonna grab a shower."

Rix in my shower. After he spent the night in my bed. And we'd decided we were keeping each other. Things were becoming awfully domestic all of a sudden.

The rational voice inside my head whispered this couldn't last, so I might as well enjoy it while I could. I quieted that voice, but decided the advice about enjoying it wasn't a bad idea.

I pulled on some clothes and made my way downstairs as I heard the shower water kick on. I wanted to rush back to the bathroom and make sure he was properly caring for whatever kind of injury he had, but I stopped myself cold. Rix's body was not only tattooed, but scarred. I'd never asked any questions, and it seemed that was exactly how he liked it. He was a capable, grown man and didn't need me fussing all over him.

He also didn't need me killing him off with my cooking. I

racked my brain for the fastest breakfast places around that might deliver if promised a hefty tip, but the thoughts died when the scent of food hit me.

Bless that girl, she was getting a raise. A big one.

Steam rose from the waffle maker and Trinity scrambled eggs on the stove.

I crossed to the espresso machine and pressed the button, watching as the dark liquid poured into a shot glass.

"I have a waffle maker?"

"It was in the pantry, still in the box. I took a chance, assuming you actually like waffles and didn't know how to operate it."

"I'm sure it came with directions . . . I just didn't try to figure it out."

"You know you've got at least six other appliances in boxes in your pantry. What gives?" She turned and shot me a laughing grin as I sipped my espresso.

"My mother. She thinks I'm going to become a housewife who cooks one of these days. Actually, she's hoping I'll start pinning recipes and DIY vertical gardens on Pinterest, and get so caught up I start pinning wedding ideas. She's crazy, because that's never going to happen."

Trinity raised an eyebrow. "You planning on more of a courthouse gig? Your daddy officiating?"

I jerked my head back. "Whoa, let's not even go there. A wedding is not part of my plans anytime soon."

That's the moment Rix decided to walk into the kitchen, hair still wet.

I swear he just took the shortest shower in the history of the planet.

"Good, because I ain't got a ring."

I choked on the last sip of my coffee and started coughing.

Trinity's eyes lit up, and Rix opened the fridge, ignoring both our reactions in favor of orange juice.

Again, this whole scene was wildly domestic. And somehow . . . easy. Except for the fact that my espresso had gone down the very wrong pipe called *what the hell did you just say*.

Rix held up the OJ. "You want some, duchess?"

I nodded. "Please."

"Trinity?"

"I already have some, thanks."

And so our morning started with Trinity cooking to keep us all from getting food poisoning and keeping Rix from knowing about my complete lack of skill in the kitchen.

Conversation was light as we ate, mostly about the Saints and Trinity's plans for art school. She was strangely silent on the Derrick front, but I didn't bring him up. I was assuming that she and Rix knew way more about what was going on with him, and for once, I didn't want to know.

There, Rix. I can play your game when I choose to.

As much as I loved hearing Trinity going on and on about art school, I was a little concerned what would happen when Derrick was back in the picture—if he came back. She was still a very young eighteen, and that boy had clearly melted enough of her brain that she didn't make the best decisions.

On the other hand, if she hadn't gotten wrapped up in him, I wouldn't be sitting at my kitchen table with his "boss" either. Which was another situation that was only half-resolved and didn't seem to have any easy answers.

Rix's phone buzzed in his pocket, and he stood to take the call. As soon as he'd left the room, Trinity turned to me.

"You're gonna marry that man. I already know it. You better learn how to cook, girl, because he's the kind that comes with quite an appetite." She winked at me.

I wasn't going to touch that statement with a ten-foot pole, especially not with Rix only one room away. The deep rumble of his voice carried just enough for me to lose the easy feeling I'd had most of the morning.

"I want patrols 24/7. We're not fucking around. They'll be back for blood."

Chills ran through me at his prediction to whomever was on the other end of the call. Trinity's face went blank and she gathered up the dishes. I decided to follow her lead, because I didn't know what else to do. Any questions that I had would be met with silence or a refusal to answer.

If someone was coming back for blood, I didn't think I wanted to know when or how or who, so long as they stayed far, far away from me. And I wanted them to stay far, far away from Rix. I was not okay with him needing more bandages. The idea of him hurting made me want to draw blood from someone else.

Whoa. When had I turned into this woman? Being around Rix had some very unexpected side effects.

When he ended the call and walked back into the kitchen, his face was set in an implacable expression. "I gotta go. Be back when I can. I'll take Trinity home too."

"Can I talk to you for a minute? Alone."

He turned, and I followed him back into the living room where he'd taken the call. Only this time I shut the French doors behind me.

"I wasn't eavesdropping, but I heard some of what you said anyway."

"And?"

"And I want to know if Trinity is going to be safe at her gran's. The woman is elderly and not in the greatest health. If anyone is looking to use her as leverage again, won't they just break in and grab her?"

"I guess you did hear plenty." He lifted his hand to my face and tucked my hair behind my ear again. It was an intimate gesture, and one that was at odds with his stoic side. "I'm not gonna let anything happen to her. She'll have someone watching out for her around the clock. I don't expect they'll retaliate that way, but I'm prepared for it regardless."

"Good. Thank you."

He shook his head. "You don't need to thank me, duchess. I take care of the people under my protection."

"So does that mean someone's watching me too?"

Rix's stare intensified. "I've had my guys on you for a while. Now, you're never unprotected."

Surprise rippled through me, but it wasn't altogether unpleasant . . . until I recalled the dates I'd been on with Rhett. I wondered if he'd heard about those. My thoughts must have been written on my face, because Rix frowned.

"I didn't always like what I heard, but I heard it anyway."

Well, that answered that.

"You opening the gallery today?" he asked.

"Of course. Why wouldn't I?"

"Because you have a plywood front window and you need to learn how to take a break."

I stiffened at the second part of his statement. "I don't tell you how to run your . . . business, so I don't think you get the right to tell me how to run mine."

He stepped closer, leaving no space between us, my breasts pressing against his chest. "Working six or seven days a week is gonna burn you out, duchess. And I want you smiling. Besides, tonight I got plans for you."

He was right about the burnout. As much as I loved the gallery, threads of resentment were starting to form. My life was dictated by my work, which was completely normal for a small business owner, but I was starting to feel the weight of it more than I ever had in the past. Maybe because in the past I hadn't had anything else competing for my attention like I did now. I hadn't had a life outside my business.

"Now that Trinity is back and if you've got people staked out for security, I can see if she's interested in taking on a few more hours a week. Remy already asked for more hours."

Rix slid his hand into my hair and closed his fingers around it. The gesture was so him, so possessive, it unleashed butter-flies in my stomach. "Good. I like that. So, tonight I'm gonna send you a text with instructions, and I want you to follow them to the letter."

"What kind of instructions?" I asked.

"The kind I want you to follow without question. I may not be able to sit across a table from you at a fancy restaurant, but I can still take you out and show you a good time."

My curiosity bloomed wildly. "And you're not going to give me any hint of how you plan to show me a good time?"

A seductive smile slid across Rix's face. "No. None at all. Follow the directions, and I promise you'll enjoy yourself."

With his grip on my hair, he tilted my head and lowered his lips to mine. The first passes were sips at my lips, and then when I opened to him, he took more. The kiss turned from simple to demanding in moments. Rix pulled away first.

Did I ever pull away first? *No, because you're completely lost in him whenever he touches you.* How long had it been since I'd felt this comfortable with a man? Years. And some-thing told me it was unique to Rix.

He released my hair and stepped back.

"Every time I taste you, I don't think I'm gonna be able to stop. You test my control, duchess." He brushed his lips across mine one more time and then he opened the French doors. His eyes met mine. "Tonight."

THIRTY

VALENTINA

Remy was scheduled to work with me today, and for that I was happy. I didn't want to be alone with my thoughts all afternoon if we happened to have a slow day for customers.

Rix's promise about tonight and the text that was sure to come with the instructions I was required to follow was constantly on my mind. He was right. We couldn't exactly go out in public and do anything normal couples did together, because we weren't a normal couple by any stretch of the imagination.

I scoured my brain for what else we could possibly do and came up with mostly nothing. It was hard to imagine Rix setting up a private dinner for two somewhere off the beaten path. Me and him and candlelight and roses seemed out of character. But still, my mind jumped from one outlandish possibility to the next. I was not good at surprises. I wanted to know all the things, right now.

Instead, I got to watch my new window be installed and deal with my insurance company.

The text came as I waved Remy off and flipped the OPEN sign to CLOSED.

RIX: Short skirt. Button-up blouse. Heels. Walk out of your house at 10 and get in the black Escalade.

How did I reply to that? With the only answer I wanted to give.

VALENTINA: Okay

Anticipation lit my system. Things were changing again. Tonight. I had five hours to get ready, and that meant it was time for a little pampering.

Manicured. Pedicured. Freshly trimmed and blown out. Showered. Shaved smooth. When I slid my feet into one of my favorite pairs of heels—black patent leather Louboutins—I felt like the woman I'd been all those years ago who wasn't afraid to hit the bars by myself and take what I needed for the night. Confidence and intent made all the difference in the world.

From my front window, I watched as a black Escalade drove up the street. I left my front porch lights on as I slipped out the portico door and strolled down my driveway to my path, an extra sway in my hips.

The blacked-out SUV slowed to a stop and the back door opened from the inside. I pushed through the gate and crossed the sidewalk to the curb before placing my foot on the running board. I climbed up inside, pulling the door shut behind me.

The Escalade rolled forward, but my eyes were on Rix. He was dressed as I'd never seen him before, in a charcoal-gray three-piece suit, a crisp white shirt, and a silver tie that matched his eyes.

Wow.

"Am I underdressed?" I asked, glancing down at my black mini and royal-blue silk blouse.

Rix's gaze started at my feet and slowly rose to my face. *Devouring.* That was the word for what his eyes were doing to me.

"You look beautiful."

His simple compliment filled me with warmth and even more excitement for the night ahead. "Thank you. You look . . . wow."

The smile on my lips came easily, naturally, and even though I had no idea where we were going or what we were doing, I was ready—because I was with him.

"I clean up all right once in a while."

"I'd say more than all right."

Rix curled two fingers toward me, motioning me closer. I moved to the middle seat and he slid a hand into my hair, closing his fingers around the back of my neck. It was becoming his habit, and I was getting used to it. More than used to it, I was growing to crave it.

"I need a taste, but your lips look too perfect to touch."

Instead of kissing my very shiny red lips—a bold choice for me—his mouth skimmed my jaw, the shell of my ear, and then down to my throat. Shivers rolled through my body, goose bumps prickling my skin with anticipation of more. I pressed my thighs together as his teeth scraped where his lips had trailed.

My movement wasn't lost on Rix, and his hand slid to my thigh. "Fuck, you're a hot piece, duchess." His words curled around my ear and added to the shivers.

And then I remembered the driver. I jerked my head up and swung it toward the windshield. The man looked straight ahead, his sunglasses in place, even though it was after dark.

Rix squeezed my thigh. "Johnny Doe doesn't see anything I don't want him to see."

We were already slowing in front of a large warehouse before I could reply.

"That was quick."

Rix's smile flashed. "And yet even with it being only minutes away from your house, I bet you've never heard of this club. Which isn't a bad thing."

"What club? I've heard of clubs," I protested.

"Not clubs like this."

I lowered my voice. "Is it a sex club?"

Rix's laughter filled the cabin of the SUV, but Johnny Doe didn't turn and look. "Do you want it to be?"

Did I? Tonight I was feeling like a new woman, but was this new woman *that* bold?

"Umm." I flicked my gaze up to Rix's flashing one. "I've never been to one before, so I can't say I would even know what to expect."

"We'd ease you in."

My mouth dropped open and I blinked at him. "So it *is* a sex club?"

"Guess you'll have to come and find out."

Rix climbed out of his side of the SUV and came around to my door. My mouth was still hanging open when he offered me a hand, and we crossed the short stretch of sidewalk before reaching a black steel door. When the door opened without Rix having to knock, and a woman in a red dress stood inside, I remembered to shut my mouth.

"Right this way, sir."

As she led us across a shiny black-lacquered floor to an elevator bay, also painted black, it was anticipation and not trepidation filling me. With Rix by my side, I didn't feel fear. Maybe that was the upside of knowing that wherever you went, you were with the scariest SOB in the room.

The woman in the red dress didn't follow us into the elevator, but she did press a button and the doors slid shut.

"So, you're not going to tell me."

Rix shook his head. "No. You get to experience."

He pulled something from his pocket and dangled it from his fingertips. It was a mask. Lace and satin, embroidered in silver thread and studded with crystal gems. Black ribbon ties fluttered down.

Oh my God, we really are going to a sex club.

"Is that necessary?"

Rix nodded. "Even I'll wear a mask. It's required tonight."

"Is this—"

"I promise you'll enjoy it, so stop worrying." He held the mask out, carefully laying it in place, and tied it around the back of my head before sliding a much simpler black mask over his face.

The doors opened then, and my first impression was of low music, clinking glasses, and hushed conversations. We stepped into a large room filled with dining tables and large, round velvet columns lining both sides. The floor was the same black lacquer as downstairs.

There were no whips. Or chains. Or naked people.

Instead there were men dressed in suits, women in skirts and dresses, and all were masked.

Everything was set up facing a large stage with a black velvet curtain. Ornate silver light fixtures hung from the ceiling.

"What is this place?" I asked, my voice quiet.

"Tonight, it's the hottest burlesque club you've never heard of before."

Burlesque?

"Really?"

Rix nodded and led me to one of the velvet columns, which was actually a private booth of some sort. Raised several feet off the floor, the table sat in the middle with a half-round black leather upholstered bench seat. It had a perfect view of the stage, and was concealed from view unless you walked right up to the opening. Candles flickered on the table, and a bottle of champagne chilled in a bucket.

Rix gestured to the rounded stairs. "Ladies first."

I climbed the stairs and slid across the smooth seat with his hand heating the small of my back. The lights began to dim almost immediately.

"Just in time," Rix said as he reached for the champagne. Popping the cork without hesitation, he poured two glasses. I accepted one, and he clinked the rim of his to mine. "Cheers, duchess. I think you're gonna like this."

The house band started to play, which was coincidentally when I noticed there was an orchestra pit. The curtains split to reveal two black wrought iron beds made up with silky black sheets.

A woman leaned against the frame of one, dressed in an elaborate red-and-black top and skirt, and a man against the other, wearing simple black slacks, a white dress shirt, and a black tie.

I'd watched burlesque before, but never anything completely scandalous, only the run-of-the-mill sassy strip-tease. I'd seen the LIVE SEX SHOWS signs on Bourbon Street but hadn't thought they were legit. More a scam to lure in drunk tourists willing to hand over money for the real NOLA experience.

But this . . . They started to move with the music. The woman pretended to ignore the man, who, even from our vantage point, looked hungry for her.

Was that what someone else would see when Rix looked at me? I glanced over at him, taking my eyes from the stage for just a moment, to find him watching me, his silver eyes intent.

Ah . . . so that's what this was about. See how the straight-laced chick reacts to naughtiness. I slid closer to him on the bench and pressed a fingertip to his jaw, intending to turn his head back toward the stage.

"You're here to watch the show," I whispered when he kept his eyes on me.

"You're the one I'm watching, duchess. Every chance I get."

My cheeks heated, but so did other strategic parts of my body. "Rix . . ."

"Valentina."

The music, sultry and sexy, picked up a deeper bass beat, and I looked to the stage and back to Rix.

"Watch the show."

I complied and was captivated.

The woman was teasing the man. She sat on one of the beds, fluffing her hair, checking her lipstick in a compact. The man came closer, but she stood and bent to fix her shoe, popping her rear out in his direction, but rose before he could touch. And then the clothes started to come off.

His first. He pulled off his tie and tossed it on the bed he leaned against before unbuttoning and rolling up his cuffs.

Her attention dropped to the tie, and she flipped her hair before unsnapping part of the front of her sequined top and shimmying it off. Instead of revealing skin, it gave way to a deep V-cut strapless number. She tossed the discarded layer at his face, but he caught it in midair. The act unleashed him.

He stepped forward, wrapping her long hair around his fist and grasping the back of her head. His lips found her neck, her chin, her ear . . . much like Rix had in the SUV on the way here. The man was ravenous.

The woman arched back, grasping a handful of his shirt. The man didn't stop for long moments, and when he did, it was to tear his shirt off and spin her around. Pinning her to the bed, he shackled both wrists above her head and kissed her again. Every move was more erotic than the last.

When he released his hands, she pushed at his chest, and he bounded up from the bed. She rose and pushed him backward until his knees hit the other bed and he sat. She climbed on his lap and with a snap of her wrist, the skirt of her outfit fell away, leaving bright red cheeky panties with a black bow on the back. This time it was her turn, pressing him down, pinning him, and taking what she wanted.

Both of his hands wrapped around her ass and squeezed, bringing her closer until she was directly above his face. He tore her panties in half, revealing a tiny red thong. She moaned, riding his face, and I couldn't stop myself from looking back at Rix again.

His eyes were trailing down my body to where my nipples were puckered and pressed hard against the silk of my blouse.

He must have felt my stare because his gaze cut to mine, and in that moment I wanted him to unbutton my blouse and touch me. I wanted him to tear my clothes off the way the couple were onstage. I wanted him in a frenzy for me where what he wanted most in this world was me.

But that couldn't happen here. Yes, the booth was semi-private and I was wearing a mask, but still . . . I just couldn't. I might be finding my inner vixen, as evidenced by the slickness gathering between my legs at watching this show with Rix at my side, but sex in a semi-public place was pushing my limits too far.

Wasn't it?

His gaze was on me, but now the fire was banked and concern was visible.

Crap. Me and my overactive brain were killing the moment. I looked back to the stage, the woman straddled the man, lower now, so she could tear at his belt with her teeth.

I wanted to be the aggressor for once. The instigator. But I wasn't sure if I could do that here.

I leaned close to Rix's ear. "I need to use the ladies'."

He narrowed his eyes on me, but slid out of the booth so I could pass. "You okay?"

I nodded. It was a lie. I wasn't okay, but I would be.

Walking toward the back of the room, I found a server, and he directed me to the ladies' room.

Instead of going inside, I walked past it, looking for another door. There had to be something. I pushed open a door marked PRIVATE.

Bingo.

It was a storage room of some kind. Flipping on the light revealed stacks of chairs, a few tables, and shelves of linens. There was no lock on the door, but I was turning over a new leaf. Pulling my phone from my clutch, I slowed when I saw my reflection in its glass screen. My mask hid the nerves, anticipation, daring, arousal, and a hundred other emotions rioting, but at least if we got caught, it would hide my identity.

Was that why I was being so daring tonight?

No, I decided. It wasn't the mask that had freed me from my inhibitions and given me this plan. It was Rix.

I swiped my screen and punched in my passcode incorrectly. Three times. *Get it together, Valentina.*

Finally unlocking my phone, I clicked open a text to Rix.

VALENTINA: Need you.

It was the truth. I did need him. Now.

His response was instant.

RIX: On my way.

I waited thirty seconds before I pulled open the door a crack. Rix was striding toward the ladies' room, one hand in his pocket, the other holding his phone. Concern marked his expression.

He slowed near the ladies' room. It was time.

"Over here."

Brows furrowed, he jerked his head in the direction of my voice and strode toward the door.

"What—"

I pulled the door open the rest of the way and grabbed the soft wool of his suit coat to yank him inside.

"What the—"

Shutting the door with a click, I flipped off the lights and pushed him toward an empty wall.

"Shhh. You don't want anyone to catch us, do you?"

I wished I could see his face, but I worried the light would draw attention to us, and there was nothing in the world I wanted interrupting exactly what I was doing right now. Which was shoving the jacket off his shoulders, tossing it on the table to our left, and threading my fingers through his. I lifted both of his hands up over his shoulders and pressed them against the wall. He didn't fight me.

"My duchess is feeling naughty tonight," he whispered to the dark room.

"Maybe just a little." I caught his bottom lip between my teeth and tugged before flicking and soothing it with my tongue. My mouth closed over his, my tongue sliding inside. I loved his taste, his scent, everything about this man.

I just love him.

The realization struck me and I released his hands, wanting to touch more of him, wanting this scene to play out like it had in my head. A fantasy I never knew I had until I'd watched the show onstage tonight.

"I want you," I told him as I reached for his belt buckle and slipped the belt free.

"I always fucking want you."

"Right now. Right here."

He lowered his hands to glide down my sides and he squeezed my hips. "Thank God."

The next words I wanted to speak stuck in my throat. They were dirtier, filthier than I'd ever spoken before, but they were exactly what I wanted. So I found the courage to say them anyway.

"I want you to fuck me against this wall. My legs wrapped around your waist, you holding me up until we both come. And then I want to straighten my skirt and your jacket and walk back to our table with no one having any clue what just happened."

I imagined his eyes flaring with heat. His hands squeezed my sides in approval.

"I'll give you whatever you want, duchess. Especially that."

His hand dropped lower on my leg until he found my bare thigh and slid up it. He paused when he didn't feel any panties.

Once again, I wished I could see his face, because the shock had to be perfect.

I'll shock him again someday.

His groan filled the room. "Killin' me." Rix's hand closed around my bare ass and slid low between my cheeks. "Soaked. Perfect. Mine."

One finger circled my opening, teasing just enough to bring out my own moan. I wanted more. Needed him filling me.

As soon as the thought entered my head, he plunged one finger inside.

"Oh God. Yes." I rocked my hips against him.

"Wish I could watch you fucking my finger. So damn perfect."

"More."

His forehead lowered to mine as he continued to thrust his finger in and out. "You want me? Here? Where anyone could walk in and see us?"

The recitation of the discovery we could face did nothing to chill my desire. If anything, it fed the flames.

"Yes, here. Now."

"Then I better give you want you want."

His hand left me, and I heard the hiss of a zipper. I reached out, palming his cock and closing my hand around it to stroke.

"That what you want?"

"Yes."

Both hands wrapped around my ass and he lifted me. "Legs around my waist, duchess."

I followed orders, and his cock fit between us perfectly. Frissons of pleasure scattered through me as I ground against it, going higher each time to push the head against my entrance. Rix lifted me, helping my purpose along. Seated against me, he lowered me slowly and his cock sank inside me, inch by inch until I was filled. Gloriously, amazingly filled.

The sounds of our breathing and my whimpered moans eclipsed the silence as Rix lifted me slowly before lowering me back down. I savored every movement. Reveled in his touch. My clit brushed the fabric on his dress shirt, and each time it sent me higher and higher.

"Oh God. Like that."

Rix moved me effortlessly as I clung to his shoulders. It wouldn't take me long to go over the edge. I was already close.

Thrust after thrust, I moaned louder, digging my nails into his shoulders where the muscles bunched and rippled as he lifted me.

I squeezed my eyes shut as I felt the orgasm draw together and then . . . it splintered into a thousand shards of pleasure radiating from my center out through my limbs. I knew I wouldn't be able to hold back the scream, so I pressed my lips against his shoulder to silence the sound.

Rix paused, letting me revel for a few moments before he continued. Stroke after stroke, faster and faster. His ragged breathing clued me in to his quickly approaching orgasm.

I wanted it. Wanted him to let go. With me. Because I did this. This was my daring move, and I loved knowing that it brought him to the brink.

Rix didn't silence his roar as he came. His forehead dropped to mine as his chest heaved with each breath he sucked in.

"Gonna kill me, woman. But what a way to go."

Kill him? I couldn't stop the giggle that escaped. He made me sound like some kind of skilled seductress, and that couldn't be further from the truth. But then again, I had been tonight.

Rix pulled away, and that's when it hit me. We hadn't used a condom.

Oh. Shit.

He stiffened, and I knew he'd just had the same realization. He reached around the stack of linens beside us, producing a cloth napkin, and I quickly cleaned up. I'd just finished blindly setting my clothes to rights when the door swung open and the light flicked on. As soon as my eyes adjusted, they swung to the young server standing just inside the door, shock stamped on his expression.

I glanced to Rix as he was buttoning his suit coat.

"Uh, you shouldn't be in here, sir."

Rix grabbed my hand and pulled me along behind him. "Thanks for the heads-up. We'll be on our way."

The curtains were drawing closed as we stepped out into the main room, and the lights were coming up.

"End of the first act," Rix murmured to me. "You want to stay? Or go back to your place?"

What did I want? More Rix. But in a private setting.

"I'm ready if you are."

He nodded and we moved toward the elevators. "We'll come back another night, and you'll get the full experience."

Another giggle escaped me. "I feel like I got the full experience tonight."

"Not yet, but you will." Rix's silver eyes flashed as we entered the elevator, and he pulled out his phone. A quick text and he tucked it back in his pocket.

"Johnny?"

"Letting him know to get us."

This driver business was kind of convenient, but still very strange. I waited a few beats before speaking again.

"Are we going to talk about the fact that I jumped you without a condom?"

Rix grinned. "Couldn't wait for even a second, but I can't say it bothers me."

"So you're not freaking out?"

He shook his head. "Are you? You're on the pill, right?"

"The shot, so we're good. And I've been tested. I'm clean."

Rix slid his arm around my waist and pulled me close. "Then we're fine. I wouldn't put you at risk in any way, and certainly not that. I've never not used one, and I can't say I'm in a hurry to start using them again after that."

The lingering *so was it good for you* question was put to rest in my head. Of course it was. I stood a little taller, pride straightening my spine. For whatever reason, Rix had the same fascination with me that I had with him. I still didn't understand it, but I wasn't going to question it. Too many questions would dull the shine, because I was sure I didn't have answers for most of them.

For right now, I was going to live in the moment and enjoy every bit I could. I knew all too well that everything could be snatched away in an instant, and I refused to miss appreciating this experience.

Rix led me out to the car, one hand on the small of my back. It reinforced the feeling of safety I always had in his presence. Like nothing could touch me. I craved that feeling almost as much as I craved him.

We slid into the SUV, and Rix gave instructions to Johnny as we rolled forward. "Back to my woman's place. Take a different route than we did before, and make sure we aren't being followed."

Being followed?

I waited until he settled back in his seat before asking, "Are you worried the other gang would follow you?"

Rix shrugged. "It's always possible. I don't need to lead anyone directly to you. We took a long, backassward route on the way there just to be sure."

Every time he said or did something that put me and my safety first, I fell a little further, a little harder. Honestly, though, who was I kidding? I was already past the point of no return.

Instead of taking a few minutes, we drove for twenty-five, and when we passed my favorite little hole-in-the-wall restaurant for po'boys, I asked Johnny to pull over. Rix didn't raise so much as an eyebrow when he had Johnny run in and get us some. We devoured them before we even made it back to my house. Which raised the question . . .

"Are you going to come in the front door?"

"Your neighbors would be scandalized."

My neighbors were good friends of my parents and kept a fairly close eye on my house at my father's request.

"I don't care." It was the closest I'd come to a declaration.

"You might."

"I don't."

Rix had Johnny slow the car two blocks away from my house. "I think this will be more fun." He pulled the door open and hopped out.

"What are you doing?"

"I'm gonna race you."

"Race me?"

"Whoever makes it inside first calls the shots tonight."

This got my attention. But there was no time to respond because Rix was already shutting the door.

I slapped the back of the empty passenger seat. "Hurry!"

Johnny chuckled, low and rusty, indicating that while he might not see anything Rix didn't want him to see, he certainly heard plenty.

He turned a corner and slowed at the next stop sign, the car seeming to move at a snail's pace. I stemmed the urge to smack the seat again. Barely. Instead, I scanned the yards of the neighbors' houses, my mind filling in images of Rix scaling brick walls and hopping garden gates.

When Johnny pulled up at the stop sign at the corner of my street, I yanked open the door and jumped out.

"Wha—"

"Thanks for the ride!" I tossed over my shoulder as I shut the door and took off down the broken sidewalk on my heels. I made it through my gate and flipped open my clutch to find my key. Unlocking the portico, I hurried to the inside door and unlocked it. I waited for the beep of the alarm, but it was silent.

"No freaking way. He couldn't have—"

"He couldn't have what?" Rix said, leaning against the wall near my stairway.

"How did you?"

I studied him closer, looking for tears in his jacket or smudges on his crisp white shirt. The only stain I could see was a red lipstick smudge on his collar, peeking out from beneath his suit coat. *Oops.*

I crossed to him and reached for the button. Rix's eyebrows rose, but he didn't protest as I unbuttoned his suit coat and slid it off his shoulders.

When I'd used him for a sound-dampening device, I'd wrecked his shirt. But *maybe* if it didn't set, the dry cleaner could still get it out.

My hands went to the top button, and Rix's fingers covered mine. "Whoa, duchess. According to the rules, I won, and I'm calling the shots."

"Shhh. I'm trying to save your shirt."

He looked down at the collar, a smirk tugging at the corners of his mouth. "I'm pretty sure I know where that came from."

"Which means it's my responsibility to make sure the stain doesn't set." I moved his fingers aside and unbuttoned the placket, then peeled the shirt off his arms.

Rix said nothing, but I could feel his eyes on me as I

paused, remembering to unbutton the cuffs before I tugged the shirt free.

"I'll just be a few minutes," I said, turning in the direction of the laundry room and my utility sink.

Rix's big hand closed around my arm before I could take a second step. "Wait."

I glanced over my shoulder, and the expression on his face wasn't what I was expecting to see. It was intense, but unreadable. It wasn't heat so much as . . . I couldn't place it. Rix plucked the shirt from my hand and tossed it on a stair.

"What are you—"

He pulled me close until our bodies touched.

"No one has taken care of me for longer than I can remember. No one has wanted to. Thought to. And you do it instinctively. My wound last night," he gestured to the small bandage that still covered his side, "and now my shirt. That means something to me, and it tells me a lot about you. Makes me want things I shouldn't let myself want. A future I can't stop myself from picturing you in. I like when you throw attitude my way, when you're being stubborn, how you feel when my cock is deep inside you, and there's nothing I want more than to stare into your eyes and blow both our minds. I don't know how this is gonna work, but it's gonna work. I'm not settling for less. Not with you. For once in my life, I'm gonna have it all."

Rix slid both hands under my ass and picked me up, much like he had in the storeroom, and carried me up the stairs. I'd forgotten all about his wound then, but now that he'd reminded me, I was worried he'd hurt himself carting me around.

"You got shot, so you shouldn't be carrying me," I protested. "You probably hurt yourself earlier. I was such an idiot. We should look at it."

Rix smiled down at me but didn't stop climbing the stairs. "I didn't. But I'm glad you care."

"But—"

"Your turn to hush now. The only words I want from you are more, and yes, and right there."

I squeezed the back of his neck, where my hands held tight. "You're such a man."

Pushing his hips against me so I could feel the solid length of his erection behind the zipper of his suit pants, he smirked. "Damn right, I am. And you love it."

And I did. Love him, that is. The words were in my throat, but I couldn't form them into syllables and vocalize them. They twisted inside me, wanting to break free, but this wasn't the moment.

I knew the adage that if you loved someone, you shouldn't wait to tell them because you might not have another chance, but something was holding me back. Did he feel the same way about me? I shoved the words down, rocking against him as he reached the top of the stairs.

"So does this mean you're claiming your prize for being first? You're not going to concede and let me take the reins tonight?"

Rix slowed as he approached my room, stopping completely at the foot of my bed. "You want the reins, duchess?"

I did. This I knew without hesitation. I'd taken the lead in the storeroom, and I wasn't done. If I couldn't tell him how I felt, then I could show him.

"Yes. I do."

"Then my calling the shots means I'm handing the reins to you." He lowered me to the bed and stepped back. "Where do you want me?"

"Right there."

I rose to my feet and reached for the buttons of my blouse. One by one I unfastened them, my gaze on Rix and his on my hands. His absolute captivation with my movements rekindled the boldness I'd felt earlier tonight. I wanted to be on my knees before this man.

I laid my blouse on the bed. Stepping forward, wearing nothing but my skirt, heels and bra, I lowered myself to the floor, placing my hands on his thighs to steady myself.

"What are you doin', duchess?"

I looked up to see the softest hint of a smile on his lips. I let my own curve up, channeling my inner temptress. Yes, I was on my knees, but he'd handed me the reins, and that meant I had the power.

"I think you know what I'm doing." I reached for his belt and slid it from the buckle before going for the button and zipper and pulling his cock free.

In the storeroom, I'd wrapped my hand around him, but I hadn't had a chance to get my lips around him. Ever since the day in my studio when we'd been interrupted, I'd been aching to do this. My fingers didn't touch as I closed them around his thick shaft, but still I stroked up and down.

My tongue darted out to join the game, and Rix groaned before tangling his hands in my hair. But he didn't try to guide my movements. Didn't try to push himself deeper into my mouth when I just closed my lips around the head.

"Fuck, you're beautiful. And not just because I love watching you take my cock."

I moaned as I took him deeper, working him with my tongue and my mouth, loving the sound of his groans and murmured praise. They spurred me on and I grew bolder, wanting to make him lose control.

I could tell I was getting close when his hips bucked unconsciously against my face before he drew back, pulling his length from my mouth.

"I wasn't done," I protested.

Rix kept his hold on my hair and tilted my face up to meet

his gaze. "I don't want to come in your mouth. I want to sink into that tight pussy of yours again with nothin' between us. Haven't been able to stop thinking about it."

I considered pouting, but I could work with that. "Then I want to be on top."

A lazy smile spread across his face. "I did give you the reins, so it's only right that you ride me."

He shoved his pants the rest of the way off his hips and moved to sit on the bed. Sliding up to the head, he propped himself on a pillow, right in the middle.

I couldn't get over how beautiful he was. He'd hate that I called him that in my head, but it was the truth. The caramel tone of his skin, the black and gray ink covering his arms and chest. The heavy muscles underlying it all.

He was a masterpiece in his own right. It only made sense that I'd been compelled to paint him, and my hands were once again itching to hold a brush.

Later. Right now, I was going to take my pleasure and make this man see stars. Maybe forget every woman who ever came before me.

"You waitin' on something, duchess?"

Shaking my head, I reached behind me for the zipper on my skirt and slid it down. It fell to the floor and I stepped forward. My bra was next, discarded beside the growing pile of clothes.

Crawling up the bed to straddle him, I pressed a kiss to his chest, over his heart. Another to his neck, his jaw, and then his lips. All that leashed strength beneath me, and it was mine.

He was mine.

THIRTY-ONE
RIX

S he didn't look like the duchess I called her. She looked like a queen. Hair, black as night, spilling down her shoulders. Her breasts were high and firm, the perfect size for my mouth.

I'd told her she could take the reins, and I'd meant it, but I couldn't stop myself from touching her. My hands on her hips as she settled her pussy over my cock. Hot, slick heat had me fighting the urge to lift her and impale her on my dick.

Yes, I'd wanted women before, but never had I wanted one like this. With Valentina, all bets were off. All rules were broken. All standards crushed. She was just so much more. And she was mine.

Her fingertips started at my jaw and trailed down my neck, skimming across my collarbone to my chest, down my abs and then over to my fingertips, before sliding back up my arms to my shoulders. She curled her hands shut, gripping me as she shifted forward and rocked on my cock.

Fuck. I wasn't going to last nearly long enough to do this justice. She'd already had my dick in her mouth, and when she'd done that, I'd been almost unable to hold myself back. A lifetime of fucking her wouldn't be enough, especially one predicted to be as short as mine.

That thought pushed from my head, I kept my grip on her hips, helping her move against me, angling my hips so her clit dragged along the head of my cock. She was already flushed, her pupils dilated, and her breathing heavy. My woman was close to the edge too, which meant this might not be the longest ride ever, but it would be fucking explosive all the same.

"I want you," she whispered, releasing my shoulder to wrap her hand around my cock and angle it toward her entrance.

The perfect searing heat stole my senses, and it took everything in me to let her keep control when all I wanted to do was lift up and plunge deep inside her. But Valentina didn't make me wait long. She slid down my cock, inch by fucking inch, moaning and squeezing with every move.

The moment took on a sheen of perfection I'd never before experienced. Valentina's beautiful face, flush with passion, her need for me and my cock written on every feature. Everything about her tied together to make the sexiest package I'd ever encountered.

My thoughts scattered when she froze, my cock buried in her tight little pussy, and she began to rock forward and back, working her clit.

Oh, we can do better than that.

I reached out a hand to wrap around her hip, my thumb centered on her clit and pressing down. It was like hitting a detonator.

"Oh my God." She moaned, hips bucking into my hand as her muscles clamped down around me. "I can't stop it."

"Don't stop, baby. Come for me."

With her head dropping back and muscles shaking, I tightened my grip on her hips with both hands, keeping the pressure on her clit as I lifted her and lowered her on my cock, my hips pumping up with each movement.

"Can't stop," she whispered, her nipples tightening just before she tensed again. I wanted to make her come over and over again, just so I could see her face like that.

My own climax slammed into me without warning, and I couldn't hold it back.

"Fuck," I roared into the room, pulling her down hard on my cock as I came.

I loved her.

And that changed everything.

THIRTY-TWO
VALENTINA

Rix had unleashed some kind of wildness inside me, and I didn't want to rein it in. I fell asleep wrapped in his arms, but didn't stay asleep for long because it seemed I'd unleashed something in him as well. He woke me twice in the night, the first time with his mouth on my breasts, and the second time as he slid inside me. I loved it. Loved him. And I didn't want to spend another night without him in my bed.

The third time, it was the sun streaming through my window that woke me. Flicking my eyes open, I noticed the lack of heat at my back immediately. All night, I'd been held inside the safety of Rix's arms, and I missed it.

Has he left?

Still half-asleep, I rolled out of bed, my muscles languid. I found my robe on the back of my bathroom door and slipped it on. My house was quiet. Making my way down the stairs to the kitchen in search of coffee and the man who should have still been in my bed, I stopped short when I saw a note on the counter.

Had to go take care of something. I'll be back when I can.
Didn't want to leave you this morning.

It was unsigned, but Rix didn't need to sign a note for me to know it was from him. The timer on my coffeemaker tripped and the delicious scent filled the kitchen.

While I sipped, my brain sped from one possibility to the next. The daring woman who'd made an appearance last night wanted to come out to play again, and I was embracing her. I'd finally shed the remaining threads of victimhood and I was whole. Rix hadn't healed me, but he'd given me the motivation to heal myself.

For that I would always be grateful, but it wasn't why I loved him.

───

Eight hours packed with customers and sales later, there was still no word from Rix, and I was frustrated by the silence. I wanted to celebrate this amazing day, and I wanted him to celebrate with me. I understood that much of his world would never exist for me, but at times like this, I felt completely in the dark.

But that didn't mean I couldn't tempt him to finish whatever he was doing by sending a helpful text. I flipped the OPEN sign to CLOSED and considered my alternatives.

According to Rix, I had an unseen man watching over me, so I fearlessly walked the streets toward a club on Bourbon Street that I knew would be packed with tourists even at this hour. The chances of me seeing a single familiar face were slim to none. I sent the text as I settled onto one of the few free bar stools.

The text included three pieces of information. Where I was, the fact that I wasn't wearing panties, and how badly I wanted him inside me right now.

If that couldn't shake the man loose, I didn't know what could.

Several tough-looking guys filled the bar, and I surreptitiously glanced over them, wondering which one was my babysitter for the evening.

What if I didn't have any? What if I was riding on a false sense of security and completely vulnerable to Rix's enemies?

No, this was where trust came in. He could assess whatever threats were out there better than I ever could, and I absolutely trusted he wouldn't leave me unprotected against something he could prevent.

Still, I kept my guard up.

I was nearing the end of my first margarita when a prickle of awareness skittered over my skin. Tossing my heavy hair over my shoulder, I looked to my right. Dark, tattooed arms leaned against the bar.

"Can I buy you another drink?"

Rix's deep voice wrapped around me like rough silk.

"I don't usually let strangers buy me drinks."

One dark eyebrow went up at the word *strangers*. Yep, I wanted to play, and he got the message loud and clear.

"Then I guess that makes you a pretty smart lady, because most strangers are just trying to get you liquored up so they can cop a feel in an alley and take you back to their hotel."

Pushing my empty glass forward, I met his gaze. "But not you?"

Rix signaled to the bartender, and he appeared within seconds. Nothing like the five minutes it had taken me to get service when I'd first sat down. "Another margarita for the lady, and I'll take a double shot of Patrón."

He didn't respond until the drinks were in front of us and he'd slid a large bill to the bartender.

"I already know what's gonna happen, so there's no trying involved," he said.

"Is that right?" My tone was flirty and full of challenge as I accepted the margarita on the rocks he offered up. The sweet liquid hit my tongue. "Do I look like a sure thing to you?"

Rix knocked back his shot and set the glass on the table behind him. Turning my bar stool to face him, he slid between my legs. My skirt inched up my thighs. The movement had me hyperaware of my lack-of-panties situation. The hand that landed on my knee and slid up under my skirt kicked my awareness into extreme need. I drank deeply, draining half my glass.

The beat of club music thumped around us while tourists partied and laughed, paying no mind to what we were doing. It made me bold, made me want him to touch me in ways I shouldn't want to be touched in public. I thought of the enclosed booth last night, and how if I'd been bolder, I would have grabbed his hand and pushed it under my skirt and let him touch me while we watched the erotic scene onstage instead of luring him into a storeroom.

Heat slicked my center, and I wanted him to feel how wet I was for him even now. One more gulp and I finished my drink. Liquid courage coursing through my veins with the need, I scooted forward on my bar stool, my legs spreading further around his knees, and Rix's eyes widened for a fraction of a second before he slid his hand higher.

"You tempt a man, duchess."

"Good thing he's the man I want to tempt."

His fingers were within an inch of where I wanted them, but

still he didn't touch me. The bartender's voice interrupted, but I didn't move.

"Another round?"

"Yes." Rix reached his free hand into his pocket and tossed a bill on the bar top. He used the movement to get closer, and I bit my lip as one finger slid across my slit and stroked.

Silver fire flashed in Rix's eyes, and I wondered if mine sparked darkly. I wanted him. Needed to feel him.

When the bartender returned with our drinks, Rix nodded to the money. "We're all set."

He ignored his shot as he handed me my drink.

"You're never gonna think of margaritas again and not remember how I finger fucked your tight little cunt until you came against my hand," he whispered in my ear.

I took a sip, willing my hand not to shake as he slid a finger inside me.

Oh God. I tightened my grip on the glass as he teased me, thrusting his finger in and pulling it out.

"Is that right?" I murmured, trying to sound saucy, when what I was truly doing was fighting to keep my hips from grinding into his touch.

"That's right. I'm gonna have you biting that lip as you come, trying to keep from crying out, before you finish that drink."

That's when Rix's thumb joined the action, finding my clit.

All the noise in the bar was drowned out by the blood pulsing in my ears. My field of vision shrank to only Rix, and every sensation swirling through my body centered on his touch. My orgasm was quick, intense, and blinding.

I squeezed my eyes shut, slammed my glass to the bar, and gripped his arm. My nails dug in, but I couldn't loosen my hold. My lip stung as my teeth pressed down. I willed myself not to cry out, and almost lost the battle when he thrust again and pressed.

Pleasure licking at every inch of my insides, I tugged at his arm, a silent plea that I'd had enough and any more would make me a public spectacle. Rix mercifully pulled his hand free from between my legs. In the shafts of neon coming from the club lights in the ceiling, the skin of his fingertips glistened. From me.

Instead of wiping it away, Rix sucked his finger and thumb clean.

"You ready?" he asked, as if I hadn't just watched one of the most erotic acts of my life.

All I could do was nod. I'd come in ready to play, and the game had been turned on me in the best way possible.

Rix led me out of the bar, his hand on my lower back. Johnny was parked on a side street two blocks away in the Escalade. When Rix opened the door and then followed me inside, the SUV rolled forward. Around and around we drove until apparently Johnny was sure there was no one following us. This time, he pulled alongside the curb in front of my house.

I looked to Rix, and the expression on his face told me he wasn't coming inside.

"I got some work to finish up and I'll be back."

"What kind of work?" The question was out before I could stop it. I knew I wasn't getting an answer. Heck, I wasn't even sure if I wanted an answer.

Rix's expression was guarded. "Just work. I'll be back when I can."

"I interrupted you." Guilt lanced through me, but I wouldn't give back this last hour for anything.

"You're never an interruption." His words were clearly a lie.

"Why did you come if you were busy? You didn't need to."

Rix lifted a hand to my face. "If my woman says she's drinking alone, I'm not the kind of man to leave her to it."

"Still—"

"Don't worry about it. I'll be back soon." He leaned in and pressed a kiss to my lips before reaching past me and opening the door. "Don't wait up."

"Be safe," I whispered, pressing my lips to his cheek. I had no idea what he was going out to do, but I was sure of one thing. "I don't want to lose you."

"You won't."

I could only hope he was right.

THIRTY-THREE

RIX

Drugs. Money. Guns. They'd been my world for years, but I was ready to get out. Valentina wasn't the kind of woman I could keep while doing what I did, and I wasn't willing to let her go. What I could let go of was drugs, money, and guns. But when you were as bound up in the game as I was, nothing was ever simple.

Johnny and I rolled on the warehouse where I had a meet set up. Hennessy was still sniffing around, looking for evidence that his brother wasn't dirty. I'd offered up a reward for the wire tape, and wouldn't you know it, money talked.

I was getting my hands on it today, from another employee of the NOPD, ironically enough. In this world, no one and nothing were ever what or who they seemed to be. The good guys weren't all good and the bad guys weren't all bad. Just one more lesson about life.

And why the fuck was I getting philosophical? I was here to get something Hennessy wanted, and then I was going to warn him off Valentina once and for all.

The warehouse was dark and quiet when I walked in. Abandoned twenty years ago after a main Mardi Gras parade route change, the old brick building still held random pieces of broken floats that had never been moved. It was very NOLA.

Gregory Herman waited inside, arms crossed, wearing thick-rimmed glasses that magnified his eyes. From the way he was jumping at every sound, he had to be hopped up on something, because there was no way he could be that nervous. Could he? A tech nerd at the precinct for less than a year, according to my sources, he didn't do much fieldwork, but he was a savant when it came to computers and surveillance and all that shit.

Johnny was at my back as I approached Herman. "You alone?" I asked. I hadn't taken the time to search the building, but that was the other thing that could have him so jumpy. "Because if you ain't, you and whoever you brought are going to have a rather unpleasant evening."

He shook his head violently, almost dislodging his glasses. Resettling them on his nose, he stuttered, "N-n-no, sir. Just me. I didn't want anyone to know what I was doing."

"Because you're breaking the law and could end up in jail for doing this yourself."

I wanted to make sure the consequences were clear to him before I handed over the money. I didn't get the *set-up* vibe from him either.

"I guess. I mean, it's just a file. It's no big deal."

His lack of remorse would be troubling to his superiors, but it was fine by me.

"Exactly. And you're getting a decent bonus for your assistance. No harm, no foul."

Herman nodded. "Right. Exactly."

"So let's hear it."

"Hear it?" he asked.

"The recording." At his confused expression, I added, "Did you think I'd pay for shit before I heard it? You could be scam-min' me, Herman, although I think you're too nice a guy to be trying that."

"I swear I'm not. It's all here. I thought you'd want to listen to it in private. I mean, this could be big stuff. I don't recognize the voices, so I'm not much help."

"We're listening to it now, and then we'll both be on with our day."

"Oh, okay. I guess that's fine." He pulled a USB drive out of his pocket. "Do you have a computer?"

Taking it from Herman, I turned to Johnny. He already had the laptop out and open in his hands. I slid the USB drive into place, found the file, and hit PLAY.

Static was all I heard at first, and then a conversation started.

"I told you I'm done."

"And I told you I'm not. We've got at least three or four more runs before I'm going to be ready to call it quits."

"You're taking a lot of fucking chances, Hennessy."

Well, fuck. We listened to the end of the recording, even though I didn't need to hear any more to have my answers.

I held out a hand and Johnny placed an envelope in it.

"For your good work," I said.

Herman grabbed the envelope and folded it in half before shoving it in his pants pocket. "Guess I'll be on my way."

"You do that."

He left the warehouse, and I waited several long moments before my curse echoed through the room.

Fuck. As much as Hennessy was pissing me the fuck off right now with his dogged determination to get my woman, I didn't want this for him. This wasn't the kind of news I wanted to deliver to any person. It also wasn't something I was going to keep from him.

"Let's roll," I said to Johnny before we turned to leave the warehouse. A shuffling sound caught my attention before we got too far. We both drew our guns in the direction of the noise before taking another step.

"Come out or you're dead." My tone was casual, but my words weren't.

D-Rock materialized from the shadows.

"What the fuck are you doing back in town?" I demanded, lowering my piece.

He was lucky I didn't shoot him instead. He was supposed to be laid up in his aunt's guest room, not allowed to step foot in Louisiana again without my express permission. His recklessness had cost people their lives, and had caused me a huge pain in the ass.

"I needed to talk to you."

"That's what phones are for, genius."

"Nah, man. I needed to get back here. Gotta see my girl."

"Your girl is done with you. Most women don't appreciate getting kidnapped and staying kidnapped for a week, and on top of that, they're not big fans of being rescued by people who aren't their man."

"But I—"

"All you did was start a war. You need to get the fuck out of town before you cause me more trouble. Told you I didn't want to see your face anytime soon."

"But Trinity—"

"Is fucking going to art school, and she doesn't need a gangbanger like you to fuck with her life any more than you already have. The girl is bright. She's going places. You're not what she needs."

D-Rock's face twisted into an ugly scowl. "Ain't that the pot callin' the kettle? Fuck, you're so far up that rich bitch's ass, you can't even see that you're fuckin' draggin' her down like you're accusing me of doin' to Trinity." He laughed bitterly.

"You're a gangbanger and she's practically fuckin' royalty. You've got no business touchin' her, but you don't seem to get that, do you? What do you think is gonna happen with you two? You're gonna move into her fancy digs and live happily ever after?"

If my gun were still drawn, I would have been tempted to pull the trigger to shut him up. "None of that shit you spewed is any of your goddamned business, so I suggest you buy yourself a bus ticket and get back to Bumfuck where I sent you, and wait until you're called."

D-Rock's face twisted with rage. "You don't get to fuckin' tell me what to do. I'm not some punk kid anymore, Rix. I've paid my dues. I get a say."

I stalked toward him. Enough was enough. "You don't get a say unless I tell you you do. You're still a punk kid because you can't make a damn decision without putting what you want first. You need to grow the fuck up before you get yourself killed. Or before I kill you."

"Fuck you, Rix."

Enough of this little fucker. I closed the distance separating us and grabbed him by the throat, lifted him off his feet, and walked forward until his back slammed into the concrete wall. If my crew didn't respect me, then they weren't part of the crew any longer. Because he was a stupid fuck, I'd given him more chances than he deserved, but this was his last.

"You ever talk like that to me again, I will fuckin' kill you with my bare hands. I won't waste a bullet on your sorry piece-of-shit brain because you've wasted too much already. You're done with the girl. No need to explain. I'll take care of that shit. And if you talk about my woman again, you'll wish you were dead long before I get around to ending you."

And I meant every single fucking word of it. My hands weren't clean. But in my world, the ends justified the means, and I got shit done. A few more steps, and I could walk out on this life.

I could already taste the sweetness of freedom on the other side. Not long now.

D-Rock gurgled against my hold, and I shook him hard.

"You get me?"

He nodded with jerking movements before I lowered him to his feet.

"Do not test me again. This is your last chance. Now, get the fuck out of my sight."

He fixed his shirt and glared at me. All his thoughts showed on his face, but he was smart enough not to open his mouth.

"I'm gone," he spat, before turning on his heel and stalking out of the warehouse.

"Let's get the hell out of here, Johnny. This place is pissing me off."

"Sure thing, boss."

THIRTY-FOUR
VALENTINA

The press of the mask on my face brought me right back to earlier this week. Rix. The club. It was everything I could do not to shiver when I remembered the storage room.

Tonight's purpose was much more mundane, but still worthy. My mother had helped organize a masquerade at the New Orleans Museum of Art to raise money for a new children's art program that was to be offered to any city resident under the age of fourteen at no cost. A noble cause, and one I couldn't turn down given my own passion for the arts, even if my mother hadn't co-chaired the committee.

I thought of little girls like Trinity. When I'd first met her at twelve and she'd been assigned as the Little to my Big, she'd been quiet and shy. Pulling words from her had been like pulling teeth. But when I'd brought out art supplies on a whim, she'd blossomed. I wanted that for all the other kids out there who might not otherwise discover a talent and become the next George Rodrigue with his famous blue dogs.

Tying my mask a little tighter, I stared into the mirror and laughed at the irony of an event to raise money for children but didn't include a single child. No, tonight NOMA was full of glittering dresses and expensively cut suits with deep pockets. A silent auction of certain donated pieces was being held to raise funds on top of the hefty price of a ticket.

I stepped out of the ladies' room and began circling the ball-room, searching for my parents. I knew plenty of other people in attendance, although the masks hid the identities well enough that I wasn't able to place many of them.

As was the norm in this town when you pulled on a mask, people felt free to dress more risqué, laugh louder, act bolder. I'd already been on the receiving end of a very handsy gentleman who'd apparently hit the open bar a too hard. Which wasn't a terrible idea, I supposed.

I strode up to the shortest line. Tonight would go much faster with a drink in my hand. I might support the cause they were raising money for, but that didn't mean I was endlessly entertained by the event. I'd rather be home, in my studio, waiting for a certain man to break into my house.

Rix had been MIA all afternoon and evening, and as much as I wanted to text and ask where he was and what he was doing, I hesitated. The only thing I was pretty certain of was that he would find his way into my bed tonight somehow.

A glass of red acquired, I circled the room, catching sight of my father. Even from here, it was obvious his eyes were on my mother as she gestured to one of the silent auction pieces, no doubt giving excellent reasons why the last bid was dreadfully underpriced and how someone could still grab it for a steal. She was an expert at that.

I made my way to my father.

"You're looking dashing in your mask this evening."

His smile was quick, but softened when he realized it was me. "Darling daughter. You look beautiful."

My emerald-green dress was long and fitted, with a slit

243

running up the back just past my knees. Without it, I wouldn't have been able to walk in the thing. The V-cut of the front wasn't exactly plunging, but rather the daring edge of flattering. I'd bought it months ago, and when I'd seen the event on my calendar for tonight, it had seemed like the perfect choice.

The looks I'd drawn since I'd walked in the door had me reconsidering whether I'd pushed the daring edge a further than necessary, but I didn't think so. It was the masks allowing more emboldened stares than one would normally encounter at a charity event. And apparently my father didn't think it looked scandalous.

"You look handsome yourself."

He lifted his highball glass to clink against the rim of my wineglass. "Your old man can still pull off black tie when necessary." He winked at me and sipped.

It was no secret that my father hated wearing a tux. Bow ties were his nemesis, and no amount of black-tie events would ever make him see differently. In his position, especially with all of my mother's causes, he'd been to a ridiculous number.

I glanced at my mother, still pushing the bid on a gorgeous abstract skyline of the city. "She's in her element."

"Of course. She's emptying pockets for the good of the children of this city. You know there's nothing she loves better than repurposing people's funds."

Repurposing people's funds. A great way to describe it.

"Harold! Is that you under that mask?"

A man's voice cut through the background music and chatter as he strode up to us. He was younger than my father by at least twenty years, with hair as black as night except for a little gray at the temples. He'd also opted for a suit and not a tux, and it fit him to perfection. His own mask hid parts of his face, but not his dark eyes and chiseled jaw. I didn't think a woman alive would be able to argue he wasn't handsome.

"Garrett Hughes, I haven't seen your face in a long time. Heard you moved out of town."

The men shook hands, and Hughes replied, "Business took me to the West Coast for the last year, but this place is always home." His eyes fixed on me. "And who is this stunning woman?" His dark eyes sparkled with interest.

Oh no, I need another interested guy like I need another hole in my head.

"This is my daughter, Valentina. I believe I've mentioned her before."

Hughes held out a hand, and I placed mine in it. He lifted it to his lips.

"Charmed." His next words were directed at my father, but his attention never left me. "If I'd known the daughter you'd casually mentioned was one of the most beautiful women I'd ever seen, I would have pressed for an introduction and reconsidered leaving town for so long."

My father's laugh rang out from beside me. "I think there's a good reason I never made more than a casual mention. A man like you would try to steal her away from us for good."

Hughes's smile widened. "Obviously."

"But you might have missed your window, Hughes. Valentina's got a man in her life."

Hughes's eyebrows rose above his mask. "Isn't that the reason for the saying *may the best man win*?"

I finally joined the conversation. "I'm so sorry to disappoint you, Mr. Hughes, but I'm of the opinion that the best man has already won."

"Whoa-ho!" My father chuckled. "She is serious about him. Sorry, Hughes. One thing is certain about my girl—she knows her mind and she doesn't waver from it."

If my father only knew where my mind was these days, he'd probably push me off on Hughes as fast as possible. He had no doubt I was talking about Rhett Hennessy, an upstanding member of the justice system, not a man on the wrong side of the law.

How was I ever going to tell my parents? But I had to. I would make them understand. Somehow.

"Well, at least grace me with a dance to let me down gently?" Hughes hadn't released my hand.

I saw no easy way out of his invitation. At least a dozen couples were dancing in the center of the room to the strains of the jazz band providing the entertainment.

"Of course, Mr. Hughes. My pleasure," I replied, a polite smile on my face.

"The pleasure is all mine, I promise."

He led me out onto the dance floor, and I placed my wine-glass on the tray of a passing server. Hughes's dark gaze sharpened on my face as he placed a hand at my side.

"How serious is it?"

"As serious as it gets," I replied without hesitation. I recognized a determined man when I saw one, and the only thing I could do to quell his interest was to be firm in my convictions.

"That's a shame."

"Maybe for you. I have to say I'm quite happy about it."

His lips quirked. "You could at least pretend to let me down easy."

Laughing, I followed his lead easily on the dance floor. "You just met me, and three minutes isn't long enough to get your hopes up that high. I'm sure you'll survive."

"True. But still, missed opportunities are my least favorite kind."

He slowed, and I stumbled as a deep voice came from behind me.

"I believe this is where I cut in."

I swung my head around to see Rix standing beside us on

the dance floor. A mask obscured most of his face, but I would know him anywhere.

Hughes released his grip on me. "Ah, *as serious as it gets* has come to stake his claim. Fair enough, sir. If she were mine, I wouldn't let another man hold her either."

With that, Hughes bowed off and Rix pulled me into his arms before we slid back into the dance.

So many thoughts jumbled in my brain, but the one that floated to the surface was probably the most ridiculous. *Rix knows how to dance?*

I couldn't even speak for a full minute because I'd somehow lost the ability to form words. When I finally pulled it together, I whispered, "What are you doing here?"

"Thought I'd see what the fuss was all about with these fancy events."

"Are you insane?"

His silver gaze locked on me. "Crazy about you, but I wouldn't claim insane."

"How did you even know I was here?"

He flashed a smile. "You know I've got eyes on you everywhere, duchess. I always know where you are."

I did know that, but apparently I'd forgotten in the shock of seeing him here. "And you wanted to know what the fuss was about."

A nod. "Didn't much like what I saw."

Hughes. He was talking about Hughes.

"I don't even know him."

Rix swept me in a turn. "You make a habit of dancing with guys you don't know?"

"When they know my father and I have no graceful way to decline, I do. And where did you learn to dance?"

"My cousin liked to play cotillion when she was five or six, even though there was no way in hell she'd ever be going to one because we were all dirt poor. She never would've even heard of cotillion if not for Old Lady Able across the street telling stories about how her mama had gone to one. She had these footprint sheets showing the steps, and tapes of Fred Astaire and Ginger Rogers, and told my cousin she needed to learn like a proper young lady. I got roped into being her partner. I was all of eight or nine at the time. One whole summer, my cousin wanted to practice every day."

I pictured a young boy, probably lanky and tall, if Rix's height was any indication, stepping from footprint to footprint with a small girl. It was an endearing image.

"Guess there are some things you just don't forget. Can't say I haven't used it to my advantage before."

His last comment got my attention. "You like to take the ladies dancing? Wow them with your skills?"

"Don't need to wow them with my dancing skills. You know the others are better."

This entire moment was surreal. We shouldn't be having this conversation. We shouldn't be dancing to this song. He shouldn't even be here. And yet, I wouldn't trade this moment —even with the possible consequences—for anything. Every glimpse into Rix's past was precious.

He spun me into another turn that took us right to the doorway, and pulled me out of the room.

"What—"

Rix didn't respond, just crossed the lobby and stepped around a white curtain blocking one of the few sections closed for tonight's event. It was a sign of how much I'd changed that I followed him without question or hesitation.

The room was lit only by the glow coming through the white curtain, and was empty of people. Scaffolding and white sheeting indicated this was the section currently being remodeled, and the lack of art on the wall confirmed my assumption. My mother had mentioned it before.

But thoughts of my mother evaporated when Rix's hand slid through the slit in the back of my dress and he palmed my ass.

"Fuck. I knew you'd be wearing a thong with this."

"I almost wore nothing under it."

"Not unless you're with me." His words were pure alpha decree.

I could have pretended otherwise, but instead I went for the truth. "Why do you think I didn't?"

Rix groaned and I shifted, already wet and eager for him to touch me. We could hear the band playing from rooms away and the sound of the party, but it didn't occur to me to care. When he touched me, I lost all sense of reason.

His lips found mine, tasting, taking, spurring me on. Heat bloomed over my entire body. I wanted him. Now. Here.

Insanity. But I didn't care. The urgency wasn't only in me.

Rix pulled away and spoke low. "Turn around and grab the scaffolding, duchess. Bend forward."

The newly found scandalous side of me reveled in his order. I gave no thought to anything beyond him, his touch, and how much I wanted him.

I turned and grabbed the scaffolding. "Hurry," I said over my shoulder. My voice was barely a whisper.

"You gonna be able to stay quiet?"

Quiet? I'd have to be. I had no choice. But the reminder was a forbidden thrill of what we were doing.

Who am I?

A whole new woman. One who wasn't afraid to push boundaries and take chances and *live*. And I really liked the new me.

Rix pushed my dress up, the slit up the back making access easier. Who knew I'd picked the perfect dress for tonight? His touch sent prickles of sensation across my skin as he slid my feet apart and tugged my panties to the side.

Wasting no time, Rix plunged one finger inside and groaned.

"Always ready for me. Fucking love that."

I pressed back against him, loving it just as much. His finger slid out, swirled around my clit, and then disappeared. The quiet clink of a belt buckle met my ears, followed by the hiss of a zipper.

I can't believe I'm doing this. But there's no way I'm stopping.

The insanity of the moment ceased to matter when Rix pressed inside, filling me completely. A moan rose to my lips, but I bit it back.

Quiet. Be quiet.

As much as the thought of potentially getting caught was adding a forbidden edge to the pleasure thrumming through my body, I didn't *actually* want to get caught. So I stayed quiet.

Rix shoved my dress further up, reaching around to cover my clit with his fingers. In this position, he hit my G-spot with every thrust, and there was no way I'd be able to hold on. My orgasm was already building and Rix increased his pace, silent as he pushed me to the edge.

I bit down on my bottom lip hard enough to sting as the pleasure overwhelmed me. I wanted to scream. Instead, I fractured from the inside out, shaking as the orgasm rocked through me. My body clenched down on his, and Rix's low groan signaled that he was close. A few more thrusts and he stilled.

The sound of our heavy breathing was all I could hear above the soulful sounds of jazz sneaking in from beyond the curtain.

Oh my God. I can't believe we just did that. Oh my God.
Insanity. Complete insanity. Mind-blowing insanity.

Rix pulled away, and wetness slid down my thighs.

Crap. Reality set in. "I gotta get to the ladies' room to repair. And, um, clean up."

"Shit. I should've . . . I didn't even think. Fuck. I didn't come here for this, regardless of what you're thinking."

My eyes met his in the darkness of the room. "Why did you come?"

"Same reason I always come. I can't stay away."

THIRTY-FIVE
VALENTINA

As I lay in bed, Rix's body curled around me, I couldn't help but relive the events of tonight. We'd gone our separate ways once we'd left the closed-off room. Luckily, no one had seen me make my way to the restroom or his exit out a side door.

When I'd returned from the ladies', Garrett Hughes hadn't approached me again, but I'd felt his eyes on me. I'd stayed close to my father, wondering what he would have done if I'd brought Rix back into the room with me. How would I have introduced him?

Daddy, this is the guy I'm in love with. I don't know his full name because I don't ask questions. It's better that way. I think he might love me too, but I don't know because I'm afraid to bring it up.

I would sound like an idiot. Who gets into a relationship with someone they know virtually nothing about?

Tomorrow. I would ask all my questions tomorrow. Including the most important one—did we have a future?

Rix was gone when I woke, foiling my plans. No note. No text. Nothing. Did he have some kind of man-radar that went off when he knew I wanted to talk about something serious? Like questions he might not have answers to?

I busied myself getting ready for the day and arrived at the gallery an hour early. My new window sparkled in the sunlight, and I rearranged a few pieces. I had a gap on one wall and didn't know what I wanted to use to fill it. A quiet voice inside me told me that it was where my work should go.

This new Valentina Noble was brave enough to take risks, but did those include baring her heart and soul, and letting the world know she was an artist as well? Did I have thick enough skin? Could I handle the comments that my work was amateurish and not high enough caliber to be displayed on my own walls?

I supposed I would find out.

I locked the door, set the alarm, and headed back home.

My Tesla wasn't ideal for transporting artwork, but I fit three small pieces in the front seat. It had taken me nearly forty minutes to decide which ones to pick. I'd ended up selecting three that were similar in style to the one Yve and Lucas had bought. Which reminded me, I needed to honor my promise to notify them before I put these up for sale.

Trinity waited at the door, head ducked to stare at her phone, as I approached with the canvases.

"Would you mind giving me a hand?" I asked, happy to see her in the spot she'd waited for me so many times before. It was like the world was righting itself again.

Her head jerked up and she took in my full arms. Scurrying over, she lifted the paintings from my hold. I didn't normally show up with an armful of canvases, so the confusion on her face was justified. Normally our pieces were shipped in or dropped off by the artist.

"What are these?"

She looked down at them as I reached into my purse for my keys.

"They're new pieces I'm going to sell."

"Who's the artist?"

Here it was, my opening. I swallowed and gathered all the strains of confidence floating around inside me. "Me."

I expected shock. Instead I got a big smile.

"It's about time."

"Excuse me?"

Finding my keys, I pushed one into the lock and opened the door before turning off the alarm.

Trinity followed me inside. "You forget how many times I've been to your house. It's not like you lock the door to your studio."

No, but I definitely kept it closed. Then again, she was a curious girl.

"So you went snooping?"

"I smelled paint thinner, and I'm an artist. What would you have done?"

Good point. I pulled open the drawer to my desk and dropped my purse inside.

"Where are we going to put them?" Trinity asked.

"I'm debating. I . . . kind of sold one of my pieces already as an anonymous artist, and the buyers asked to be notified if any other pieces by that particular artist came up for sale."

"Guess I missed out on a lot while I was watching Netflix and stuffing my face with Cheetos."

She left out the part about being scared to death and locked in a room. I'd texted her several times over the last couple of days to check in, but her responses had all been along the same lines. *I'm fine. I promise. No worse for wear. Actually, I'm lucky as hell it wasn't worse, and I'm going to put it out of my mind.*

Clearly, Trinity didn't want to talk about it. That I could understand. I didn't ever want to talk about what had happened to me either after I'd spilled it all to the police, a rape counselor, and finally a psychologist. That had been enough.

I had the psychologist's card in my desk, and I'd be giving it to Trinity before she left for the day, along with the knowledge that the bill would be on me for as long as she wanted to go.

She walked to the wall with the empty space. "They'd go nicely here, but you already planned that."

I had, but now I couldn't kick the idea that I should call Yve and offer them to her before I put them out. But it wasn't like I was going to hang them on the wall and have a mad rush of customers after them. They'd probably gather dust for months before I gave up and took them home.

Then I remembered how quickly Yve and Lucas had snatched up the last one. My decision was made.

"Why don't you put them up, and I'll call Yve and let her know I've got more for her to see."

Yve wasted no time coming to the gallery. Dirty Dog was only a few blocks away, and she always had at least one employee manning the place with her.

When she walked in the door, the skirt of her retro canary-yellow dress swirling around her legs, her eyes tracked the walls and landed on the canvases before I could even say hello or point. She stood silently for long moments studying them, all depicting a dark-haired woman wrapped in a red silk sheet in three different poses. It was me, but no one would ever know because her face was turned away in each.

Yve didn't turn to look at me when she spoke. "She's beautiful. They're beautiful. Lucas's birthday is coming up, and I have to have them. The one we already purchased is amazing, but lonely. These will look perfect with her, and I can't wait to surprise him."

The words wrapped around my artist's soul like a balm. She'd said them without knowing it was me, but I had to tell her. I couldn't keep this a secret.

"I'll take them all," she said, her eyes still fixed on the wall where they hung.

And then I remembered one little detail. "Don't you want to know the price?"

Yve finally turned to me. "You looking to gouge me after the last one?"

"Of course not. I just thought you might want a price before you said yes."

"Nope. You're not going to charge me enough regardless."

I thought quickly and named a price that was near what Lucas had insisted on paying for the last one—multiplied by three.

Yve nodded. "Can I take them now?"

Wow.

"If you want. I can wrap them for you. Or crate them if you'd prefer."

She considered. "Wrapping them is fine. I'm not going far. I've got my car at Dirty Dog, so I can put them right in it. I can't wait to see the look on his face. You saved me a hell of a lot of trouble because I had no idea what to get the man who has everything for his birthday."

I thought Lucas might agree with that sentiment, because now he did seem to have everything—he had Yve.

"Then I'll ring you up and you can get back to work."

Yve turned her shrewd gaze on me. "Are you going to tell me who the artist is?"

"Does it matter?"

Another shake of her head. "Not at all, but for future reference, I'd like to know."

"You're not going to find her work anywhere other than here."

"Exclusive?"

"Something like that." With a deep breath, I took the plunge. "I painted them."

I had no idea what kind of reaction I would get, but Yve's wide, brilliant smile was a perfect one.

"Are you freaking kidding me?"

"No. Not kidding."

"That just makes it even better." Yve's excitement colored her tone. "I have *your* artwork on my wall and I didn't even know it. That makes me so damn happy, I can't even tell you." She strode toward me and I found myself on the receiving end of an unexpected hug.

"Thank you," I whispered.

She pulled back and looked me in the eye. "Now, tell me why your walls aren't covered in your work and why you're not advertising it as your own."

"I wasn't ready yet. This was a big move for me. You and Trinity and one other are the sum total of the people I've told."

"One other . . . the mystery man, am I right?"

Hesitantly, I nodded before explaining that he'd pushed me into it by moving the painting she'd purchased from my house to my gallery without me being aware.

"No wonder you were so damn shocked."

"It wasn't exactly what I expected to see here."

"I like him on principle. He goes after what he wants, pushes you to succeed. Those are both pros in my book."

He didn't take no for an answer. He routinely broke into my house against my wishes until he'd worked himself into my life such that I couldn't go five minutes without him crossing my mind.

What would Yve say if she really knew who he was?

The words were on the tip of my tongue to ask her when I swiped her credit card. But I couldn't get them out.

Yve wasn't done with the subject either. "You ever going to tell us who this guy is?"

I worried my lower lip. "He's not someone my parents will ever approve of."

Yve shrugged. "Does that matter?"

"Not exactly, but I'm just saying that as a way to . . . I don't know, Yve. He's not someone I should probably even know."

Her eyebrows went up, and her interest was well and truly caught. "But you can't stay away . . . Now this sounds like an even better story than I thought."

The door opened and I looked away, expecting a customer to save me from this discussion, but it was Trinity returning with the coffee she'd just had to have. No rescue from that quarter. And Yve thought one step faster than me.

"So, how hot is this guy Valentina can't keep her hands off of?"

Trinity paused with her coffee partway to her mouth and answered before I could intervene. "Rix? He's hot. Like *dayum, thank the day his mama was born* hot."

My stomach twisted as soon as she said his name.

Yve's gaze swung from Trinity to me. The cat was officially out of the bag. "Rix? Not the Rix who put some serious interest into Elle when she started working for Lord at Chains? Not the gangbanger Rix."

I cringed at her description of him. First, because I didn't know he'd put any kind of interest into Elle, let alone *serious* interest. And second, I *hated* the word gangbanger. It didn't apply to him. Right?

When I didn't immediately respond, Yve's eyes widened further and her mouth hung open. "No. Freaking. Way. I don't believe it."

Trinity, realizing she'd let the cat out of the bag, whispered, "Sorry. I thought she knew."

And that just confirmed it.

"Holy. Shit. I hate sayin' shit like *I can't even,* but right now —I can't even." Yve lifted a hand to her mouth and shook her head.

I'd never seen her look so stunned. But if I'd just been told what she'd been told . . . I would probably look like a gaping fish out of water too.

"Wow, girl. You've definitely been holding out on us. Hard core."

I wasn't even sure what I should say, but I knew I needed privacy to say it. "Trinity, could you give us a few minutes? Maybe go grab a beignet to go with that coffee?"

She nodded and shot me a sheepish smile. "I'm so sorry. I thought—"

"It's okay, hon. Don't worry about a thing. It was all going to come out eventually."

Yve cocked a hip. "Damn right it was going to come out. It should've come out already."

Trinity slipped out the door, and I walked around my desk and sank into my chair.

"I have no idea what I'm doing. None. Maybe less than none."

Yve took one of the slim, modern chairs I had for clients and dropped her big purple purse on the other. "I'm getting that. How did it even start?"

I nodded toward the door Trinity had left through. "Trinity."

Then I told her an abbreviated version of the story, complete

259

with the role Rix and Rhett had played in it. When I was done, Yve's mouth gaped even further than before.

"Damn. When you got back in the game, you got back in the game *hard*."

"More like clueless."

"Do you love him?" she asked. "Because at the end of the day, if you love the guy *and* you're willing to do whatever it takes to be with him, you're going to be fine. But if either of those two pieces are missing, you should run like hell now . . . that is, if he'd even let you run at this point. From what I've heard about him, when he finds a woman, he *owns* them. *Claims* them. He's got quite the reputation, from what I hear."

I didn't want to hear about his reputation or how he'd been with other women, regardless of whether there was any truth to it. He'd never minced words with me. Actually, his favorite word did seem to be *mine*. So maybe his reputation was accurate and well deserved.

Doesn't matter.

"He makes me feel safe. Alive. Basically, he just makes me *feel* when I thought I'd never feel anything again."

Yve's smile was understanding. She'd been through hell too, although hers had lasted much longer than mine. "I know what you mean. Even if all you feel is the urge to punch him in the throat, feeling *something* is better than feeling nothing."

"Exactly. I thought I was broken, but he opened my eyes. I was waiting for something to force me to start living again. He may be one of the bad guys, but he's a good man. And he's mine."

"Sounds like you're just as possessive as he is."

"Maybe I am," I said.

Rix was mine. I was his. We would figure this out. Any other alternative was completely unacceptable.

Yve had taken the painting and left me with too many swirling questions and no answers. Brisk business made the next several hours slide by quickly, and I took comfort in Trinity being back to her normal chatty self, less mentions of Derrick. I still wasn't sure what had happened there, but every time I went to ask, I bit my tongue. If he was out of her life for good, I wasn't going to start bringing him up.

I volunteered to make the run for lunch, and left Trinity holding down the fort. But I wasn't going out only to pick up some salads. I had another task to take care of. One that was long overdue.

Rhett Hennessy was also a good man, but he wasn't the man for me. I'd lied to him about . . . well, everything, and it was time to tell him as much of the truth as I could.

I made my way to the precinct, but luck, if you could call it that, was with me. He was heading in at the same time, white paper bag in hand with delicious scents wafting from it. Apparently I wasn't the only one who was starving.

He lifted his chin and smiled when he saw me. "What a coincidence."

My smile was less enthusiastic than his. "You could say that. Do you have a minute?"

"If I'd known you were coming looking for me, I'd have offered to take you to lunch."

"I don't need that much of your time. Just a few minutes will do."

His smile faded and a harder, shrewder expression replaced it. "What do you need, Valentina? Another missing and reappearing employee? Some other mysterious crime the NOPD can assist with?"

I dropped my gaze to the ground and stared at the gum and

other substances that the scrubbers hadn't managed to remove this morning, gathering my courage. When I looked into his face again, one raised eyebrow dared me to spill. It was time.

"I'm sorry. I lied to you. I know that's unforgiveable, but I had a good reason. And . . . I have to tell you, in all fairness, the other guy won before the game even started, and I just hadn't caught up yet. I didn't mean to lead you on. I really, truly didn't. You're a nice—"

Rhett held up a hand. "You can stop with the apologies. I might not lose the girl very often, but I'd already picked up on that clear as day. The lying? Yeah, that pissed me off, but I figured you weren't the type to do it without a good reason. Wish you could've trusted me, but that isn't always the case. Call it water under the bridge."

He was making this easier than I'd expected. "I really am sorry."

Rhett shrugged. "So am I. We could've been good together."

This was the moment when I was supposed to add in the *letting him down gently* part. Where I said, *If it doesn't work out, I'll let you know*. But I couldn't do that. I wasn't even allowing for the possibility that things wouldn't work out between Rix and me.

"I'm sorry," I repeated.

"Don't worry about it, sweetheart. But if things don't go the way you plan, you know where to find me."

Damn it, I hated that he'd put that out in the universe. I dropped my gaze back to the sidewalk.

Rhett reached out a hand and tipped my chin up. "You don't have a clue, do you?"

I frowned. "What do you mean?"

"You're one hell of a prize, and don't forget it. Make sure

this guy appreciates you for what you are." He leaned in and brushed a kiss across my cheek.

Shit. Rix was undoubtedly going to hear about that. I stepped back and surreptitiously looked around for whoever might be babysitting me today. There were too many people on the streets to pinpoint who it could be.

Rhett was watching me carefully when I dragged my gaze back to him. "Something wrong?"

I shook my head. "No. Sorry. I'll let you get back to your lunch."

"Take care, Valentina."

I hoped he found someone. Someone who didn't lie to him and wasn't wrapped up in another man. He was a good guy and deserved better than I'd been able to offer him. But there wasn't much left to offer when your heart was already taken.

I turned and headed down the sidewalk, my phone buzzing in my hand before I made it three steps.

Rix: We're gonna have words, duchess. Only lips on you are mine.

I raised my hand in the air and saluted my mystery babysitter with the middle finger. Such a tattletale.

THIRTY-SIX
RIX

Normally I never showed up to a meet by myself, but since Johnny was MIA with the Escalade, I fired up my 1970 Chevelle SS that I'd picked up off Lord Robichaux over at Chains. It hadn't been my first choice at the time, but now I was in love with the car. No one drove her but me, so Johnny checking out gave me the perfect excuse to get it out of the garage.

Still, it wasn't normal for him to disappear like that.

"Can't say I was surprised you wanted to meet today," Hennessy said. "But it wasn't necessary. I know where I stand. That shit is clear."

"Ain't here about that, and if I were you, I would pretend it never happened." The fucker had known I would have eyes on Valentina when she went to meet with him.

Hennessy laughed, his smirk fixed firmly in place. "I bet." His phone buzzed in his pocket, and he pulled it out and read something before glancing up at me. "You've got a blacked-out Escalade, don't you?"

I frowned. "Yeah, why?"

"Cops tried to pull one over but it hauled ass and disappeared. They catch up with it, you gonna need to bail someone out of jail?"

I pulled out my own phone and tried Johnny again. It went straight to voice mail.

Something was off, but I didn't know what. I tried Evo next. He had eyes on Valentina today and would follow her until she was home. Hennessy watched me while I made the call.

"What up, boss?" Evo answered.

"She home safe yet?"

"Just pulling in."

"See anything off tonight?"

"Nah, not a thing. Why?"

"No reason. You got plans tonight?"

"It's my girl's birthday. Taking her out to the club for table service. Fancy shit."

Fuck. Part of me wanted to tell him to cancel and babysit Valentina, but I was overreacting. As long as she was locked up tight in her house with that alarm set, nothing could touch her. The cops would be there in minutes if someone tried, and I'd be right behind them.

The feeling in my gut settled. I was just overreacting.

"Enjoy your night, man. Pick it up in the morning like normal."

I hung up and texted Valentina.

Rix: Make sure you lock up and set the alarm. I'll be by later. If you're going out, let me know.

"What?" I asked when I looked up to see Hennessy shaking his head at me.

"I wanna give you shit for keeping eyes on her all the time, but I can't. I respect that you're keeping her safe. If I had to lose her to anyone, at least I know you'll make sure nothing touches her."

"Damn right. And that nothing includes you."

Hennessy raised his hands. "I conceded. Hands off. Tell me that's not why you dragged me down here. I got better shit to do than gossip like old ladies."

I sobered. "No, it's not."

Hennessy's easy smile disappeared. "You found the recordings from the wire?"

I nodded. "Got them from one of your guys." I held up a USB drive.

"You listen to it?" Hennessy asked as he reached for it.

I jerked my hand back out of his reach.

"Some shit you need to know before you listen, because I'm not sending you into this blind. You're not gonna fucking believe me, but I'm not making shit up here. It ain't what you want to hear. It's gonna tear up the world you know, and you're gonna have choices to make."

Hennessy narrowed his eyes. "Fucking give it to me, and stop with the warnings and tell me what you know."

I took a long breath and released it. "Your brother wasn't dirty."

Relief flashed on his face. "I knew that."

I prepped myself to deliver the blow that would rock his world. "But your pop is."

Other than the blink of his eyes, Hennessy went completely still before lunging at me. "Watch your fuckin' mouth."

I held up the USB drive. "I'm not making shit up. I'm just the messenger."

"No fucking way. I don't believe you." His jaw clenched and unclenched in time with his fists, and I wondered if he'd take a swing at me.

I offered the USB drive to him, and he snatched it out of my hand. "I wouldn't want to give anyone that news. Ever. But it's the truth."

"No fucking way." He stared at the drive as if it were going to grow fangs and strike his hand.

"I'm sorry, man." And I was. I hadn't known my pop so I couldn't relate, but the way his face twisted with pain would sink deep into anyone's gut.

"Won't fucking believe it until I hear it. No goddamned way." His words were ground out from between teeth clenched so tight, he'd be taking a trip to the dentist if he didn't ease up.

"I got a laptop in my ride, if you want." I didn't know why I offered. He wasn't gonna want shit from me for help.

Hennessy rubbed a hand over his face. "Fuck. *Fuck*. I'm not using my department computer to listen to this shit, because that's what this is—*shit. Bullshit*."

I said nothing. There was nothing I could say he'd want to hear right now. Or ever, probably. His life was getting fucked in a way he never saw coming.

I jerked my head toward the door where I parked outside. I had no idea where Hennessy parked, but he wasn't a moron, so I doubted it was anywhere someone would connect him to being here. He followed me, the thump of a fist slamming into the metal door and the crash of the door into the brick of the building trailing us.

I popped the lock on the Chevelle and reached inside to pull a small laptop out of my backpack. I held out my hand for the USB drive, and Hennessy slapped it back into my palm.

I booted it up and slipped the drive in. Neither of us spoke as we waited for the recording to start.

I'd listened to it a dozen times, so I knew exactly how it went. Hennessy listened in silence, fists clenching, deep creases furrowing his forehead. I wished I hadn't been watching when he recognized his pop's voice. *Crushing*. That's what it was.

Lifting both hands to his face, he slid them up and over to grasp the back of his head, breaths coming fast and uneven. *Man on the edge*.

"Again. Play it again," he demanded.

So I did.

Six times.

After the last time, Hennessy spun and strode to the door, punching it with the force of the rage clawing its way out of him.

"Fuck."

He was going to break his hand if he did it again—if he hadn't already. When he bent at the waist and reached for his ankle, I tensed, instinctively going for the gun tucked into the back of my jeans.

The pistol flashed out of the ankle holster, but Hennessy never turned around. He unloaded it at the brick wall, chunks flying everywhere.

Ears ringing, and ducking to dodge the brick shrapnel, I watched as the man battled with the demons I'd just unleashed in his life.

When the gun was empty, he threw it at the wall and roared.

Reminding me of a wounded beast, he spun, veins popping from his skin, tendons strained as he continued to bellow at the sky.

"Fuck!"

He needed to pull his shit together before he came completely unglued. Or he needed to take it like a man and get wasted.

"Whiskey, bourbon, vodka, or tequila?" I asked.

"Bourbon," he bit out.

"I'll meet you at the Saint."

For a moment, I thought he'd tell me to go fuck myself, but he didn't.

"I'll be there."

THIRTY-SEVEN
VALENTINA

I followed Rix's instructions, locking the house and setting my alarm before settling down with a glass of wine and a book to wait for him. One glass turned into two, and then three.

It was all the book's fault, I swear. Angsty love-triangle nonsense. She just needed to pick one, but I couldn't stop reading. I laughed at myself. I was just as bad as this heroine, but at least I'd made my decision. I hoped my happily-ever-after was coming next.

Headlights cut across my front windows and into the house. I followed them as a vehicle pulled up to the gate at my drive. I waited, and then the lights flashed. Moving to another window, I squinted. The Cadillac emblem shone on the big silver grill.

A smile spread across my face. When the high beams flashed again, I hurried downstairs and slipped my feet into flip-flops before turning off the alarm and rushing outside. My front gate had been fixed, on Rix's orders, so I unlocked it and pushed it open. I strolled toward the SUV, a huge smile on my face. The door pushed open partway and I slipped inside—and froze.

It wasn't Rix.

It was a man I'd never seen before. And the barrel of his gun was pointed directly at me.

THIRTY-EIGHT

VALENTINA

The nightmare was so vivid—being tossed over a shoulder, the taste of blood filling my mouth, men barking orders and slamming doors. I jerked awake, thankful it was just a dream.

My head pounded against the cushion.

Why am I sleeping in a chair? How much wine did I drink?

I yawned, rubbing a hand against my aching temple. It came away wet and my brain snapped into gear. It wasn't a dream.

The Escalade. The guy with the gun. Everything going black.

Fuck.

Rix is going to kill them.

And he wasn't going to be very happy with me either. I'd gotten myself kidnapped.

Feelings of helplessness swirled inside, fighting to break free. *Keep it together, Valentina. You are not a victim. You are not going to fall apart. You're going to save yourself.*

Rising to my feet on shaky legs, I studied the room I was in. It was dark, but the carpet was plush and a fresh, clean scent tinged the air. I walked to the window and tugged aside the curtain. In the darkness, I could see lights reflecting off the surface of water. A lake? Maybe Pontchartrain? I craned my head, trying to get a better look, but in the darkness any landmarks were impossible to make out.

I flipped the latch on the window. *Could it be this easy? Just climb out the window and slip away into the night.* I shoved at the sill, but it didn't move.

So that's a no for easy.

I ran my fingers along the frame. It wasn't painted shut . . . and then the pads of my fingers touched the screws.

Seriously? Complete fire hazard! But could I break it?

Scanning my surroundings, I spotted a floor lamp near the chair I'd woken up in. Crossing the room, I bypassed the lamp for the door. Sheer curiosity had me trying the knob. Locked. Obviously. But I still had to try.

Rounding the chair, I pulled the plug free and hefted the lamp. It was solid and would work for my purpose. The window was about shoulder height, and I'd be able to haul myself up and over and be gone before they even knew I was missing. I hoped.

Using the lamp base like a battering ram, I slammed it into the window.

It bounced off.

Crap.

Readjusting my grip, I rammed it into the window again. Glass shattered and I spun, avoiding the flying shards.

Setting the lamp aside, I searched the room for something to clear the glass away so I could climb out without slicing myself to ribbons. The recliner I'd woken up in had two cloth covers over the arms. *Those'll work.* Grabbing them both, I was almost to the window when the door burst open.

"Fucking bitch!"

The guy with the gun was back. And he looked even more pissed this time.

I reached for the window anyway.

Metallic pops sounded, and something hit the wall to my left.

Bullets.

Holy. Crap.

I dropped to the floor, hands over my head, not caring that glass sliced into me. If I caught a bullet, I might not live long enough to heal anyway.

The room quieted, but fear kept me curled up in a ball.

The man spoke, triumph in his voice. "They told me not to touch you. Told me I couldn't fuck you. But all bets are off when you start causing problems, you little bitch."

His words echoed in my pounding head. *Told me not to touch you. Told me I couldn't fuck you. But all bets are off . . .*

No. No. No. Not again. I couldn't go through that again. Never. Again. I would fight. As my hands squeezed into fists, I found a shard of glass clenched in one palm. I would kill before I'd let someone make me helpless again.

"Get the fuck up."

I forced myself to look up at him. The long barrel of the gun stared back at me. I shook, swallowing back bile rising in my throat.

He could kill me and no one would even hear it because even I'd seen enough movies to recognize a silencer. I shook and the glass sliced into my palm. The pain helped me hold on to the thin shred of my sanity.

"Get the fuck up," he ordered again.

I pushed up onto my knees, my eyes never leaving the gun. Rising slowly, I fought my trembling muscles to stand tall.

Don't show fear. Never show fear.

"Get the fuck over here." He gestured with the gun.

The last thing I wanted to do was walk a single inch closer to a man who'd said he wanted to rape me. When I didn't move, he snarled and strode toward me. As soon as he was within striking distance, my hand shot out, the shard of glass held like a dagger.

But I'd moved too soon. He dodged, roaring at me when my makeshift weapon sliced a path across his shoulder.

"You cunt!"

His fist swung, once again catching me in the temple. The blow sent me to my knees, the glass flying from my hand.

I wasn't too proud to admit that I cowered as he grabbed me by the throat and dragged me to my feet.

My hands went to his, clawing at the grip cutting off my oxygen supply and unleashing flashbacks of the last time a man had pinned me down against my will.

You stupid whore. What kind of slut leaves with a man she just met? I'm gonna give you what you're begging for. Make you beg for me.

I could feel his breath on my face as blackness edged around my vision. For a moment, I hoped for unconsciousness. But then I wouldn't be able to fight back.

I fought harder. Clawed deeper.

He lifted and shook me until my arms dropped to my sides. "Stupid bitch. Fighting will only make it worse."

The words were too similar. He slammed me into the wall again, my back cracking.

"What the fuck are you doing, man?"

Another voice penetrated the static rushing through my head. My eyes slid shut as the blackness crept closer and closer.

The man released his grip before I lost my hold on consciousness. I hit the floor, sucking in lungfuls of air. When the blackness receded, I stared up at the men as they shoved each other and argued.

The man with the gun grunted and threw his hands into the air. "Fine! Fucking take her! Cunt's more trouble than she's worth." He shoved the door open and left.

The other man crouched in front of me, a hand wrapping around my arm. "Get up. I'm moving you." When I jerked away, not wanting his touch on my skin, he only gripped harder and said, "Don't fucking fight me. I don't want to hurt you, but I will if I have to."

Tremors racked my body as he dragged me to my feet.

"Let's go."

I stumbled behind him as he led me around a corner and up a set of stairs. In my peripheral vision, I caught sight of two men standing near a table piled high with black packages shaped like bricks. Black duffel bags were mounded on the floor to the side.

Drugs. The obvious answer penetrated my brain beyond the fight-or-flight instincts vying for supremacy. I snapped my eyes forward, not wanting anyone to realize I'd seen anything. I didn't need to give them another reason to want me dead.

The man hauling me up the stairs turned right and shoved open a door to reveal a nursery.

"You make a sound, you're dead. You try to climb out that window, you're dead. You piss me off, you're dead. And if Hernandez gets you, you're probably worse than dead."

Worse than dead. Going back to the world where every sound terrified me and I couldn't close my eyes without being haunted by nightmares would be worse than death.

He shoved me inside and I stumbled to the wall, pressing a hand against it as I slid down before wrapping my arms tight around my legs to present the smallest target possible.

"You try to leave this room, I promise you'll regret it."

He didn't need to spell it out for me again. I got it. He

turned and left the room, and I didn't even hear the sound of the door locking.

But his threats would keep me from testing that handle. Who was I kidding? His threats would keep me curled into a ball on the floor while my memories battered me and I lost control over the tears welling in my eyes.

Rix. I need Rix.

THIRTY-NINE

RIX

Watching a man drink wasn't my idea of a good time, but something kept me sitting on the bar stool beside Hennessy as he ordered his first bourbon. He hadn't said much since he walked in the door, but words weren't necessary.

I checked the time again. Just after seven. I wanted to get to Valentina's before eight. The way Hennessy was staring at the bourbon placed in front of him without touching it had me wondering how long this would take. I tried Johnny three more times with no answer. Something was off.

My phone lit up with a message from an unknown number. A photo.

I opened it and froze. I'd recognize Valentina anywhere, and the sight of blood dripping from her temple sent burning fires of rage bursting through my veins.

What. The. Fuck.

A text followed.

UNKNOWN NUMBER: *She's a fighter, but she ain't getting away from us. She'll get a bullet to the head if you don't cooperate.*

I wouldn't panic, but I sure as fuck would rip the limbs from someone's goddamned body for touching her. For daring to take my woman.

I closed out the message and called her phone. There was no goddamned way the FNDs had her. No fucking way.

It rang and rang until the voice mail picked up and her cheery voice answered. *"You've got Valentina. You know what to do."*

That was the fucking problem—I didn't have Valentina. Someone else did.

I shoved away from the bar and stalked to the corner of the room. Leaving a message was probably pointless, but I didn't care.

"I'm gonna get you home safe. Stay strong, duchess. I love you. Just hold on, and I'll be there. I'm coming for you."

I ended the call and slammed a fist into the wall. *How the fuck did this happen?* She was supposed to be locked up safe inside her house.

Didn't matter. All that mattered was getting her back.

My phone buzzed in my hand. A call. My first thought was Valentina. But it wasn't.

It was another unknown number.

I answered. "This is Rix, and if you got my woman, then you're gonna die."

A dark chuckle met my ears. "I'm not worried about dying today, but you should be worried about how long she'll live. She's a feisty one. I can see the appeal. You don't cooperate, then I'm gonna let my guys feel the appeal when they fuck her

279

on her hands and knees, tied up and screaming for you. They like the fighters."

He would die. They would all die.

There was no other alternative.

I didn't care what he wanted, but I held back my threats because I needed to know where he was. The voice, I recognized. Same piece of shit who'd be been running weak game for years. He'd stepped up, and now he would die. Trio, a lieutenant of the FNDs, would not live to see the sunrise. He didn't need to identify himself because I'd recognize his rough voice anywhere.

"What the fuck do you want?"

"What I've wanted since you left two of my guys dead and three as good as dead. Blood."

"Then you come after my blood, not someone else's, cocksucker."

He laughed, and I gritted my teeth. Hennessy was off his stool and leaning against the pool table beside me.

"Hers spills just as easy."

"Fuck you, you want a trade? Is that what you want?" I demanded. I wouldn't let her bleed another drop for me.

"You know I'll take your blood any day, but tonight, if you want her back, you're gonna bring me money too. A fuck ton of it. I know you got it. You got two hours."

The amount he rattled off was big. So fucking big that if he'd given me a couple of days, I could get my hands on it, but not in two hours. No fucking way. *Shit.*

"You bring it or she dies. Slowly. Painfully. Bloody. After my guys have had their fill. Your choice."

Rage roiled through my veins like napalm. I would destroy him.

"If anyone touches a single hair on her head, I swear to God I will gut you all like the spineless fucks you are."

His laugh met my ears again. "I got all the cards here. Bring the money or I'll leave her body in the gutter."

"Where?"

The address memorized as soon as it was out of his mouth, I walked to the bar and grabbed a napkin and pen off someone's credit card folder and scribbled it down. I wouldn't take a single chance of getting this wrong.

It was a familiar street. On the lake. I knew the general vicinity, and it didn't make sense for the FNDs to be setting up shop in such a nice hood. They were trash. Crack houses were more their style than lake houses.

But the step up gave credence to the rumors I'd been hearing on the street—the ones I knew Hennessy would be very interested in. The FNDs were running the drug ring he was trying to bring down, and they had to be in bed with the cartel. The only reason Trio would need to get his hands on that kind of cash was if some serious bad shit was going down and he was fucked without it.

"I'll be there."

The line went dead and I lowered my phone to the bar, fighting the urge to smash it and follow it up with my fists the way Hennessy had with the door at the warehouse. I glanced at the wall I'd already punched. I hadn't left a mark, but I would now. I would tear this place down with my bare hands if it would get her back, but right now I couldn't afford to waste the energy. Right now, the only thing that mattered was getting Valentina back. And vengeance.

"What the fuck is going on?" Hennessy asked from beside me.

I had a decision to make. Go it alone, bringing half the cash and as many guys as I could assemble in the next two hours, or let Hennessy in on what was going down. I would do anything to get Valentina back quicker and safer. I knew the moment I told him the FNDs had her, he'd make this his problem and the problem of the NOPD.

I made my choice.

The FNDs would never expect a SWAT team.

I turned to Hennessy. "We're going back to the station, and you're gonna get that promotion you've been after because you're gonna bust a drug ring and help me get my woman back."

At the mention of Valentina, Hennessy's eyes narrowed. "What the hell did you get her into now?"

"I'll explain on the way."

FORTY
VALENTINA

tay still. Don't break.

The words repeated like a mantra in my head as my body shook and I dug my nails into my shins, willing my body to stay curled into the ball I'd wrapped myself in. I needed the pain.

Memories and flashbacks of that night bombarded me. The dark, deserted road. When he pulled off onto the shoulder. My questions. His hand across my face. The door wrenching open and my nails clawing at the seat as he dragged me out and threw me in the back, tearing at my clothes.

Tremors of fear rattled my teeth with their strength. Tears mixed with the dried blood on my face and hands. I was pathetic. Helpless. Useless. Defenseless.

I stared at the wall, seeing the scene replay over and over.

Smears of blood. Broken nails. I'd fought him, and it hadn't helped.

My eyes constantly darted to the door.

Would they come? Would I fight?

I will survive. Even if I want to die.

I tried to find the strength I'd fought for all these years, but there was nothing left.

My mind shifted, dragging thoughts of Rix to the forefront. I wanted to be strong. Wanted to be the girl who could save herself. But I was foolish. Broken.

He can't see me like this. I can't take seeing the pity in his eyes. It would be worse than seeing it in Rhett's. I couldn't take it.

God, listen to yourself, Valentina. Stop.

The voices inside me were strong and adamant from both sides. The battle played out in my head as I waited silently with tears streaming down my face.

My sense of time was warped as I stayed curled unto my ball. It could have been minutes or hours that had passed before I heard glass shatter, a crash, and men yelling.

Good guys? Or bad?

Weak threads of hope twined together in my belly.

"Go! Go! Go!"

Gunshots.

More yelling.

I squeezed into a smaller ball as doors slammed open.

Footsteps thundered up the stairs.

Oh shit.

"Clear!"

"Clear!"

Something rammed into the door, and the handle flew off on the inside.

I gripped my shins tighter, my gaze fixed on the door. *Good guys or bad?*

SWAT. It was the first thing I saw when the man in the

black vest, helmet, and goggles charged through the doorway, his gun sweeping the room.

The good guys.

"Got her!" He lowered the gun, pressed an earpiece, and spoke quickly. "Hendrix, I'm bringing her out!" The man turned to me. "Come on, Ms. Noble. Let's get you out of here. Hendrix will be happy as fuck to see you're okay."

Hendrix?

And *okay?* What was okay? Blood dripped from my face and my hands. *It could always be worse.* I nodded, my head bobbing. I was sort of okay.

But who was Hendrix? My brain struggled to free itself from survival mode, but I couldn't answer my own swirling questions. Instead, I just latched onto the fact that he was one of the good guys.

The man helped me to my feet. One of my flip-flops was missing, but I didn't care. I wanted out of this house. Right now.

"You want me to carry you, Ms. Noble?"

I shook my head and didn't spit out the words I wanted to. *Don't touch me.* Digging deep and grabbing hold of some fleeting reserve of strength, I followed him out of the room.

Bile rose in my throat at the dead bodies on the living room floor, blood seeping out around them into the beige carpet.

Tearing my gaze away, I searched for the door. *Out. Now.*

Men with SWAT vests swarmed the house, and confusion dogged my every step. *Who called in the SWAT team?*

One of the men slung his gun over his shoulder and rushed toward us. "Thank fuck," he murmured as he grabbed me and pulled me into him.

I jerked back. "Don't touch me," I whispered, my voice harsh and broken.

He pulled away, his hands cupping my jaw before I could shove away. "I got you, duchess."

My eyes met silver ones through the goggles.

Rix.

In a SWAT uniform.

What? My brain couldn't keep up.

"Let's get you out of here. Come on."

He bustled me out the front door hanging drunkenly off its hinges. We reached a black Suburban, and Rix shoved the goggles up off his face and onto the helmet.

"Are you okay?"

That question again.

I nodded, but my heart rate accelerated. Tears stung my eyes at the concern in his gaze.

I wanted to turn away. Didn't want him to see me like this.

Be strong, Valentina. Don't break. Don't let him see you break.

I tried to focus on him, not on the pathetic mess I knew I was. "Why are you wearing a uniform?" My words came out faint and shaky.

Rix ignored my question and ran his hands over my face, hair, arms, and hands. "Fuck. You got some cuts." I opened my mouth to ask my question again, when Rix returned to the tender spot on my temple. "Already bruising, duchess. Dammit. We need to get you to the ER to get checked out."

I couldn't think about my injuries or I'd fail in my promise to myself not to let him see me break. Instead, I grabbed his hand as he smoothed my hair away from my face.

"Why are you wearing a SWAT uniform?"

The man who'd brought me down the stairs joined us at the SUV. "Good to have you back, man. Just like we trained at the academy."

Academy?

"You want to get her out of here? No one needs to know you were here. Don't want to blow your cover." He dug keys out of his pocket and handed them off to Rix.

Blow your cover?

Even in the chaos of my mind, it all slid together. My gaze shot to Rix. His face was hard, but one thing was clear.

Rix wasn't Rix.

And he'd been lying to me since the day we met.

The knowledge rocked me as the confession bled into his gaze. I didn't need him to reply to know it was true. *Rix isn't Rix.*

Jerking out of his arms, I stumbled back. He let me go— another confession of guilt.

"Who are you?" My voice shook, and the mess of my emotions rammed together like fists to flesh.

I was going to break. I was going to lose it. He was my safety. The one solid thing I could count on. And he wasn't real. He was a lie.

"Thank fuck, you got her." Another familiar voice joined the rush of static in my head.

Rhett came around the SUV. Rhett. The man who'd seen me at my worst before, and it had changed his opinion of me forever, no matter what he'd said.

"Who are you?" I demanded again.

Rix's mouth tightened. "Beauregard Hendrix. NOPD. Undercover."

The words were like a kick to the gut, shattering my ability to hold it together. *Everything was a lie.*

"I don't even know you."

His silver gaze pierced me. "I'm the same man I was before, duchess."

I swallowed as hot tears spilled over. "I can't do this right now. I can't do this."

I tore my eyes away from Rix, or whoever he was, and found Rhett. I spun and threw myself into his arms.

"Get me out of here," I begged. The whole of me was falling to pieces. A full-on breakdown was imminent, and that wasn't something I wanted anyone to see.

Rhett closed his arms around me. "Shhh. It's okay. You're fine. You're just fine, honey."

"Get me out of here," I said again, my voice raw with the sobs I was holding back. "Now. Please."

"Okay. We're going." Over my head, he spoke to someone else. "I'm taking her to the hospital."

The thought of once again finding myself battered and bruised in a hospital bed, Rhett sitting across from me, shredded the remainder of my control. Sobs broke free, racking my body. He held me tighter, and I wanted to curl into myself and never come out.

I'm broken. I'm truly broken.

FORTY-ONE
RIX

Watching as Valentina shrank away from me and threw herself into the arms of another man ripped at my insides. *Fuck*. I wanted to tear her away from Hennessy and hold her close to make sure she was okay, but the look on her face told me everything I needed to know.

She didn't want me touching her.

That knowledge was enough to bring a man to his knees. But to fight for her, I'd stand strong.

And there's no way in hell I wasn't following them to the hospital. I wasn't letting her go. I'd make her understand.

Fuck. I would not lose her. Not over this. Not over any goddamned thing.

I watched as Hennessy loaded her into his Jeep and rounded the hood. When he met my eyes, there was no triumph in his gaze.

I nodded at him. He knew I wasn't backing down.

The taillights lit up, and he drove away the only woman who'd ever own me.

Be ready, Valentina. I'm coming for you. Every fucking time.

FORTY-TWO
HENNESSY

I'd seen her crumple before, but this time it was worse. Valentina Noble wasn't a woman on the edge; she was a woman who'd fallen off a cliff.

I'd seen it more than once. Victims of trauma, especially rape, who were faced with another traumatic experience often regressed dramatically due to flashbacks. Valentina wasn't just battling the situation we'd pulled her out of. She was battling herself. And in her case, it was the strongest enemy she had.

Dried blood marred her arms, legs, and face. I wanted to clean her up, but that could wait until she was in the ER. Her safety—not her appearance—was all that mattered.

Her sobs had subsided, but I didn't take that as a good sign. Tears still streamed down her cheeks.

"Honey, you just hold on. We're gonna get you all fixed up again, and the last few hours will be like they never happened."

She didn't respond for several minutes, and when she did, her voice was quiet and shaky. "You can't change the fact that I love him, and all he's ever done is lie to me." Her breaths came out ragged and harsh.

Fuck. How did I deal with this?

She kept going, and her words lit a fire of guilt inside me. "I guess I should've picked you. At least you never lied to me."

Maybe not outright, but I'd known exactly what she'd been facing with Rix. How did I tell her that? I couldn't push her further over the edge. Not right now.

"Things aren't always what they seem, but that doesn't make them bad."

When she laughed, it was edged with hysteria. "I thought he was bad. I was okay with bad." Valentina shook her head. "What the hell was I thinking? I can't even trust myself."

And that was why she was breaking. She'd lost the confidence in herself she'd clawed back.

"You're going to be just fine. Keep trusting your gut and you'll be okay. You trusted yourself with him before. Do you really think you would've fallen for a criminal, Valentina? You're not that woman. Whether you realize it or not, your judgment is better than ever."

Her gaze cut to me, sharpening, and some of the brokenness faded away.

"You knew." Betrayal laced her tone. "You knew I was seeing him, didn't you?"

Fuck.

We were only minutes away from the hospital, and I'd hoped it would take her longer to put the pieces together in her state, but Valentina had never been stupid.

"You're a cop. He's an undercover cop. You had to know." When her voice shook this time, it was with anger. The truth must have been written on my face, because she spoke again, the words coming out even harsher. "Let me out of this car. I can't—"

Fuck it. I kept driving, but I didn't hold back.

"Yeah, I knew. And you can be really fucking certain that if I hadn't known he was on the right side of the line, I would've locked you down and kept you away from him. I get that you're feeling raw and betrayed, but over what? The fact that the guy you fell for isn't going to end up in prison someday because he's a gangbanger? You should be happy as hell right now to find out that he's on the right side of the line."

Her head jerked back with surprise that I'd dropped the kid gloves I'd worn with her so many times before. But this was what she needed. A dose of reality to drag her back together and get her head straight.

"But—"

"No fucking buts. Maybe you didn't see it, but when you turned from him, he was gutted. The man is head over ass in love with you, and he's been doing his job this whole time. And guess what? Part of his job was not being able to tell you what his job was. And you know what else he made part of his job? Keeping you safe from everything that came along with it."

"But—"

"Dammit, Valentina. He's exactly the same guy you've always thought he was. He just happens to be on the right side of the law. Doesn't change anything about him. Since day one at the academy, he's never played by the rules. He's always been on the edge. You think he's dangerous? That's because he *is*. But he's dangerous in a way that helps people—including you."

The sign for the ER came into view, and I glanced at her as I turned the corner, wondering if my words were sinking in. The frown on Valentina's face told me they were.

Silence filled the car, and neither of us spoke as I parked and helped her out and up to the door of the emergency room. She had plenty to think about now, and I hope it helped. Maybe

I could fix this for Rix, because there was no way in fuck anyone could fix my own life.

My brother would be vindicated. And the world would know my father was a dirty cop. My life as I knew it might be fucked, but maybe the one good deed I could do was help Valentina find her way back to Rix.

FORTY-THREE
VALENTINA

My brain was slipping close to shutdown territory again. That stage where all you wanted was an empty room, a bottle of wine, and to be left alone to come to grips with whatever was consuming you.

Instead, I was in the ER, and my mother burst through the door.

"Oh, honey, what happened?" She rushed inside in full tizzy, and only stilled when she had my face cradled in her smooth hands. "Oh, your poor head."

I'd looked in the mirror and seen the dark bruise marring the skin of my temple. The dried blood matting my hair had been rinsed away, and the wound had stopped bleeding. The nurse who'd just left hadn't thought the cut was deep enough to need stitches. I'd taken in all of this and built a wall of clinical detachment. It was the only way I could deal with people poking and prodding me anymore.

My father was usually right behind my mother in situations like this, but he hadn't yet come through the door.

"Where's Dad?"

My mother pressed a kiss to my forehead and released her

hold on my face before stepping back. "He's talking to the police. They wanted to fill him in on what happened, and he definitely wanted answers."

"Where?" A trickle of apprehension pooled in my belly. "On the phone?"

My mother shook her head. "No, in the lobby. Well, now they're in a private room because they needed to get out of earshot of everyone else."

Who was my father talking to? Rhett? Or was Rix here?

Everything Rhett had said in the car while I'd been barely holding on had played through my mind the entire time I'd sat in this room.

He's exactly the same guy you've always thought he was. He just happens to be on the right side of the law.

The cut on my hand where I'd squeezed the glass shard had been the deepest and needed a few stitches. Everything else was fine.

I was fine.

My head had been cleared by the doctor, but that didn't mean it wasn't still jammed full of questions.

My mother stepped out of the room, and I pulled on a clean *Love NOLA* T-shirt my father had bought from the gift shop at her request. I'd cried when he'd delivered it to the room and hugged me. He'd also told me I wasn't allowed to get kidnapped again because his old heart couldn't take it.

I promised him I wouldn't.

Both my parents had given me space, and I was taking it.

What was I going to do?

What did I want?

Trust your gut. That was what Rhett had told me.

I swallowed, standing with my hand on the door. Hesitating for long moments, I pulled myself together.

I am not a victim. I am a survivor. I am whatever I want to be.

And I wanted to be Rix's.

Did his name matter when I knew his heart?

Did which side of the line he stood on matter when he made me feel safe either way?

I gave myself a mental slap. He was one of the good guys. Someday, maybe we could be seen together in public. We wouldn't have to sneak around anymore. We could have a normal life. Together. Out in the open. I could introduce him to my parents. I could have it all.

The epiphany washed over me.

I can have it all.

I opened the door and stepped out to find my future.

FORTY-FOUR

RIX

Valentina and her mother walked into the lobby side by side. Harold Noble stopped midsentence.

"There's my girls." He crossed the room to them and hugged Valentina.

I wanted her in my arms. Needed her in my arms.

Fuck, I just needed her.

When her father released her, her eyes finally met mine. For long moments, no one spoke.

Noble broke the silence. "Valentina, have you met—" He paused when she ran to me and threw herself into my arms.

I wrapped them around her. *Thank fuck. So good.*

"I'll take that as a yes," Noble murmured.

Tears wet my shirt, and I pulled back to see her dark eyes shining with them. Using my thumbs, I wiped them away.

"No more tears, duchess. It guts me to see you cry."

She sucked in a breath. "I'm so sorry. I shouldn't have gone outside. I thought it was you. I'm such an idiot. It was all my fault."

Her words didn't make sense. "What are you talking about?"

"The Escalade. It stopped in front of the house. I thought it was you. I went outside. You told me not to, but I didn't listen."

That answered the question of how they'd nabbed her, but I didn't care anymore. Not when she was back where she needed to be. "Doesn't matter."

But she kept going. "And I'm sorry. I—I let them break me. I lost my grip, but I don't want to lose you."

"Shhh, duchess. You can't lose me. I'm here. No matter what. And they didn't break you. No one can break you. You're the strongest woman I know."

"But I walked away from you."

I shook my head. "You threw yourself into my arms just now. Does that sound like you walked away from me?"

"I love you," she whispered. "Don't ever let me go."

"Never."

"Does someone want to explain what's going on here?" Noble asked, his confusion obvious.

Valentina's mother tugged at his arm. "I think it's obvious, dear."

FORTY-FIVE
VALENTINA

I pressed P<small>LAY</small> on the voice mail for the fourth time.

"I'm gonna get you home safe. Stay strong, duchess. I love you. Just hold on, and I'll be there. I'm coming for you."

Squeezing my phone tight, I blinked back tears. Happy tears this time.

He loves me.

I'd finally said the words to him at the hospital, but he hadn't said them back. I'd been in the shower when that realization had struck. I'd been drying my hair, robe wrapped around my waist, when I'd seen my phone on the dresser next to my purse. The voice mail icon had lit the screen when I touched it.

Rix pushed open the bedroom door, a white take-out bag in one hand. "You feeling better now that you're cleaned up?"

I did. There was something cathartic about watching the remnants of dried blood wash down the drain. I might have cried a few more tears, but with the rush of the water, you couldn't ever tell.

I nodded. And then my words came out quietly, colored with wonder. "You love me."

Rix eyed me, confusion on his face. "Of course I fucking love you, duchess. I would've taken every bullet fired in that house today if it meant they never would've touched you."

"But . . . you never said it."

He lowered the take-out bag on the dresser and walked toward me. "I've been living it. Feeling it with every breath I take. Always on my mind. In every beat of my heart in my chest."

I bit my lip as his words washed over me. "We should probably send a thank-you to D-Rock."

Rix huffed out a laugh, shaking his head. "I'll pass. That punk isn't coming around your girl again." He pressed a knee to the bed and leaned forward until his lips brushed mine. "You don't have to worry about that."

One less thing to worry about was certainly welcome. But what about the rest of it?

"And you being undercover? What happens next with that?"

Rix pulled away and stared down at me. "NOPD crushed the FND ring. I'll stay under long enough to wrap up anything else I need to, and then I'm out. Done."

"How does that work? Is it safe? Do you . . . have to leave town?"

I thought of the gallery and everything I'd have to leave behind to follow him. I would. I pictured living on a beach somewhere, a paintbrush in my hand as I stared out over the sparkling water of some tropical vista. I could do that.

He didn't answer me immediately. "Depends on what you want. I'm not walking away from you. I can stay with the department. I got an offer to head up the gang task force when I'm ready for it."

I can have it all.

"Do *you* want to stay?"

"I want to be where you are. If that's NOLA, then I'll stay

under until the enemies I've made are off the streets and you're not gonna be in danger."

"How long will that take?" I couldn't help but wonder if we were talking weeks, or months, or years.

A smile curled the corner of Rix's mouth. "I got a hell of an incentive to wrap it up pretty fucking fast."

"And then?"

"And then we start the next chapter. You and me. Out of the shadows and into the light."

"That sounds perfect to me."

"Good. Because it's happening, duchess. You're mine. Not giving you up for anything."

"I'm not giving you up either."

He leaned down and pressed another kiss to my lips. "I love you, Valentina."

The words glued back together my remaining cracked pieces. "I love you too. Rix or Beau, or whoever you are."

"Yours. That's who I am."

FORTY-SIX
HENNESSY

One week later

I laid my badge and gun on the deputy chief's desk, and it took only seconds for me to feel wrong without them. I'd only ever wanted to be a cop, and now I didn't know what the fuck I was going to do with my life. But one thing was certain—I couldn't stay with the NOPD.

"Don't think I need to explain why I'm doing this."

The truth about what my father had done had made it up the chain of command, and an investigation had already been launched. My mom was shattered, and there was no way my dad wouldn't end up in prison.

The deputy chief's face was solemn. "No, I don't need an explanation, but you don't have to do this."

A harsh laugh scraped its way out of my throat. "We both know that's bullshit. I'm done."

He nodded. "Then I accept your resignation. Best of luck to you, Hennessy."

I turned and left his office, the entire precinct seeming to go silent as I grabbed the box on my desk and walked out the door for the last time.

To protect and serve. It was all I knew. But that life was over.

EPILOGUE
RIX

S tanding in the back hallway of the courthouse, I fought
the edge of nerves moving in.

He won't say no.

Harold Noble had made it clear in our passing conversations
that he was waiting for this visit.

The opinions of other men had rarely mattered to me, but
Valentina's father was a different story. He would give his
blessing, but it went deeper than that.

Acceptance. Family. The things I'd never really had before.
The Nobles had let me into theirs, and now I wanted to make it
official.

I knew I wasn't good enough for Valentina the first day she
showed up on my porch, looking fine as hell in her skirt and
blouse and fancy heels. But for some reason, she didn't care.
Not then and not now.

But her father should. Any father should.

The door to Harold Noble's chambers opened, and he met
me with a smile and an outstretched hand.

"It's about time you showed up here, son."

304

Son. I'd never had that, and this man gave it to me.

"Good to see you, sir."

We shook hands, and he motioned me into his chambers before he shut the door.

"Have a seat."

I did, and he settled into the large leather chair behind a wide desk.

Not wasting a beat on small talk, he said, "I think we both know exactly why you're here."

I nodded. "Yes, sir. I'm going to marry your daughter."

"Not asking for permission?" He raised a bushy brow.

"Stating my intentions. I don't believe in asking permission, but I sure would like your blessing."

He narrowed his gaze on me. I fought the urge to shift in my leather club chair. I was probably going about this all wrong, but I was doing it the only way I knew how.

"And if I don't give my blessing?" he asked, crossing his arms.

"I'm marrying her either way. She's the best part of my life, and no man will ever love her more than I do. I'd take a bullet for her. Die for her."

"How much of this has to do with the fact that she's carrying your baby?"

I wasn't surprised he knew. I figured Jo had caught on when Valentina had stepped away twice during dinner last week, because the smell of beef was setting off her nausea lately.

I met his gaze, much like Valentina's dark one. "Not a damn thing. She's been mine since the day I first saw her. The baby is just one more miracle I didn't think I deserved in my life."

"I worried about you when she first told us. Worried that you'd been under too long and too deep to be able to surface. That lifestyle becomes ingrained in you. You don't just play along, you live it every day." He uncrossed his arms and leaned forward, elbows on the desk. "Do you miss it? The rush?"

I didn't answer right away. Did I miss it? Life as the king of my own empire? Power, money, and everything that came with it?

"I'd give it all up again to be with her. If you don't think I know how rare a woman your daughter is, you're wrong. She's worth everything."

He nodded. "I can't disagree with that. I just worry about you getting bored trying to live the civilized life. A wife, kid, house in the Garden District."

I leaned forward and rested my forearms on the edge of his desk and met his gaze. "A woman who loves me, a kid I never thought I'd have, and a home? That's the kind of life I would never even let myself dream of before, and now it's mine. You think I'd ever fuck that up?"

Noble didn't answer as he rose, hand outstretched. "Welcome to the family, son. You set the date and I'll officiate. Glad she picked a man worthy of her."

Worthy of her. That was my hope. I'd do my damnedest to prove it.

I clasped his hand. "Thank you, sir."

When I turned to leave, I paused at the door. "You and Jo going to pretend to be surprised when we tell you about the baby?"

Noble's smile transformed into a grin. "My first grandbaby? Damn right we'll pretend to be surprised."

"Good man."

I walked out of the courthouse, the weight of my task off my shoulders and approval of Valentina's father lightening my every step.

Damn, but life was sweet. Now to pick up the ring and get to the gallery for Valentina's big night.

THE CROWD IN NOBLE ART QUIETED AS VALENTINA MADE HER way to the center of the room. Her royal-blue dress hugged her curves and reminded me of the shirt she'd worn the night I'd taken her to the club. That had been six months ago.

Six long months of me continuing to sneak in through the back way, and no one being the wiser about our relationship except for a very select few close friends. Not Hennessy, though. He'd disappeared without a word after he resigned from the NOPD.

Sorting shit out and bringing the existence of the NODOs to an end had taken longer than I'd expected, but my woman hadn't complained. As long as I found my way into her bed every night, that was all she'd cared about.

The delay had grated on me, though. A woman like Valentina wasn't meant to be kept in the shadows. She was destined to be standing in the middle of an elegant gallery, surrounded by friends and family, a champagne flute in her hand and a smile on her face that came straight from the heart.

She was meant for nights like tonight, and I would make sure she had hundreds of them.

"Thank you all for coming."

That smile of hers was wide and easy, hiding the trace of her nerves from everyone but me. I could see them in her, but I was proud as hell that she was doing this.

"Tonight is very special to me for several reasons. First, the gathering of friends and family is always a reason to celebrate. Second, tonight is a night I never thought I'd have the courage to see through. And finally, because tonight is about giving back to the community that I love."

She reached for a cord attached to a black drape that sepa-rated the original gallery space from the newly remodeled other half of the building she'd taken over when the antique store had given up its lease a few months back. She'd waited months, refusing to take this step and host this event without me being able to be present. I'd protested, but there were certain arguments a man had to know were pointless to keep pushing.

"So without further ado, I give you Noble Art's newest collection, *Beauty and the City*, offered for sale by me and Trinity Rodgers."

With a tug of the cord, the drape slid to the floor, revealing a room with two distinct styles of artwork hanging on the wall. The crowd began to murmur in approval.

"All profits from the sale of these pieces will benefit the *Teach Life Through Art* program, offered to the children of this city at no cost by the New Orleans Museum of Art."

The crowd clapped loudly, shrill whistles filling the air. I glanced toward the sound, and Elle Snyder had two fingers in her mouth as she blew. Her man, Lord, laughed and tugged her into his side, interrupting the whistle.

"Cheers to Valentina and Trinity," I said, raising my glass high. "An amazing project to support an amazing cause, which is nothing less than I'd expect from such an amazing woman." Glasses lifted in hands all across the room.

"To Valentina and Trinity," everyone echoed.

Trinity held her glass of sparkling white grape juice in the air as well, then curtsied.

Remy gathered the blue curtain up from the floor as people crossed the room into the new section to view the pieces.

A hand clamped over my shoulder.

"You've significantly added to the courthouse docket, son." When I turned to see Harold Noble standing beside me, he added, "Proud of your work, and congratulations on the promotion."

Seeing approval in Valentina's father's eyes meant more to

me than I could explain. She was close with both her parents, and being inducted as an honorary part of their family was something I hadn't expected. *Family*. It was something I hadn't had in years.

"Thank you, sir. I'm definitely excited for the next challenge."

I'd accepted the position as head of the gang task force, which put all of the knowledge I'd gathered undercover to work in a more direct way. Being able to think like a gangbanger made it easier to take them down tactically, which put fewer officers at risk. It was still strange to be cleaning up the streets in such an overt fashion, but I didn't miss living in the shadows.

My gaze wandered to Valentina. Especially not when it meant that I could see my duchess in all her glory.

Elle and Lord joined me and Judge Noble near the edge of the room.

"So, when are you going to make an honest woman out of her?" Elle asked.

Noble and I exchanged a sideways glance before he adopted an amused expression. "That's an excellent question."

Jo smacked his arm. "Shush, Harry. These kids will get around to it when the time is right." She smiled at me. "You don't listen to anything he has to say. He thinks that everyone should propose within weeks of meeting, and that when it's right, you just know." When I just smiled, she winked at me knowingly before adding, "I'm excited for a few grandbabies, though."

I wasn't confirming or denying that fact. Tonight was about Valentina and Trinity's art.

But the reality of it still hit me hard as I watched her work the room. No bump visible yet, but still . . . A kid. A perfect combination of me and Valentina that would probably raise hell regardless of whether it was wearing pink or blue. Not only had

I escaped the shadows to step into the light, I'd gotten more than I could have ever imagined.

Hours later I lay in bed, Valentina's head on my chest and her fingertips tracing the ink on my pecs. The picture I stole from her all those months ago hung on the wall.

"Proud of you, duchess. Really fucking proud."
She curled into me closer, and squeezed. "It felt good to see them all on the wall. And Trinity, you'd think she'd won the lottery."

"Did good with that girl. You're gonna be a hell of a mom."

"I hope so."

"No doubt about it."

"When should we tell my parents?" she asked.

I slid a hand through her hair and met her gaze. "I think they already know, but maybe hold off until you tell them we're getting married."

Her chin jerked up as her hand stilled. "Are you proposing?"

I shook my head. "No, because that would make it a question, and there's no doubt that it's happening."

Valentina's laugh met my ears. "So you don't want to hear me say yes?"

I rolled out from under her and pinned her to the bed. "The day we walk down the aisle is good enough for me. You want your pops to give you away and officiate?"

Her eyes sparkled. "Yes. I always wanted that. Exactly that."

"It's my job to give you everything you always wanted, duchess." I lowered my lips to hers, stealing a kiss. "Since you've given it all to me."

"You already have," she whispered.

"Not yet, but I will."

Her arms wound around my neck and squeezed. "I love you."

"Always, duchess. Love you always."

THE END

AUTHOR'S NOTE

Want more of the Beneath series?
There are still more deliciously addictive alpha males and
strong, sassy women in the Beneath world to devour:

Beneath This Mask (Book #1 - Simon and Charlie)
Beneath This Ink (Book #2 - Con and Vanessa)
Beneath These Chains (Book #3 - Lord and Elle)
Beneath These Scars (Book #4 - Lucas Titan and Yve)
Beneath These Shadows (Book #6 - Bishop and Eden)
Beneath The Truth (Book #7 - Hennessy and Ariel)

ACKNOWLEDGMENTS

Book number nine! How did this happen? Many long days and late nights, crazy ideas that ran wild, and an amazing team.

Special thanks go out to:

The Meghan March Runaway Readers Facebook group, for being the most fabulous collection of ladies I've had the pleasure of (virtually) meeting. Your support and dedication blows me away every day. I'm so thankful for you.

My readers—I'm infinitely grateful that you've picked up this book. Without you, I wouldn't be living my dream. I will always work my hardest to bring you books I think you'll love.

All the book bloggers who take the time to read and review this and any of my other books. Your time and dedication are truly appreciated.

Pam Berehulke, editors extraordinaire, for once again helping me deliver the best story I'm capable of writing.

Natasha Gentile and Jamie Lynn, my fabulous beta readers, for not asking any questions when I sent you this book to read. Wasn't it better that way?

My family, for their constant support of big dreams. I love you all.

ALSO BY MEGHAN MARCH

MAGNOLIA DUET:

Creole Kingpin

Madam Temptress

LEGEND TRILOGY:

The Fall of Legend

House of Scarlett

The Fight for Forever

DIRTY MAFIA DUET:

Black Sheep

White Knight

FORGE TRILOGY:

Deal with the Devil

Luck of the Devil

Heart of the Devil

SIN TRILOGY:

Richer Than Sin

Guilty as Sin

Reveling in Sin

MOUNT TRILOGY:

Ruthless King

Defiant Queen

Sinful Empire

SAVAGE TRILOGY:

Savage Prince

Iron Princess

Rogue Royalty

BENEATH SERIES:

Beneath This Mask

Beneath This Ink

Beneath These Chains

Beneath These Scars

Beneath These Lies

Beneath These Shadows

Beneath The Truth

DIRTY BILLIONAIRE TRILOGY:

Dirty Billionaire

Dirty Pleasures

Dirty Together

DIRTY GIRL DUET:

Dirty Girl

Dirty Love

REAL GOOD DUET:

Real Good Man

Real Good Love

REAL DIRTY DUET:

Real Dirty

Real Sexy

FLASH BANG SERIES:

Flash Bang

Hard Charger

STANDALONES:

Take Me Back

Bad Judgment

ABOUT THE AUTHOR

Making the jump from corporate lawyer to romance author was a leap of faith that *New York Times*, #1 *Wall Street Journal*, and *USA Today* bestselling author Meghan March will never regret. With over thirty titles published, she has sold millions of books in nearly a dozen languages to fellow romance-lovers around the world. A nomad at heart, she can currently be found in the woods of the Pacific Northwest, living her happily ever after with her real-life alpha hero.

She'd love to hear from you.
Connect with her at:
www.meghanmarch.com